WHITE SCAR

WHITE SCAR

JILL PETTS

The Book Guild Ltd

First published in Great Britain in 2021 by
The Book Guild Ltd
9 Priory Business Park
Wistow Road, Kibworth
Leicestershire, LE8 0RX
Freephone: 0800 999 2982
www.bookguild.co.uk
Email: info@bookguild.co.uk
Twitter: @bookguild

This work is entirely fictitious and bears no resemblance to any persons living or dead.

Typeset in 11pt Adobe Jenson Pro

Printed on FSC accredited paper
Printed and bound in Great Britain by 4edge Limited

ISBN 978 1913913 618

British Library Cataloguing in Publication Data.
A catalogue record for this book is available from the British Library.

For Peter and Chloe, who inspired me, and still do.

For Tony and Yass who helped me, and still do.

And for all you soon to be White Scar cavers –
the witch is waiting for you.

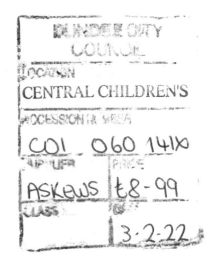

THE CAVE

Ralph is in a huge cave. A strange orange glow illuminates the cave, casting shadows that seem to be taking part in a macabre dance. He feels clammy and cold. Panic seems to creep up his throat, but he can't shout for help or run. This part of the dream never changes.

His eyes are always drawn to the cragged face of a woman, which is etched into the cave wall, shrouded in darkness, highlighted by the flickering light. Arched brows of stone overhang hate-filled eyes, tinged orange like two burning orbs. A sharp chin juts beneath mean lips. Water swollen with mineral deposits has formed copper and brown ringlets, which frame the face. *Perhaps it was a pretty face once*, dreams Ralph. A taste of blood is on his tongue, salty and metallic, the taste of the cave. He watches a drop of the heavy water trace its way along the ridge of a crooked nose, before suspending itself at the tip of a stalactite emerging, without hurry, from the limestone nostril. The sluggish liquid will someday extend itself into a droplet and fall, stroking the arched back of the cat embedded in the rock beneath its mistress, the feline tail and hackles raised in eternal, motionless anger. All is quiet, black, still, just as it has been for a century. Then, from the very core of the limestone, comes not a murmur nor even a whisper, but a thought given sound, floating in the quietude: '*We'll soon be free, Pusskin, we'll soon be free.*'

Ralph is now gasping for breath. He is running but not moving. The witch's breath is on his neck, her whisper in his ears. He reaches out to touch the cave walls, anything solid. He expects to feel dampness. Instead his fingers touch softness and warmth. He lies still, panting. He is in his bed. There is no cave, no cat and no witch. He peers through the panes of his bedroom window. There's the full moon, shining on the white scar on the hillside, the grazing sheep like little boulders in the grass. This part of the dream doesn't change either.

CHAPTER 1

INGLESET, MAY 2150
THE EVENING OF THE CONCERT

Ralph Milway willed his eyes open. Grit was scratching his eyeballs. When he managed to peel his eyelids back all he could see was whiteness. He shut his eyes again, but the whiteness went searing to the centre of his brain, stinging his nerves. After a minute, or perhaps it was an hour, the stinging subsided and he coughed. A fine powder, mixed with saliva, dribbled from his mouth, sticking to his chin. He tried to move, but a heavy weight, solid and unyielding, pinned his right shoulder down. The weight stirred of its own accord.

'Dad?' said Ralph. The word sounded muffled, as if spoken through water swishing inside his head. With his left hand he touched first his left ear, and then his right. Both ears were still attached.

His father's weight shifted from him. Ralph pushed himself up, so he rested on his elbows, blinking through the fog. He wasn't sure if the fog was inside or outside of his body. Perhaps it was both.

'Ralph. Are you all right?' His father's voice pushed through the fog.

'I think so. What happened?' Ralph said, sure that his mouth was crammed with mushrooms.

He felt his dad stand up. The white veil settled. A sound like a church bell tolling crashed against his eardrums and rang inside his head. He slowly stood up, a strong pair of hands clasping his arms to help him. Then clarity arrived.

'Easy does it,' said his father.

Ralph surveyed the hillside on which he stood. Hadn't there been bright green grass across it a few moments before? Now it was covered in greyish rocks and dust, except for one area, about five metres or so to the left of where he and his father were standing, where a gaping black hole had been gouged out of the hill. Then he remembered the explosion. He felt his stomach knot in a tight cramp. His mouth filled with bile and then he threw up.

Wiping his mouth with a dust-covered sleeve, Ralph stood gawping at the black hole. His father's hands once again tightened around his shoulders.

'Come away from the edge,' said his dad.

Ralph felt himself being guided down the hillside, to a point below the hole.

'What have I done?' Ralph's throat felt like it had needles at the back of it, and his words came out in a croak.

'It's okay, son.' Ralph felt his dad squeeze his arm.

'Dad, I'm sorry, it's completely my fault. I did check everything before the concert. I'm sure I wrote everything down properly, but when I checked the bit of paper, it definitely said three hundred grams of Blowamyte.'

'I checked everything you did, except the quantities. I should have watched you measure it out,' said his dad.

Ralph crouched down and ran his hand over what used to be grass, but now looked and felt like a covering of abrasive snow. How could he have got this so wrong, *again*? A gnawing sensation started up in the pit of his stomach, and he started to sweat. Inside his head he felt as if a pair of eyes, glowing orange and narrow with hate, were staring right into his brain, but when he looked up, all he could see was the grey shroud still descending on the hillside, and his dad looking down at him with worry and love etched across his face. Ralph felt himself lurch. The orange eyes faded and darkness closed in on him.

Somewhere close by, he could hear his twin sister, Alba, calling to him. 'Ralph. Where are you? Are you alive?' He teetered on the edge of oblivion.

'Ralph! Ande! You're alive, thank God.' A woman's voice sliced into Ralph's brain. He revived, and scrambled to his feet.

He looked down the hill and saw his mother covered in dust, like a moving statue, scrambling up the hillside, ignoring the debris as she stumbled over it. Next to his mother, he saw Alba, also ghostly white, striding towards him and his father. His mother reached him and enveloped him in her arms, kissing his forehead and ruffling his hair. Beneath the dust he could smell her scent: baked cakes, honey, lavender soap. He choked back a sob. Alba clung to her father, her head buried in his woollen shirt.

'We're both fine, Shelia,' said Ande to his wife. 'Has anyone been hurt in the valley?'

'I'm not sure. Once the rocks had stopped hailing down, Alba and I came straight here. None of the people around us seemed harmed in any way though,' said Shelia.

Alba moved away from her father and edged towards the chasm.

'Alba, don't go near. I'm not sure how safe it is,' said Ande.

'I'd rather fall in the hole than step in that,' she said, looking at the pile of sick, but she moved towards her father, and gave him another hug.

Ralph was still feeling shaky. His mother was fussing, giving him a drink of water from a ceramic flask which she had carried in a canvas bag slung across her body. He saw movement further down the hill.

'Dad, the villagers are coming. Let me speak to them. It was my fault. You can't take the blame again this year.'

'Don't worry, son. Let's position ourselves around the hole. We don't want anyone tumbling in.'

The sun was beginning to lower and a full moon hung like a lace cobweb in the cobalt sky. Ralph watched the flaming torches, held aloft by the villagers, flickering up the hillside. The first of the folk arrived at the scene, and stood with mouths open. More people soon arrived, craning to see what had gone on. The innkeeper, a farmer and the vicar stood alongside the Milway family to act as guards.

Ralph shielded his still-tender eyes with the back of his hand as sudden flashes lit the scene. He rubbed his eyes and blinked to refocus.

'Arfur, do you mind? Show some respect. There's been enough

blinding lights for the evening.' Ralph heard the voice of Judge Tara-Zed. She was talking to Arfur Sendal, the local reporter.

Tara-Zed was a tall, elegant, black lady. No one knew how old she was, but Ralph guessed she was quite old, perhaps in her thirties. He felt himself blush and hoped the white dust would mask the redness.

'Certainly made up for last year,' said the innkeeper.

There was a nervous chuckle from the crowd. Ralph squirmed.

'What exactly has gone on here now eh, Mr. Milway?' asked Arfur.

'Once again I got the charges wrong,' said Ande.

'Dad, I...' said Ralph, but his mother placed her arm around his shoulder and squeezed him to her.

'Not now, Ralph. Let Dad sort this out,' whispered Shelia, kissing her son's forehead. Ralph rubbed his head, but felt too overwhelmed with tiredness to resist his mother.

'It would appear I have blasted a rift in the side of the hill. Night is falling and I do not know how safe the surrounding soil is. I suggest we leave the hillside immediately and carefully, so as not to cause any landslides, and meet in the village hall as soon as possible,' said Ande.

'I agree with Ande. Please leave the hillside quickly and safely,' said Tara-Zed. She smiled at Ralph. He hoped she wouldn't notice the vomit.

His mother peeled away from Ralph and he watched her talking in whispers with Ande and Tara-Zed.

Ralph and his family were the last to leave the hillside, waiting for Arfur Sendal to be long gone into the village. Ralph walked next to his father.

'Let me talk to the people,' said Ralph.

'It's okay, son. I take full responsibility,' said Ande, placing his arm across his son's shoulders.

'What is all the fuss, anyway? I mean, nobody got hurt and it was more realistic than ever before. There was a hole there a hundred years ago, so why can't there be one now?' said Alba.

Ralph noticed the quick glances his parents exchanged.

'Shut up, sis,' said Ralph. Alba furrowed her brow for a moment and looked at her parents. The children would normally be reprimanded for any rudeness, whatever the circumstances, but they seemed not to have noticed.

Alba stared at Ralph and gave a quick shrug of her shoulders. A light drizzle began to fall.

'That's strange. I really didn't expect any rain tonight,' said Ande, as clouds obscured the moon.

Ralph and Alba both shivered and pulled their jackets around them, as the family continued their journey in silence.

CHAPTER 2

INGLESET: ONE HUNDRED YEARS EARLIER, MAY 2050
THE MORNING OF THE TRIAL

'Silence in court.' Rigela Kent heard the shrill voice of Silas Morte, the court usher, penetrate the oak door, behind which she stood. The usher, dressed in his high-collared black suit and stiff cravat, always reminded her of a bony, black bird.

The entire population of Ingleset had squeezed into the wooden courthouse, their hubbub muffled by the door. Rigela knew the villagers would ignore Silas, and she smiled to herself as she thought of him standing upon the dais in the court room, sticking out his scrawny neck and poking his sharp nose this way and that, flapping his hands as if preparing for flight.

'Silence! Silence! The judge is about to enter.' Silas was shrieking. His arms would be flailing like a propeller by now, but she heard the voices drop.

Rigela was standing in a small antechamber at the side of the courtroom, usually used as a storage room for the judge's robes. Along with a pageboy, there were four other people in the room with her. From the back of the room came a flurry of movement and a short, round figure dressed in judge's garments bumped into her leg. There was no apology, neither did Rigela expect one.

'Open the door, boy,' said the short figure, prodding the pageboy with a podgy finger. The lad, who already had his hand placed on the door latch, pulled the door open, and stuck out his tongue at the back of the robed figure, before shutting the door so it just nudged the judge. Rigela widened her eyes and stared at the boy, but this was not the occasion to chastise him.

She smoothed out an imaginary crease in her black velvet dress, her hands making the silver thread woven through the cloth shimmer.

Rigela turned towards a hag who was dressed in tattered clothes, standing in the centre of the room. The hag's skin was as cracked as an old leather bag, and her grey and ginger hair was matted with dirt. Her wrists were bound together with a fine silver thread, which looked as if one tug would break it, but it was made from indestructible moonsilver.

'Please, Aster, it's not too late. Tell us what really happened and we'll direct the court accordingly. Say nothing and you will face an awful punishment,' said Rigela.

A pair of orange eyes burnt into Rigela's, but Aster said nothing.

'Save your breath, Sister,' said another woman standing to the left of Aster.

'I know, Sister Altair, but I find it so hard to believe,' said Rigela, addressing a flame haired woman, with milky skin and green eyes.

'Rigela, we've all tried to help her. It is time to accept she is beyond redemption. Punishment is the only recourse,' said the last woman standing to the right of Aster.

'You are right, Sister Deneb, but how can one so perfect fall so badly?' said Rigela.

Rigela Kent, Altair and Deneb were the Sisters of Antares, a mystical order; one of their duties was to guard the accused and ensure a fair trial.

There was no time for further discussion, as Silas Morte's voice once again breached the door. 'Bring in the accused.'

As the pageboy pulled back the door, he bowed low. Around their waists the three Sisters wore delicate belts made of finely spun gold. Attached to each belt was a thin gold scabbard, each decorated with intricate patterns depicting winding ivy, fire-breathing dragons, and the sun, moon and stars. The women placed their hands on their scabbards and each withdrew a silver wand. The tip of Rigela's wand emitted tiny zigzags of lightning, which spluttered into nothing. From Altair's wand emerged tiny, crackling flames, and from Deneb's wand came droplets of ice, like crushed diamonds, which evaporated before they reached the floor.

Rigela heard the villagers inhale as she led the cortège into the courtroom, Aster behind her, flanked by Altair and Deneb. The room was stifling. To the right of the door was the dais. She could see the judge in profile, on his high chair, propped up further by cushions, peering through his pince-nez over the top of his lectern, mopping his brow beneath his periwig with a red and white spotted handkerchief.

Silas Morte was seating himself at his desk, next to the dais, flourishing his coat tails behind him and fidgeting like a bird getting comfortable in its nest. Behind him, on a stark wooden bench, three figures, a middle-aged man and a woman, with an older lady, sat grim-faced, clutching hands. Rigela looked away from them and walked forwards. As if she were an arrow slicing through flesh, the silent crowd parted before her. She knew that the people at the sides of the courtroom must be pressed against the wall, but still there was no sound. Even the high rafters had ceased creaking and the mice, who conducted their daily business across the beams, remained in their nests.

Now that Aster was on the move, an aroma of rotten fish pervaded the room. People buried their noses in aprons and shirtsleeves, until their nostrils adjusted to the fetid stench. A few bloated bluebottles emerged from the creature's tangled locks and buzzed around before being squelched by the onlookers.

'They could 'ave given 'er a bath,' Rigela heard Hetty Seamstress mutter, breaking the silence and wafting a piece of lace, steeped in lavender oil, around her face.

In the centre of the room, in front of the dais, was the dock, a square wooden platform supported by wood paneling. Rigela stepped aside. Her face remained impassive, but she felt her stomach knot as she watched Aster drag herself into the dock. The Sisters, still with their wands drawn, positioned themselves along three sides of the dock, and then, with the villagers, faced the judge.

Rigela flinched as someone at the back of the courtroom let out a cough which broke the trance of the spectators. She looked towards the judge, and saw him glower in the direction of the unknown person, no doubt irritated that his moment of masterful gravitas had been so crudely interrupted. He stretched his squat frame to its diminutive height, but it had the desired effect of focusing the assembly once more upon him. He redirected his gaze to the hag. Rigela looked at a knot in a beam just above the judge's head, her heart now racing, willing the ordeal to be over.

'Ahem, you, Aster, sometimes witch, have been tried before the High Court of Ingleset for crimes against its country folk.'

The judge spoke in a slow voice. Rigela knew he was trying to sound important, although in truth his voice was too squeaky to carry the graveness he desired. Despite the situation, she had to stifle a smile.

'On the count of the kidnap and murder of the last of the fairies, known as Willis and Elle, I find you...' The judge paused, looking around the room at the rapt audience. As he brought his stare back to the hag, he said forcefully, '*Guilty as charged.*'

A cheer erupted from the crowd until people started to hiss, 'Shush, he's got more to say.'

Silence fell once more until it was broken by a low babbling.

'It's 'er,' said Hetty, pointing at the witch. 'She's trying to muster up one of 'er incantations.'

'Fat chance she's got,' said the village baker from the other side of the room, 'not with the Sisters guarding her.'

An approving murmur went round the hall. Rigela continued to stare at the knot of wood, sensing that Altair and Deneb would be trying to concentrate on their task. Rigela touched the belt of filigree gold around her waist, identical to that worn by the other two women. She knew the power they could wield with the wands. The chains that bound Aster were of the same metal and had been conjured from the joining of the wands.

Each time the hag fidgeted, the three wands sparked their power menacingly, to sighs of 'oo' and 'ah' from the onlookers.

The audience settled once more and the judge, after a bout of 'ahem-ing' and much jowl wobbling, continued his pronouncements.

'On the second count of the *cold-blooded,*' the judge's voice rose to a squeak, 'murder of Bishop Roland, you are found *guilty.*'

Another cheer went up. Rigela could just see one of the figures seated on the bench behind the dais, a woman, with grey hair tied in a neat bun, sitting upright in dignified silence, obscured from the general view of the court. Upon hearing the verdict her shoulders heaved and she sobbed quietly into a hankie. She was the murdered bishop's widow, Beryl. Once more, quietness descended over the chamber.

The judge, who was now fully immersed in the importance of his orations, continued.

'And finally,' he said, leering at Aster, 'on the count of the human sacrifice of Coran, only son of Marsha and Stalwart, you are found *guilty.*'

Rigela shivered as the court room exploded in a volcano of cheers, as people hugged and slapped each other on the back and shook hands heartily. She and the Sisters stood firm, as babies awoke and hollered with abandon. She saw a man, standing beneath a beam, brush a shower of mouse droppings from his face. The judge stood waving his hands as if celebrating a victory. But on the bench, next to the bishop's wife, she saw two people clasping each other's hands and her heart felt heavy for them. She saw the man, Stalwart Woodkeeper, placing a hand on his pregnant wife's swollen belly.

'Perhaps we'll get some peace now,' she saw him mouth.

'Let us pray it be so,' said Marsha, who had tears in her eyes. Rigela saw Marsha's stomach suddenly ripple as the baby moved within her.

Rigela clenched her jaw and returned her gaze to the judge. This was no time for unhelpful sentimentality.

'Order. Order,' shrilled Silas Morte, who was once more ignored by the rapturous crowd.

He really is a ridiculous man, thought Rigela as she watched Silas clamber onto his chair and again flap his hands frantically in an effort to calm the villagers.

'The judge wishes to pronounce sentence.'

As if he had cast a spell, everyone quietened, for they all wanted to know what would become of this evil creature, who all this time had stood muttering and rubbing her hands.

Once again the judge took centre stage, but was now standing, although it was difficult to tell the difference from when he was sitting.

'The crimes you have committed have been solely for your own evil purposes, which makes them more wicked, heinous and repugnant than any crime this court has ever heard,' said the judge.

This was quite true, reflected Rigela, as, until then, the most serious case the judge had dealt with was that of the mistaken identity of a herd of sheep. The village of Ingleset in the Borough of Inglevale had, until Aster began her carnage, been an idyllic place to live, especially as the world started to rebuild itself from the wars and catastrophes it had so recently endured.

'As you are aware this land has, unfortunately in this instance, I believe, no death penalty,' continued the judge.

'Shame,' shouted an onlooker.

'Pity,' chipped in another.

'Silence,' squawked Silas. 'Let the judge continue or I will remove you from the courtroom.'

No one spoke, for none of the villagers wanted to miss the passing of sentence, although they very much doubted the ability of Silas to make any one of them leave.

'Ahem, as I have said,' continued the judge, pushing his glasses further up his nose and grasping both lapels of his gown with each hand, 'there is no death penalty I can issue.'

He puffed out his chest and surveyed the room for any would-be hecklers. Hearing none, he returned his gaze to the witch.

'The village council, guided by myself, ahem, have given the matter of your punishment careful consideration. I sentence you, Aster, to eternal banishment in the black hole of White Scar. I ask the Sisters of Antares to escort you there forthwith.'

Once more, hysteria broke out.

'Oh mercy me. How terrible,' cried Hetty, swooning into Bill the innkeeper's arms.

'Fetch the smelling salts. Hetty's passed out again,' said the man.

'It's too awful,' sobbed another woman.

'You mean it's too bloomin' good for her,' said Lionel the butcher.

Rigela watched Marsha, Stalwart and the bishop's wife creep out through the rear door. She knew their thoughts mirrored her own, and those of Altair and Deneb. Banishment was a cruel punishment. No one knew what horrors lay in the cave, and she felt a shiver run through her body as she thought about the eternal night that awaited Aster, and the cold, damp sepulchral passages that would become a living tomb. The only certainty was there would be no means of escape for Aster once she was discharged into the bitter labyrinth.

Rigela looked straight ahead as the people stepped aside to make way for the witch to pass. She led the way towards the exit. Aster stepped from the dock, mumbling and looking fitfully around, as the Sisters surrounded her, their wands crackling with their separate powers upon every step.

Time had felt suspended in the courtroom, but it was just after four o'clock in the afternoon. One hundred people had crammed into the courthouse which had been designed to take half that amount. Rigela glanced behind her to see the villagers spilling out behind them like a river bursting its banks, led by Hetty who had quickly recovered from her swoon and elbowed her way to the front of the crowd. In contrast to the portentousness of the occasion, the sun was high in the sky and shining brightly on a glorious spring afternoon. People raised their hands to their eyes, as they stepped from the gloom into the light. The scene would have been comedic had it not been so grave.

'Oh, my poor back,' said Bill, placing his hands on his hips and arching backwards, making his rotund stomach look like a bass drum.

'Watch out!' said Lionel, stretching his arms above his head. 'You'll flatten someone.'

All around, people were raising their arms and bending over as they expanded into the space, slowly forming a line behind the Sisters, like a troupe of acrobats of all ages and sizes, warming up for a performance. Children scooted off here and there before being called to their parents' sides. The judge and his usher had been left behind and were the last to leave.

Silas flapped around: 'Let his worshipfulness past. Make way for the judge.'

Once again he was ignored and he and the judge struggled to catch up with the villagers, who were already being led by Rigela to the scene of punishment.

York, 2050
The Day of the Trial

Mr. Hunter sat on the edge of the bed, watching his old friend Sir Wesley die. He ran his fingers through his thinning hair and felt the stabs of arthritis across his shoulders as he waited for Sir Wesley's veined eyelids to struggle open, revealing rheumy eyes.

Sir Wesley lay in the same chamber in Clifford's Tower he had occupied for many years. Mr. Hunter allowed himself a smile as he recalled Sir Wesley's refusal to relocate to the Castle Museum buildings, when the High Council had moved from the tower several years before, once the risk of flooding had subsided. The Council had to trudge the fifty steps to the tower once a month, to include Sir Wesley in any voting.

'You have lived long, my dear friend,' said Mr. Hunter.

'I never thought I would. Certainly never wanted to.' Sir Wesley's voice was as firm as when Mr. Hunter first met him, in the aftermath of the war and the landing of the Great Meteor.

'We all pulled through,' said Mr. Hunter.

Sir Wesley sniffed.

'You never did tell me much about yourself, Hunter.'

'Not much to tell. If anything, the Global War gave me a status I never had before. I used to sell cars. Had my own business in Docklands. I was in a penthouse flat overlooking the Thames. I'd been striking a deal to import some high value cars when the tidal wave struck, not long after the Great Meteor landed in the Pacific. I was trying to carry on as usual. Like everyone else, I never believed it would affect Britain, but I watched it surge up the river, felt the building tremble as if it were having a convulsion, saw the Thames Barrier fall like dominoes, buildings collapse like decks of cards.' Mr. Hunter paused, staring beyond a crinkle in Sir Wesley's sheets at a point in history only he could see. 'I should have been with my wife and little girl. I never thought it would go that far. I thought someone would stop it. So many died.'

'Including your family?' said Sir Wesley.

'I left the flat as soon as it was calm enough. The two business people I was with, a man and a woman, had radiation sickness, so I left them with the other sufferers. I found a canoe, of all things, in a flat which had belonged to a fitness fanatic and paddled towards my home. The water had subsided there, but mud and sewage were everywhere. I found them huddled in the loft. At first I thought they were alive, they looked so perfect, but they'd suffocated. I contemplated killing myself, but I couldn't. How had I survived when billions of far better people than me hadn't? So I came north. That's when I met you and joined the High Council. But I was only ever trying to make up for letting my family down.' Both men paused.

'You were an arrogant so-and-so back then, but you have served the survivors well. I do not have much longer. Tell me, Hunter, what did Anna say?'

Mr. Hunter refocused on Sir Wesley.

'Nothing of consequence,' he said, tapping his thumbs together. Sir Wesley gave a chuckle, which rattled with phlegm.

'I have lived through awful times. I am dying. Nothing you can tell me will make that experience any worse or any better. But please don't lie to me on my death bed,' said Sir Wesley.

Mr. Hunter took his friend's hand. It felt cold and weightless.

'As you know, I paid the visit because of the events in Ingleset. The three wands will be together and I wanted to make sure she's not up to something.

'The journey was uneventful. It never fails to strike me how splendidly isolated the castle is, surrounded on all sides by sea. The sailor knew the channels well and avoided snagging the rudder on any of the buildings submerged below.

'Unlike us, Lady Anna has hardly changed. If anything she looks better than ever. The guards are still rotated monthly. She has three meals brought to her every day. She grumbled about the food, but I told her she has more than she deserves,' said Mr. Hunter.

'Did she say anything?' said Sir Wesley. Mr. Hunter shifted his position.

'The pleasantries were short. I told her the security measures would continue indefinitely. She seemed disinterested. But as I opened the door to leave, she said, almost to herself, "*I* shall outlive them all. My other child, hidden so well they'd never suspect, will restore me and Anthony. We'll show them for the fools they are."

'I tried not to show my shock. I pressed her for more information but she just sat with her lips squeezed together, stroking that wretched cross of hers with one hand, and patting the jar with Anthony's ashes with the other. I can't see how she's linked to that case in Ingleset.'

'Another child? No wonder she is such a tormented soul,' said Sir Wesley. His breathing had grown shallow.

'Anyway, Aster... the witch, is to be thrown alive into a cave, so even if she is the missing child, she'll soon be dead. She was such a beautiful creature once,' said Mr. Hunter.

'Good grief. A cave? I had hoped humanity had stopped being so barbaric.'

Mr. Hunter had to lean in close to hear Sir Wesley. 'A mother's love is a powerful force. You must be vigilant, my dear friend.' With a final rattle of breath, Sir Wesley died.

CHAPTER 3

INGLESET, MAY 2050

THE DAY OF THE TRIAL

If viewed from above, Ingleset took the shape of an eye with a round well in the centre like an unblinking pupil. Two roads led into the village hub from either end as if running into, or out of, each corner of the eye. The courthouse was positioned at the southern end of the village. The village had once had more roads and houses, but these had been destroyed in the war, or had crumbled with neglect, so the village now centred on the nucleus of the well.

Rigela led the procession, surefooted across the cobbled stones, past the schoolhouse, the inn, around the well, and by the shops and finally the church, which had been rebuilt using stone from the original church, which had collapsed during the war. She remembered Aster teaching in the Sunday school, the children's laughter often being so loud in the adjacent hall, it disturbed the service. Aster had grown flowers and herbs, and made healing remedies and had once been a familiar and welcome figure, before her body and soul had soured.

Upon passing through the narrow roadway that led to the north, Rigela always took a deep breath in as the confinement of the village centre gave way to a panorama of earth and sky, as if she were drinking in the countryside. A vast valley in the shape of a flattened letter 'u' continued as far as the eye could follow. Woodland lay to the left and grew around the back of the village. On this vernal day, bordering summer, the grass was a shimmering green as if a million emeralds had been spread across the valley. The limestone outcrops, which jutted from the ground like exposed bones, shone cleanly in the sunlight. A few sheep, their numbers ravaged by the war of a few years earlier, munched greedily on the extravagant grass. Rigela would have loved nothing more than to be riding her horse, a powerful black stallion, along the valley, feeling the breeze on her face, her long black hair flying around her head, instead of being part of this onerous, heart-rending, task.

Behind her, she could hear the chatter of the crowd.

'Fresh plumpberry tarts,' cried Alice the baker.

Rigela had seen the cart full of pastries brimming over with stewed purple fruit in their centres, the sweet aroma swirling its way to the villagers' noses, although how any person could have an appetite on a day such as this was beyond her imagination.

Alice's daughter, Rachel, with a big, gap-toothed smile, ran up to Rigela and offered her a pie.

'Not today, thank you,' said Rigela, without returning the smile, and the child shrank back and ran off.

'How much, Alice?' she heard Hetty say.

'Nothing today, Hetty dear. We've a lot to celebrate.'

Rigela winced.

Bill the innkeeper and his son Iain were pushing a little wagon with two barrels and several pitchers balanced on it.

'Inkle juice and ale. Inkle juice and ale. All on the house,' cried Bill, and she could hear a hubbub of people crowding round to quench their thirst on this warm day.

Even the judge and Silas were smiling as they caught up with the front of the party, shaking hands with several of the villagers, readily accepting pies and mugs of inkle juice, relieved that their grievous duty was almost at an end. It seemed to Rigela that only the Sisters remained impassive, as they concentrated on their solemn task.

A few months earlier, when Rigela visited the village just after Christmasnowtide, snow had lined the valley and covered the hills and it had been difficult to tell where earth finished and the heavens began, but today, as the villagers marched on, their feet sprang on the lush grass. Clumps of golden buttercups and purple orchids provided a reminder of warmer days to come, for all except the murderess.

From the corner of her eye, Rigela could see the silver ribbon of a stream appearing and disappearing along the centre of the valley floor; its abundant melt-water jumped over unmovable stones and twisted around rocky remnants left by the great glacier that had carved the landscape, and the beginnings of its myriad cave systems, long ago.

It was such a contrast to how the inhabitants of Ingleset usually lived, thought Rigela. They led a simple lifestyle, thankful that the years since the Global War had passed without further conflict. They helped each other in daily tasks and took pleasure in each other's company. Laughter came from the inn each evening, and the church of All Faith and None buzzed with friendship on Sundays.

The village well provided a fresh supply from the underground water table. The villagers wore clothes made of wool from the sheep who pastured in the valley. Timber for building and heat was sourced from the wood which grew to the west of the village, and which was managed by Stalwart. She admired the way he ensured the wood remained sustainable and met everyone's needs. Technology was limited to what could be achieved with medieval resources, but nobody minded. Aster had been so welcomed into the village not so very long before. She should have been happy. Rigela frowned.

As the group passed by the edge of the woodland, a derelict single-story cottage with a decaying thatched roof could be seen, not far from the wood keeper's home. Rigela kept her gaze steadfast, even though she was desperate to know if this scene would invoke repentance from Aster. The dried-up carcasses of once sweet flowers lined the unkempt path that led to a peeling door. A dead rambling rose clung wretchedly to the chipped, whitewashed walls and with the windows boarded up, the structure looked as forlorn and devoid of warmth as its previous occupant. This had been Aster's cottage, the scene of her cadaverous spells. Rigela looked back at her. The witch glanced sideways at her former home, the contents of her heart appearing to be reflected in the emotionless face and vacant eyes.

'We should burn it,' said Frank, the farmer.

'I've got some tinder,' came a reply.

'I say we burn it and…' said Frank, but he quietened as he looked up to see a pair of eyes boring into him.

Rigela did not speak but peeled her gaze from the man, who now hung his head and scuffed a blade of grass with his foot.

'Not today, eh, Frank? We've enough to be getting on with,' said Hetty.

From the trees came a light rustle of twigs and leaves. A small black cat with one white ear and a white chin cautiously appeared, letting out tiny mews.

'Oh look, it's 'er little kitty,' said Hetty.

'She might need some company down the hole,' shouted a shepherd.

'The cat's as rotten as she is,' cried the school mistress.

On seeing Aster, the cat ran towards her, giving a pitiful mew. She tried to entwine herself between the witch's legs, not understanding that the delicate chains that bound her mistress were not a string to be played with, and squealing as they cut into her paws. The witch seemed not to notice her new companion and shuffled on, ranting to herself.

Both the judge and clerk were now in front of Rigela, slowing her long, even stride. They strutted with their noses held high and chests puffed out. A few of the children got in step behind the odd couple and mimicked their walk, but soon fell out of line when they remembered that not only the Sisters of Antares but also the witch herself were behind them. Rigela felt her wand twitch, an extension of the frustration she was feeling with the two men ahead of her; she knew they were using this to further their careers.

About a mile from the village, the group took a route to the right. They passed an uneven bulge of earth, with a few pieces of concrete and twisted metal protruding from the ground. Rigela recalled talk that this had once been an entrance to the cave system, used before the war for people to enter the cave in safety and for pleasure. The entrance had collapsed during the many seismic shifts the world underwent after the impact of the Great Meteor. There seemed nothing pleasurable for the next visitor to the cave, she thought with a sigh.

The group proceeded diagonally up the valley side towards what looked like a large black stain in the grass, about two-thirds up the side of the hill. Aster hesitated, but a quick jolt of fire ice from Deneb's wand persuaded her forwards, her cat mewing wretchedly.

'That's not a sight you normally see,' said Alice the baker, pointing skywards.

'After the carrion, I expect,' said Lionel the butcher, for above them a large flock of crows had appeared from nowhere and started to follow the procession, cawing and wheeling, their beady eyes on the lookout for any morsels discarded by the group.

A small child dropped her plumpberry tart, but before she could bend over to pick it up, a large black bird swooped down and grabbed the food in its cruel claws, screeching scorn as it did so. The child hid in the folds of its mother's apron, crying in alarm. The presence of the crows seemed to stir up the crowd and they bayed and hurled insults at the witch, whose hands and feet were still ensnared in the silver manacles.

She stumbled, provoking jeers from the crowd: 'Banshee', 'child-eater', 'fairy-slayer'. The revulsion at witnessing violent acts during the war and enjoyment of the subsequent years of peace was for the moment forgotten as they reveled in their new-found bloodlust. Rigela knew that the chosen punishment had been thought of by the judge. He had consulted a preserved text book, and found evidence that the remains of a family from the Bronze Age had been found in a similar cave, with bones broken where they had been dropped in. It made her feel sick to think that the villagers should go along with this, but Aster had committed some atrocious crimes and deserved to be punished, but the barbarity had shocked Rigela.

Behind her, Aster cackled at the villagers. Rigela looked over her shoulder just as Aster spat a line of saliva, which narrowly missed Altair's arm. Altair instantly flicked her wrist and the wand responded with a flame spurting from its tip, prompting the witch onwards with her now-smoldering shoulder reeking of burnt fish. Rigela nodded to Altair, who she could see was flushed from her use of the wand in anger.

'Rachel, come away,' Rigela heard Alice say to her daughter. 'We need to get more pies ready.'

'Oh ma…' came the reply, quickly stifled by her mother.

'I'd forgotten what *she's* capable of. We're going back. Don't argue,' said Alice.

'We'll join you,' said a woman with a baby in a sling across her chest.

'This is no thing for the children to see,' said another.

Rigela glanced behind her again and saw a trail of women and children peel away from the group and head back towards Ingleset.

Several of the older villagers turned back too, the ascent being greater than they had remembered, for there was not even a track now as no one ventured to this area. In earlier times, sheep had strayed and fallen into the hole, but the rescue attempts had proved dangerously futile and eventually, despite the lushness of the pasture, flocks had been kept well clear of the area. Children dared not venture in this direction either, as it meant a severe punishment from the judge or, worse still, their parents. Consequently the grass rose up around their ankles, dragging against women's skirts and the judge's heavy robe.

The judge, still with his nose in the air, led the people ever more slowly on and gradually the bravado of the group abated and their earlier exuberance ebbed away. Rigela had to watch her step so as not to trip over the man and his ridiculous usher.

The walk took longer than expected and it was just after six o'clock in the evening when the makeshift parade stopped at the site where the punishment was to be executed. The sun was reluctantly setting and long shadows were cast from the occasional tree and the numerous boulders, making the landscape appear occupied by grotesque black giants. A shadow here looked like a gaping mouth ready to consume an innocent, a shadow there resembled a hobgoblin's ear. The circling crows cast the villagers' faces in and out of fluttering darkness.

Rigela stood next to the judge. She could hear him wheezing. Despite the cooling temperature, the judge mopped his brow with his red and white spotted handkerchief, the long sleeves of his gown quivering like wings.

Next to the gash in the hillside, which was the size of four large men, lay a large flat grey stone, about a quarter of which overhung the hole. It was through this rift in the landscape that Aster was to be cast to live in eternal darkness, to wander in the intestines of the hill, with only grubs or freakish algae for company. Rigela shivered and raised her wand.

'Aster, you are to ascend the stone platform,' said Rigela.

Altair and Deneb raised their wands. The hag glowered at them but struggled on to the stony precipice.

'The power of the wands will act as a rope to lower you into the cave.' This was a concession Rigela Kent had insisted on. She would not have Aster pushed by brute force into the hole.

'You will not be able to climb out. There is no other known escape. Food and water will be lowered daily by a basket. When the basket returns without being emptied for a full five days, then we shall know there is no longer need for it.' This was another concession Rigela would have no dispute on.

Aster ceased mumbling and grew quite still. Her head was lowered but she peered from beneath bushy eyebrows, her eyes a brilliant amber against her wrinkled grey skin. Rigela saw she was staring, without a trace of emotion, at the judge. Now that the witch had come to a halt, the cat rubbed up against her mistress's legs, mewing fretfully. Aster bent down and stuck one horny fingernail under the cat's chin and caressed the fur. A crusty grey teardrop slid down the witch's cheek, landing heavily on the back of her hand.

'She's shed more tears for that cat of 'ers than she ever did for 'er victims,' cried Hetty.

The cat looked at Aster and then sloped away to crouch beneath a gorse bush.

Rigela looked at Altair and Deneb, who kept glancing at the crows wheeling above in a frenzy of anticipation. They circled faster and faster like a plague of flies, till their blackness merged into one continuous circle, their violent cacophony the only sound filling the valley.

'Let us be done with this now, Silas,' the judge murmured, as he scrambled on to the rock, his short legs tired from the long walk, struggling to find their balance. Trying hard to avoid the unblinking stare of the witch, he faltered as he stood up, still sweating profusely and coughing nervously. He twisted the black ring on his chubby finger. He stood as far towards the back of the stone as he could, for he did not know what force the Sisters of Antares would use to unlock the manacles and cast the witch into the abyss.

'Ahem, by the power vested in me...' he started.

'Speak up, we can't hear you at the back,' shouted the dairy man.

'Bloomin' crows,' said Bill.

'Yes, this is the best bit,' said a teenage shepherd boy, to a murmur of approval from the throng.

Abruptly, the crows became silent, their manic flight quietening into the pulse of rhythmic wing beats.

'Ahem, as I was saying, I ask the Sisters of Antares on behalf of the people of Ingleset to cast you, Aster, into the depths of this hill for eternity.'

Rigela raised her wand in unison with Altair and Deneb. With just a twitch of her wrist, she felt a current of power surge from her arm and through the wand, from which silver flashes burst out of the tip, mixing with the blue ice and fiery flames of the wands of Altair and Deneb. The onlookers cried out and took a step back.

The shackles that held Aster evaporated in a shimmer of silver dust. At that moment Rigela saw something flash to her right, from just beneath the stone. It took her a second to realise that it was the cat, which now emitted a heart-stopping screech. It pounced at Deneb, digging its claws into her outstretched arm. Deneb flinched as a line of blood trickled along her pale forearm. Crimson droplets splashed on to her white gown. Rigela squeezed her left hand over her right as she felt her wand tremble in her grip. In that instant, she saw Aster stretch out a claw-like hand and grab the wand from Deneb's loosened hold. Aster clutched the wand to her chest. Rigela could see Altair's eyes widen and her jaw clench, but the two Sisters continued to direct their wands at Aster. Aster now extended the wand in her possession. Rigela felt a surge of resistance pulse through her own wand, but even though the Sisters' wand arms were shaking, Aster could not fight the power of the two wands and was nudged towards the opening. Just as she was about to disappear forever, she aimed Deneb's wand at the judge, who stood paralysed. Releasing its grip on Deneb's arm, the cat sprang across the stone slab and landed on the judge's back.

'Oh my, oh my,' he cried, as he overbalanced.

'Your Worship,' screeched Silas, flapping his arms and hopping from foot to foot.

The crows recommenced their squawking and several of the onlookers screamed.

The witch used her last vestige of power to send an icicle flash from the wand, which covered the judge like a shimmering blue lasso. As she toppled into the opening, Aster dragged the judge, with the cat still on his back, downwards with her into the black hole. Together with Altair, Rigela lurched forwards, hands white with effort, gripping their wands; their necks were taut, their knees bent, as they struggled with the extra weight of the judge, now joined in Aster's descent.

With one final effort, Aster sent an ice bolt tearing out from the hole, shaking the earth to its foundations and, with a terrifying thunderclap, sealed the rift above herself and her final victim. The power from the other two wands was spliced off, and Rigela and Altair dropped their arms to their sides. Rigela felt her head spin as the murderous cawing of the crows became louder, as they flitted across the heads of the onlookers before darting away. A cloud of powdered limestone, soil and grass expelled itself into the air. A vile cackle and a pitiful sob lingered over the rumbling hillside, until both sounds were borne away by a light breeze that followed the birds along the valley. As the dust dispersed, Rigela saw the faces of the onlookers, pale and petrified, as together they realised there was no longer a gaping black chasm, but instead a jagged line of white and silver rock. Like an open wound that had been crudely stitched up, the forbidding cave was sealed.

CHAPTER 4

INGLESET 2150

THE MORNING OF THE CONCERT

'And that is how the black hole became a white scar, which is funny because the hill had always been called White Scar. It used to be a tourist attraction,' said Shelia Milway, to Ralph and Alba, her fourteen-year-old twins, as she placed a warm plumpberry pie, knotted in a blue and white checked cloth, on top of an already crammed picnic basket. 'And the really funny thing,' she continued, 'is there was said to be a rock that looked like a judge, and the form of a witch and her cat could be seen on a wall. It's as if the witch and judge were always meant to be there.'

'Yeah, right, Mum. You tell us that every year,' said Ralph. 'So a hundred years ago some old witch bumps a few villagers and pixie things off, and I'm supposed to go to a stupid concert of singing flowers to commemorate it. I don't think so.'

He shoved the plate of cheese and pickle sandwiches he had been dissecting across the table where it hit the hamper, before crossing his arms in front of himself. His stomach felt like it was full of ants crawling around in it.

'It's only because you nearly ruined it last year,' said Alba. 'It's fab. We live in a village where we have flowers that perform, a gift from the Sisters of Antares so that the good judge, if he survived the fall,

25

would be comforted by its beauty and the witch and her cat would be tormented by its purity.'

'More like freaks of nature. You can be such a creep, Alba,' replied Ralph, screwing up his linen napkin.

'That's enough, Ralph,' said a stern voice.

It was the twins' father, Ande Milway, who was standing in the kitchen doorway.

Ralph slunk deeper into the chair. He always felt he was letting his dad down.

'Do not let me hear you disrespect the memory of your ancestors again. Now, have you set the firework charges correctly?'

'Sorry, Dad. It's just...'

'Ralph, there is no "just". Have you done as I asked?'

'Yes, Dad. The charges are set. Correctly, this year. It's all crucial.'

'Good, if "crucial" is a good thing. Now I'm starving and your mother's cooking is as irresistible as she is,' said Ande, hugging Shelia.

'Mum. Dad. Don't be so skank. Trying to eat, thank you,' said Alba. She had reassembled one of Ralph's rejected sandwiches and was just about to take a bite.

How could she think about eating? thought Ralph. He glowered at his parents. They were always hugging in a cringe-worthy sort of way.

'Ralph's just worried about the firework charges. Don't be too hard on him,' whispered Shelia to Ande during their embrace, but Ralph could just hear. They still thought of him as a child. 'You'll need your waterproofs by the looks of the weather,' said Shelia loudly, disengaging herself from Ande's hug, 'and, Albarea, "skank" is an unpleasant word.'

'It will be fine. There's no rain up there today,' said Ande firmly.

'So what happened to the Sisters of Antares?' said Alba.

Shelia and Ande exchanged a glance.

'The original Sisters are dead. The role is symbolic now. The present Sisters mind the two remaining wands. That's all,' said Shelia. 'Now pass me the small basket, please.'

Alba pushed the basket across the table, which Shelia started to fill with yet more food.

'But who are they?' said Alba.

'Just three ladies minding their own business,' said Shelia.

'Coran, one of the victims, must still have relatives in the village. I wonder who they are. Funny, I've never thought about this until now,' said Alba.

'That's because you're an idiot,' said Ralph, who still felt cross at his parents' patronising attitude towards him.

'Bother!' said Shelia, placing the edge of her index finger to her mouth.

'Are you okay, Mum?' said Alba.

'I just snagged my finger on the wicker. It's fine,' said Shelia, continuing to load food into the basket.

Alba rolled a crumb over the table, her brow furrowed with concentration. Ralph watched his dad spot another plumpberry pie, fresh from the oven, cooling on the oak kitchen table, and head towards it. The wisps of steam reminded Ralph of the disastrous finale to the previous year's concert when his dad had given in to his pleading and allowed him to set the charges for the grand firework finale, which symbolised the closing of the cave by the fabled witch's magic power. Because he had not laid enough charge, there was a feeble splutter, one firework was launched, and in place of the usual rapturous applause, there was an embarrassed silence. He had asked to be involved again this year, and his dad had not hesitated in saying yes to him, even though his dad had taken full responsibility for the show's anti-climax, and had checked everything Ralph had done thoroughly this year.

'Don't worry,' said Ande gently to his son. 'Everything will go well this time.'

'Yeah, whatever,' grunted Ralph.

Ralph was the older of the twins by three minutes. He wasn't sure if this was a good thing. Sometimes he felt he was expected to act more responsibly because of this. His mother often told him that he had been born with his tiny fists clenched and a quivering bottom lip but had not uttered a whimper. Alba had also arrived in a determined manner but as soon as she could draw breath had started to gurgle and cry, as if frustrated by questions on her lips which she yet had no way of forming. He often thought Alba had been born a grown up; she always seemed to know what to do.

The twins were not identical in look or character. Ralph had the same rugged looks, coal black hair and hazel eyes as his father. Alba favoured her mother, sporting thick blond tresses and blue eyes, aquiline features and rose-pink lips set against fair skin. Both were handsome children and the old ladies of the village loved to make comments such as 'they'll break a few hearts in their time, they will,' which made the children cringe. Ralph had tried a girlfriend once, Lila Monkfish. She stared at him, and trees, without blinking, and made cooing noises at babies. She hadn't been interested in caving, riding or wood carving and he had dumped her in favour of his best mates, Murgus Bellows and Davyd Baker. He thought Alba was better company than Lila, although he would never tell her that.

His mother, Shelia, was one of two teachers in the school, which stood next to the courthouse in the village centre. There were only thirty children in the village aged from five to sixteen years. When they turned sixteen, they could either leave to take up one of the village trades, which were largely unchanged in a hundred years, or move on to further education in the castle town of Skipton. Ralph wanted to learn to manage the land just like his father. He admired the way his dad knew just which trees to fell, or where to send the farmers to pasture their sheep. His dad knew how much stone to quarry in winter to avoid rockslides, or how to divert the stream so it didn't flood. Alba was a natural athlete. Her running was famous in the region. This was the first year she had been left in charge of organising the children's games that preceded the concert. She too would be quite happy to remain in the village. But his father wanted them both to attend college. 'You'll need more than knowledge about trees or how to run fast to help shape the world's future,' Ande had once said to Ralph and Alba, and the subject had been closed.

When she was not teaching, Shelia supervised the running of their home, which stood on the outskirts of the village. This had been Ralph's grandparents' house. It had at one time been a simple cottage bordered at the rear by woodland, but his grandfather had turned it into a family home. It had a clear view of White Scar Hill.

'Oi, Mr. Milway, hands off. That's for your picnic,' said Shelia. Her voice roused Ralph from his thoughts.

His dad had wandered over to the pie, picked up a fork and was wheedling out one of the steaming hot plumpberries, which had the shape of a blackberry but was the size of a damson.

'You'd better leave the kitchen now, before you get into trouble.' Shelia shooed her husband out of the room. 'The flowers haven't failed to show at six o'clock for the past ninety-nine years, so you'd better be ready.'

According to local lore, in the year following the awful event, a group of villagers had taken some flowers to lay on the white scar. They had been surprised to find a whole range of flowers, many of which were not even local to the area, growing in the valley at the foot of the hill. They were even more shocked when these plants stirred and started to produce musical notes. They sat awestruck for the next twenty minutes as a concert, the likes of which they had never heard before, was performed for them.

At the end, they rushed back to the village and told their neighbours what had occurred. By then it was dark, but at first light the next morning a group of villagers, including the newly appointed judge, went to the scene. Nothing but a few dried-up leaves were in evidence. The original group were so insistent about what they had witnessed that the following year the entire village ventured to the valley, deciding that an act of commemoration should be held in any event. At six o'clock, as the sun started to sink, the magical flowers reappeared and, to everyone's wonderment, performed their concerto. The singing flowers had never failed to appear since.

'Even if it is true,' said Ralph to his sister, 'and the good judge, the witch Aster and the cat do exist in some form of consciousness, they must be pretty sick of the concerts by now.'

'Ralph, don't be so awful. It's a really special occasion this year,' said Alba.

'Yeah, exactly. So why can't we get Meteor Queens or Dizzy-Frap up from the city, instead? Decent music.'

'Because Mrs. Grumble would faint and not be able to make honey sweets for a year, so shut up moaning, you skanker,' said Alba, flicking a crumb of cheese at her brother.

'If I'm ever holed up somewhere for a hundred years, make sure no one arranges a performance by whistling pansies, roses that la-la and dahlias that toot.'

'Don't worry, Ralph. If you're ever stuck down a hole, I shall tell everyone to forget all about you. And there aren't any dahlias in the performance.'

'Ralph. Hurry up. It's just gone two and Dad's waiting for you outside. I shoved him out of the kitchen to save this pie,' said Shelia, handing over the smaller basket with a dish wrapped in a red and white cloth on top of it. 'You'll need time to check things through. Enjoy your picnic.'

'Whatever,' grunted Ralph.

He pushed his kitchen chair back noisily on the slate floor, pulled on his waistcoat and went to join his father, who was waiting at the bottom of the garden path by the gate, a leather satchel slung across his body.

'Looks like Mum thinks we'll be up there for a fortnight, not a few hours,' said Ande spying the picnic basket, trying to raise a smile from his son.

Ande and Ralph, both walking with an easy stride, headed up the valley towards the hill with its jagged white scar in stark contrast against the green pasture. Woolly white bodies moved around the limestone outcrops, lazily viewing the visitors to their hill. Sheep had been re-established after years of careful breeding and provided a valuable source of material and food.

Ralph's mood lightened as the scenery opened up around them. He laughed when he saw a group of baby harebits hop this way and that. In the days of the war, which had ravaged the world, and after the Great Meteor had fallen, when food was scarce, rabbits had been hunted to near extinction. The few that had escaped the boiling pot had mated with the more resilient hares. The harebit had the body and face of a rabbit but the long ears and large hind legs of a hare. Consequently, the babies tripped over themselves until they learnt how to flick their ears from their faces, and rather than scampering they leapt high in the air, tipping forwards as they landed. Ralph had seen pictures of the original rabbits and hares in an old book.

'Nature got those a bit wrong,' said Ralph.

'There was a lot to sort out after the mess the world was left in. I expect they got a bit overlooked,' said his father, smiling.

As father and son walked on, the creatures tumbled over each other, racing to get away from the approaching footfalls. The overcast clouds, which had threatened rain, parted and rays of sunlight burst onto the hill. For one strange moment, as the beams merged, the scar appeared to shimmer and shake.

'Never seen sunlight do that before. Let's hope it's not a sign of things to come, eh, Ralph?' said Ande, patting his son on the back.

The Welsh Lagoons 2150
The Day of the Concert

Lady Anna sat on a high-backed oak chair, like a throne, looking to one of the five arrow slits that acted as windows. On all sides except one she was surrounded by sea, the swell and pounding of waves her constant companion these past one hundred years.

The castle, which had been her prison, had been built by Edward I several centuries earlier, eventually finding favour as a tourist haunt, before the Global War annihilated civilisation and flood water possessed the land. A few years after Lady Anna was imprisoned for her treachery, a well-meaning guard had attempted to cultivate a garden in the castle's grounds, to supplement the monthly deliveries, but the only success was with carrots and potatoes. Fish were caught daily, mainly to occupy the guards who, although they knew the story of Lady Anna's crime, could not equate it with the harmless old woman who sat in the room of the high tower and seemed to refuse to die.

Lady Anna's left hand stroked a large wooden cross, which hung on a chain around her neck, a large ruby in its centre. Her right hand rested on a black urn which stood upon a table by her chair. Next to the urn, in a gilt frame, was a faded photograph of a smiling young man, a fringe of ginger hair flopping beneath a mortar board.

'Dear Anthony. You and I will soon be restored. Sir Wesley and Mr. Hunter had no idea who they were meddling with, and neither do those fools at Ingleset,' said Lady Anna to the picture, her voice frail but clear. 'I shall pay them back for what they did to you. The three wands will soon be brought together and your sibling will secure them for us all. We can rule the world and beyond with those wands.'

She sank back in the chair, grimacing as a guard entered with a plate of baked fish, boiled potatoes and carrots.

CHAPTER 5

INGLESET, 2150

EARLY IN THE AFTERNOON OF THE CONCERT

Alba and her mother headed towards Ingleset, carrying the picnic basket between them. As they entered the village between the ageing, but strong, stone buildings, Alba felt goose bumps prickle her arms, for she could already hear the excitement growing.

The village itself still had limestone cobbles, although they had been repaired over the centuries. Many of the buildings were original. The wooden covered well in the centre of the village was now only used for drawing water for the horses of visitors, as most of the houses had water supplied directly to them.

Stalls with canopies of vibrant green, yellow and red had been set up in the centre, selling honey-apples, rattles made from papier Mache filled with seeds and painted in garish colours, and witch masks made of dried tree bark.

'Hello, Giena. How are you?' said Shelia.

'Well, the cart's well laden, as usual,' said the woman, a short, blond-haired lady in her early thirties, who was holding the reins of a chestnut pony. 'Stardust will have her work cut out, won't you, girl?'

The mare nodded its head as if in agreement.

'Hello, Miss Cygnus. We've another heavy basket to add to the cart. Sorry,' said Alba.

'Now, now, Alba. You must call me Giena when not in class.'

'Sorry, Miss Cyg... I mean Giena,' said Alba, feeling herself redden.

Giena Cygnus was the other teacher in the school and one of her mother's dearest friends. Alba had great admiration for this woman; Miss Cygnus was one of the most intelligent and resourceful adults she had encountered. She had a curved spine and walked with difficulty using a stick, and she relied on her pony and cart to travel around the village. She always wore a grey felt trilby with a wide leather headband in which she carried every useful thing: a penknife, pencil, money, whatever she needed for that day. Today, Alba saw she had a cheese knife and a small metal flint to use to light her lamp for the way home that evening, wedged in the hatband.

'Better go now, or I'll be late,' said Shelia, walking towards a building upon which a sign was mounted saying 'Ingleset Playhouse Theatre', but which was also used as a courthouse if necessary, although Alba could not recall it being used as such, apart from this annual reenactment. It stood on the same site as the wooden original, but was now made of local limestone.

The first courthouse had burned to the ground ten years after the witch's trial. Local gossip, retold over the century, reckoned that the fire was deliberately set by Silas Morte, as an act of revenge against the village. This was never proven, although he had flown the village afterwards.

'It's another good turnout, isn't it, Miss Cyg... err... Giena?' said Alba, who had spotted some school friends waving to her, but decided to stay with her teacher.

'Yes, a little too big now,' said Giena.

'Do you think the story is true?' said Alba.

'Yes, I do.'

Alba shivered, although she wasn't quite sure why.

At three-thirty, the courthouse door was opened and a strange little fellow with a hooked nose and hobgoblin ears appeared dressed in the same attire as all previous court ushers.

'Let the proceedings begin,' he said in a flat voice and straight away withdrew to the court.

A halfhearted cheer went up in the crowd until Roger, the village baker, said, 'That Jasper Corvus could make a sunny weekend miserable. Come on, everyone. Let's get this show going.'

A roar of laughter went up and those assembled started to file into the theatre cum courthouse as best they could, filling the gallery and pressing against the sides. Those who could not fit in stood outside, craning to see and hear.

Alba stayed back and stroked Stardust's nose.

'Do you want to join in, Alba?' said Giena.

'I'll stay with you,' said Alba, looking towards the people entering the theatre.

'Don't be silly. I'm happy to stay. I don't care for crowds, and I'd better keep an eye on the food cart,' said Giena.

'Okay. If you're sure,' said Alba, who was already on her way.

She squeezed in at the rear of the room, just behind Ralph's best friends, Murgus Bellows and Davyd Baker. Murgus was making squelching noises with his armpit.

Alba was in time to hear a dramatic creaking of a door at the rear of the court. The crowd, including Murgus, fell silent. Through the doorframe appeared a robust man with a red, jovial face dressed in undersized judge's garments, gesturing with his arm and bowing low.

'Behold the good judge,' said Roger Baker, and everyone clapped.

Following 'the good judge' came the graceful figure of Judge Tara-Zed. She was dressed in a dark tunic. Today she had taken on the role of Rigela Kent. Behind her came Shelia, dressed in a white tunic impersonating Deneb, and Lydia Bellows, the blacksmith's wife, was dressed in red, as Altair. A few wolf whistles went up as they approached, until the ladies pointed their wands, which the smith had made out of some left-over iron, in a mock threat. Finally, to boos and hisses, came the sound of clanking iron chains being dragged across the floor as Sam Bellows appeared dressed in a grotesque ginger and grey wool wig and old rags.

'Ah-ha,' he cried overdramatically as he entered the room, bumping into the onlookers, who shrieked with delight.

'This gets worse every year,' said Murgus Bellows under his breath to Davyd Baker.

'I know, my good man. Parents have no limits to their capacity to humiliate those they are supposed to love,' said Davyd.

'Lucky old Ralph gets to explode the fireworks,' said Murgus.

'We hope,' said Davyd.

Both boys chuckled until Alba prodded them in their ribs and glared at them.

Sam had by now dragged himself into the dock and started to poke his tongue out and pull cross-eyed faces at 'the good judge' atop the dais. A troupe of acrobats had become a regular feature of the entertainment. Alba could still recall the first time she had seen them, as a young child. She had watched in amazement as they contorted their bodies around lengths of rope, and she still felt a thrill when they appeared this time as if from the ceiling itself, sliding like snakes across the beams. There were six acrobats, three women and three men. Alba had always wondered if they were married to each other. They looked no older than when she had first seen them. They were dressed in fitted white tunics, and pale blue trousers which clung to their legs; two of them also wore wings made of delicate pink and green lace; silk ribbons and soft feathers fluttered from their tunics.

Ropes, which had been coiled on the beams, were lowered and the lithe bodies bent and spun around them, rocking gently to and fro as they did so. Alba watched as their muscles contracted and extended, trying to remember the name of the muscle groups and what exercises would give them the maximum strength and suppleness. The audience gasped and clapped as the acrobats weaved and tumbled above their heads, as if casting a spell. Farmer Matthews, as the judge, interrupted the proceedings by looking at Sam Bellows.

'Aster, I find you guilty of the murder of the two fairies, Willis and Elle.'

There were cries of delight from the audience as the two winged acrobats arched backwards and lowered themselves to the floor, head first, their legs extended above them, as if part of the rope. The audience parted, and they alighted onto the floor like a breath landing on a leaf. With less than a shudder, they slipped between the audience, seeming to melt into the courtroom walls. The remaining acrobats now swung low over Sam Bellows, tugging at the ginger wig and wringing their hands in front of his face.

'Go away, you horrid creatures,' said Sam, flapping his hands around so the chains rattled and clanked.

'I find you guilty, you bad, bad witch, and sentence you to... the cave of doom,' shouted Farmer Matthews, nearly tipping over the top of the judge's desk.

'You can't do that. I'm innocent, you big meanie,' screeched Sam Bellows as he shook his fists at Farmer Matthews and leered at the audience.

The acrobats curled themselves back towards the beams and became almost invisible as they lay down along them. Farmer Matthews stood up.

'We shall proceed to White Scar – take the condemned away,' he said.

Alba could just see through a window which overlooked the village centre. She saw Giena Cygnus, now seated on her cart, smile to herself and tap the reins. Stardust ambled off.

A procession formed. Alba squeezed out of the room and saw Jasper Corvus trying to position himself as close as possible to his real boss, Tara-Zed. He looked at her, probably hoping to see a sign of disapproval at these vulgar proceedings, but Tara-Zed smiled and acted her part along with the rest of the villagers.

The throng squeezed through the narrow road out of the village and spread out across the open valley.

Although fashions had changed, most of the fabric was still produced in the local area and there was still a certain amount of austerity and practicality in what the villagers wore. They did not look too different to their predecessors, except on this day they wore smiles and any tears were of laughter.

The children sneaked up behind 'the witch', who acted as if he was unaware of their presence. Then, without warning, he would turn around, hands clawed above his head, chains rattling, shouting: 'Children. I love children. Especially with roast potatoes and dumplings.'

The youngsters ran off squealing until they regrouped to try it all again. And so Alba immersed herself in this jolly band of players and spectators. When they arrived at the point on the valley floor where the entertainment continued, the picnic was offloaded from the cart and laid out on bright picnic rugs. Whilst the food was being arranged, Alba organised the children into various races – egg and spoon, sack races, three-legged races. During the wheel-barrow race, Murgus let Davyd fall into a pile of harebit droppings, and they stuck to Davyd's jumper like pieces of wool. Alba thought she might never stop laughing. Once the picnic was ready, the villagers shared the fayre with each other and Stardust happily munched on the lush pasture, as sounds of laughter echoed across the valley.

After leaving the house, Ande and Ralph strode up the hillside, their athletic frames making short work of the distance to the large flat stone adjacent to the scar. The fireworks were set along the length of the abrasion, which was a jagged line about three metres long and a metre wide. Three separate wires controlled a third each of the fireworks. The wires led across the side of the hill past the stone slab and merged into one main fuse about fifteen metres away, controlled by Ralph and his father.

They checked that the wires were firmly fixed into the single fuse box and that they ran uninterrupted to the fireworks, which had been loaded with the charge.

'Are you satisfied the charges are all set?' said Ande.

'Definitely,' said Ralph, although his stomach was performing somersaults.

'Let's eat then,' said his dad.

Ralph realised he was now rather hungry and helped himself to a sausagey roll, a vegetable tart, cheese, fruit, and his favourite, the traditional plumpberry pie.

'Who's there?' said Ande jumping to his feet, wiping purple juice from his mouth with the back of his hand as he did so.

Ralph looked up, rising to his feet a second after his father, dropping a half-eaten slice of pie, cross that he hadn't heard any noise.

'It's only me. Nothing to be alarmed at, is there now?' said a thin, reedy voice.

'Arfur Sendal,' said Ande. 'Typical of you to be sneaking around.'

Arfur was the area news reporter whose character was reflected in his face, which had a permanent sneer, and although he was still quite young he had greying hair and stooped, thin shoulders. He was dressed in his usual attire of a crumpled brown cord jacket, mushroom-coloured trousers and a green shirt with red cravat with what looked like an egg stain down it.

'What do you want, Arfur?' said Ande.

'Nothing, nothing. Just checking you've got everything under control. You know. Don't want another disaster, do we now?'

'Arfur. This is a restricted area. Leave,' said Ande.

'Don't be like that, Mr. Milway. Just concerned for everyone's happiness. You know me.'

'Yes, unfortunately. You milked last year's situation for all it was worth, which wasn't much but that didn't stop you. You upset my family. Now leave, before I remove you.'

'No need to be like that. I was just doing my job. Reporting the facts, wasn't I now?'

'You're so skank,' said Ralph.

'See your boy is still spirited, Mr. Milway. Any chance of a photo, eh now?' said Arfur raising his camera, which had a concertina front opening and a hand-held flash light.

'Arfur, if you know what's good for you... Ahh!' said Ande, shielding his eyes as the camera flare momentarily blinded him and Ralph.

'Oh, that's a nice one for the family album. Or the front page, isn't it now?' said Arfur as he made his oily way down the hillside, before he could find out how much force Ande really was prepared to use on him.

'You all right, son?'

'Yeah. Fine. Why didn't you just smack him one, Dad?'

'Ralph. You know the answer. It would be wrong and solve nothing and just give that weasel something more to write about. And for once it would be true,' said Ande, ruffling his son's hair.

Ralph smiled.

'Come on, Dad. We've got work to do.'

Alba saw Arfur descend the hill. His movements reminded her of an oil slick she had once seen moving up a river, smooth and insidious.

Arfur joined the crowd at the base of the hill and she saw him cram mouthfuls of food into his mouth, though he had contributed nothing himself. He buzzed about like a bee, gathering gossip instead of pollen. He hovered around groups of people with notebook and pencil in his hands, until they noticed and swatted him away.

Alba knew the folklore said that the Sisters of Antares had gifted the flowers of the valley with musical abilities. The scientific explanation was that a natural phenomenon occurred each year through a combination of wind currents and rising ground temperature, which was thought to cause the various plants to flower out of their normal season and cause them to produce melodic harmonies. But Alba believed in a third cause, that of magic; but whatever the explanation, it was still a spectacular occurrence that had never failed to happen at the same time for the past century, and it thrilled her each year.

Alba had teamed up with Murgus in the mixed pairs' three-legged race. They would have won it had the miniature whoopee cushion, which Murgus had made from oiled fish skin, not deflated in his pocket. The raspberry noise caused him to collapse with laughter just before the finish line, and Alba had to untangle her ankle from his, whilst he rolled around with tears running down his face. Alba blamed herself for agreeing to be his partner.

After everyone had feasted and the children had run their sack races, and charged around with their eggs and spoons, they settled down. The sun started its slow descent behind the crowd, seeming to hesitate so it too could witness the wonder. A hush fell as one of nature's strangest phenomena presented itself for the one hundredth time.

A hint of a breeze rose up through tiny fissures from within the hill itself, like a gentle breath. Alba felt her whole body tingle. The supernatural flowers unfurled from the ground in an elegant display of exaggerated growth. She held her breath as the tall purple foxgloves gave out the first notes of the concert: a low, bassoon-like call as if mournfully announcing a portent of doom. They were followed by the chattering of wild flowers – celandines, harebells, cow parsley, primroses and blue bells, all tinkling and chiming like the excited crowd they represented. The judge was portrayed by a hairy stonecrop, a stubby flower like a miniature thistle, that made the grumping sound of a tuba, which made Alba chuckle. Three beautiful lady's slippers, delicate pink and white orchids, depicted the Sisters of Antares, letting out the soft purring sound of an oboe.

With every note a flower made, it gave off a little puff of pollen, so the scents of the plants blended into one intoxicating perfume, hanging in the air. Bees hovered, allowing the floral dust to cover their hairy backs, their heavy wings providing a zithering musical accompaniment to the blossoming concert, before heading back to their nests drunk with the sweet abundance engorging their cells. The exceptional scents enticed ladybirds, butterflies and their moth cousins to join in the scene and they fluttered silently amongst the crowd, caught in the warm currents, their colours shining iridescently in the waning light.

A single red rose symbolised the witch, a once beautiful creature who, as she unfurled, turned bitter and, using her ugly cruel thorns, became stained red with the blood of her victims. The rose began its solo with the single, pure note of a violin, which seemed to fill the whole valley with an almost painful clarity and innocence. 'How could such perfection go so irreversibly wrong?' the rose-violin seemed to ask. But, unnoticed at first, the tone became so screeching and unpleasant it was almost impossible to listen to and Alba and the audience spontaneously put their hands to their ears and winced as one. That jarring sound ended abruptly with the introduction of three arum lilies representing the wands, letting out bugle blasts as their power was released.

The villagers sat spellbound by the disquieting exquisiteness of the performance, except for Murgus and Davyd. They had spent the performance catapulting black crowberries at peoples' backs, sniggering as they watched people glance round and brush their shoulders. Whilst the lilies performed their fanfare, the crowd's eyes turned towards the top of White Scar Hill, which was now set against a backdrop of a purple, blue and granite sky, the scar silvery in the newly risen moonlight. A stunning firework display of silver, red and blue fireworks, symbolising the power of the three wands and the closing of the hillside, would end the show.

The sounds of the performing plants could be heard clearly by Ande and Ralph high on the hillside, the sound waves drifting up, borne by what felt like the delicate sweet breath of a sleeping baby, before floating away into the night sky.

'That's the lilies, Ralph. Light the fuses.'

With one deft action, Ralph struck the tinder and the spark caught first time on the single wire. The little flame danced its way along the ground before splitting into three separate lines which led to their payload.

'Three hundred grams of Blowamyte should do the trick this year, Dad,' said Ralph.

'Don't joke about this, son. It *was* a bit of a letdown last year.'

'I'm not joking, Dad. I put one hundred grams of Blowamyte in each batch, just like you wrote down.'

'Ralph. I wrote thirty grams. Ten grams in each.'

'Dad, I'm not joking. I *have* used three hundred grams. I rechecked the paper you wrote it on and added some more. I had only used thirty grams but the paper said three hundred.'

Ande looked at his son's face, which had drained of colour and looked ghastly in the twilight.

'When did you add the extra, son?' said Ande.

'This morning. Before I came home to meet you. I wanted to be doubly sure. Is something wrong, Dad?'

'I checked the powder this morning, just after you'd set the charges,' said Ande, 'so you've changed it since.'

'Dad, I'm sorry, I thought...'

The delicate firefly flame was now sparkling off to the three separate sets of fireworks.

'It's too far to stamp out the charges. We need to hide,' said Ande.

He turned his head quickly from side to side, his eyes searching for a place of shelter on this exposed hill. He settled on the large flat rock from which the judge had been dragged to his doom one hundred years earlier, which had a shelf, like a pouting lip, on its higher side. Bramble and gorse had grown from the recess but it would be worth braving that to preserve their lives.

'Quick, son, under the rock. That's enough Blowamyte to take the top of the hill off.'

Ralph felt Ande half drag, half push him to the upper edge of the flat stone. The overhanging lip would afford some protection against the inevitable blast. Amidst the panic, he felt like a fool again.

The audience, in the meantime, were watching the white scar. Alba could sense the anxiety that they should get a good show after last year's had fizzled out in a puff of smoke. Children fidgeted and all eyes gleamed.

The first rocket whistled into the inky sky, bursting in a riot of silver stars, which disappeared into the night before they could fall to earth. The crowd gasped and a small wave of applause rippled through them. Three further rockets sped upwards, exploding in yet more showers of silver. The faces of the audience wore smiles as their eyes reflected the glittery lights. Shelia squeezed Alba's hand, a smile across her face, but Alba, who had felt a swell of pride begin to rise within her, just then felt a stab of fear run through her heart.

As this happened, a thunderous roar rolled across the valley. The spectators' smiles waned as they looked at each other, confusion replacing the happiness. The rumble continued and the onlookers instinctively crouched down, huddling together and protecting their children. An explosion erupted from the hillside above them and every firework launched into the night sky at the same time, cracking, whizzing and sending a storm of silver, blue and red glitter across the night.

'Ouch, it hurts,' cried a child.

'Take cover as best you can,' came the authoritative voice of Tara-Zed, as the ground beneath the villagers shook and shards of white rock rained down upon them. Alba leapt up and threw a picnic rug over a family who were trying to protect their three youngsters. Food went flying, but at least it afforded a small barrier from the falling rocks. A rock hit her on the side of her head, and she crouched down with her mother, pulling another picnic rug over their heads.

Yelps of pain replaced the earlier cries of joy. The rumbling lasted a full minute, but the gravel storm lasted several more before it subsided with a final dusting of crushed limestone.

Once the calamitous noise had ceased and people were sure no more debris was to fall from the sky, they looked up, blinking eyes peering out from dust-covered faces. The once bright crowd now resembled a macabre group of ghosts. Surrounding them on the valley floor was a layer of grey powder and a smattering of small stones. The awful noise was replaced by an eerie silence, the flowers' supernatural voices quietened.

Alba was squeezed in a hug by her mother, who was brushing some of the debris off her daughter. They pushed the picnic rug, heavy with small rocks, away.

'Are you okay? That was a brave thing you did,' said Shelia, glancing to where the family were emerging from beneath their picnic rug, with no apparent injuries.

'I'm fine. What about Dad?'

Alba stifled a sob. She was not worried about Ralph. Over the years she had learnt to sense her twin's feelings. Sometimes she was sure she even heard his thoughts and this occasion was no exception; Alba *felt* that her brother was alive, if emotionally shaken.

Mother and daughter looked up at the hill, which was still obscured by smoke and dust. Clutching each other's hands they set off towards the hill, stumbling and grazing their hands and knees on debris, determined to reach Ande and Ralph.

Harlech Castle
The Welsh Lagoons
Late Evening, May 2150

Lady Anna's chin lolled from side to side across her chest as she dozed in her chair. From time to time her tongue slipped between her lips to moisten the parched skin. In her mind she saw a child aged about four or five years old. His freckled face and flopping ginger hair came in and out of focus, as he rocked back and forth on a swing in a rose-filled garden, his mouth a wide smile of missing teeth. A young woman with auburn hair and a slender figure pushed the swing...

'Higher, Mummy, higher,' said the child, and chuckled as the woman flexed her arms and leant forward. They were both dressed in white T-shirts and dark blue shorts. The child's sandaled feet pushed in and out of Lady Anna's mind.

The child's chuckles turned into a croak, and then a caw, and Lady Anna jerked her head as she awoke to find a crow scratching its claws on a window ledge and tilting its head towards her. She inhaled and pushed a lock of grey hair, tinged with an occasional strand of auburn, behind her ear.

'Scavard, my dear crow. Come close and tell me all,' said Lady Anna, patting the right arm of her chair.

The bird extended its wings and, before taking off, grasped a small item, which had been lying on the window ledge, between its claws. He flapped across the short space to Lady Anna and dropped a mushroom in her lap, before settling on the arm of the chair.

'Well done, Scavard,' said Lady Anna as she picked up the mushroom, its thin stem drooping beneath the weight of its dome caplet, and held it between her paper-like fingers. 'You must have hunted hard for this.'

Lady Anna placed the mushroom on her tongue and shut her mouth. Her cheeks puckered as she drew on the fungus's nourishment. After a few moments she gasped, and silver dust puffed from her mouth. The rheumy veins in the whites of her eyes flowed like silver river tributaries on a map. Her hands tingled and she smiled as she saw silver coursing beneath her slender fingertips as if polish were being painted on the underside of her nails. After a few minutes, the silver subsided and she sat back in her chair.

Placing her right hand on her heart, she felt it beating as strong as a drum. She brought her fingers to her mouth, touched her lips and smiled a pain-free smile, her lips now plump and moist.

'This mushroom was from a ring once touched by a fairy,' she said to the crow, 'but now you have plucked it, the magic is lost from the ring forever. Are there many more sites for you to search, dear Scavard?'

The crow clicked its tongue, making sounds like Morse code. It danced from side to side as it communicated with Lady Anna, whose brow was furrowed with concentration. When the bird was silent and still, Lady Anna placed her now smooth hands together and rested her chin on her fingertips.

'So that stupid boy has opened the cave. That is good news, Scavard. The third wand will now be found and reunited with its sister wands, and then my child will unite them and there will be no more need for fairy ring mushrooms. All of us will be restored and will rule this land and the whole world if we like.'

She flung her head back and laughed, but the laughter turned into the hoarse cough of an old woman and Lady Anna fell still.

'You deserve a treat, don't you?'

The crow cawed.

Next to the urn containing Anthony's ashes was an old-fashioned dish shaped like a large slice of cheddar, decorated with a rustic scene in antique green, resting on a matching plate. Lady Anna placed her left hand on the handle of the dish. Scavard's eyes grew rounder and he strained his neck forwards. Lady Anna lifted the lid a fraction. A tiny pink nose and a few twitching whiskers appeared beneath the crack. Scavard stretched his wings. Lady Anna lifted the lid and a mouse froze for a second on the plate, long enough for Scavard to lunge and grab the rodent in his claws. The mouse was crushed before it had time to draw a breath, and Scavard flapped to the window ledge where it devoured the creature, bones, tail and all.

Lady Anna clicked her tongue against the back of her teeth. Scavard clicked a reply and flew from the window, leaving Lady Anna to return to the dream of swings and children in the flower-filled garden.

CHAPTER 6

INGLESET: ONE HUNDRED YEARS EARLIER, 2050

THE EVENING OF THE TRIAL

'Mercy me!' cried Hetty, her voice cutting the silence like scissors through fabric.

Rigela listened to the sniffs and sobs bobbing around the thick air as women hid their faces in their hands and men blinked back tears. Only the children who had been allowed to stay stood gawping, eyes shining, deeply impressed by what they had just witnessed. The sun had now set, and torches and lanterns were lit, their orange and yellow flicker turning the villagers' faces into grotesque masques.

'Get your pick-axe, Michael Stonecutter,' she heard Lionel the butcher say.

'We must start digging,' said Bill the innkeeper.

'Michael, please bring your torch over here,' said Rigela. She needed to take charge.

She walked to the end of the flat stone from where the judge had been dragged moments before. Michael stood next to her and together they surveyed the newly formed scar.

Rigela jumped off the ledge and landed on the scar. She took the torch from Michael as he followed her.

'Be careful,' screeched Hetty, hands held to her mouth.

Rigela and Michael bent down and ran their fingers across the rock. The eyes of the crowd were upon them, the only sound the crackling of the torches.

After drawing her wand from its sheath, Rigela pointed it at the stone. With a flick of her wrist a line of lightning emerged from the wand tip. She felt a power surge through her body. Holding the wand like a soldering iron, its sparks shooting up like a fountain, she ran it along the scar. A few sparks landed on her sleeve and smouldered. Altair clambered down and joined her, adding a line of fire from her wand. After a minute they stopped and replaced the wands into their golden holsters, exchanging worried glances with Michael. From their elevated position they turned to the people.

'The power of the three wands has sealed this hole and only their joint power can unseal it,' said Rigela.

'There must be another way in,' said Lionel.

'The village council and the judge himself chose this spot as a prison. Once inside, the witch would never be able to climb out and there are no other known exits,' said Michael.

'Can't you dig a tunnel through the hillside? We'll all help,' said Lionel, voicing the thoughts of the villagers.

'Before the war, yes. But not with the tools now. The limestone here is good quality. I've tried to excavate several times. I can show you the bent pick-axe heads, if you like. And I've nearly broken my arms on more than one occasion. I told the judge all this when he was deciding what punishment to give out,' said Michael.

'But what about the judge? We can't just leave the poor man to rot,' said Hetty.

'The power of the remaining two wands was cut off when the cave was sealed. There was nothing to break his descent. The cave entrance is deep. The fall would have killed them both,' said Rigela.

A loud sniff emerged from a gorse bush. Silas Morte sat with his nose immersed in a large white handkerchief. His body seemed to have withdrawn into itself so he resembled an orphaned fledgling.

By now, Hetty had fallen to her knees and was rocking back and forth ringing her hands together, until Bill the innkeeper pulled her to himself as he had done earlier. Rigela knew that Hetty was a kind woman but would also be quite relishing the dramatic role she had taken upon herself.

'We shall return to the village and appoint a new judge who will oversee the proceedings. We can do nothing more tonight,' said Rigela, so firmly that no one dared to contradict her.

The villagers nodded their heads in reluctant agreement, knowing that Rigela's words were wise, even though they could barely believe that they were helpless in the face of events. Rigela, Altair and Deneb watched as the crowd, with heads hanging low in despair, headed down the slope towards Ingleset. Their pace quickened as a light drizzle rolled in over the hills. The earlier jubilant atmosphere had been replaced by one of bewilderment, with a shining white scar overlooking the village as a reminder of the disastrous events of that evening. The Sisters of Antares strode back to Ingleset overtaking the crowd, their long hair covering their faces as they walked with heads bowed in deep contemplation.

Hetty Seamstress had gathered her wits and run down the hillside as fast as her round frame would take her, hitching her long skirts and apron almost to her waist with one hand, her chubby legs, in their woolen tights, scurrying along in a blur. In her other hand she held a lantern, which could be seen bobbing towards the home of her good friends, Marsha and Stalwart.

They were sitting in their humble, cosy cottage having supper with the bishop's wife. Hetty regaled them with the events of the last few hours.

'I can't believe Deneb lost her wand. She must feel like she's lost a limb,' said Marsha, through a fresh bout of tears shed for the poor judge.

'That poor man. He was such a comfort to me when Roland was murd... died. It's good in a way that he never married. There's no widow left behind,' said Beryl, sniffing.

'We must all go to the hall at once. They're going to appoint a new judge whilst the Sisters are here. Are you all up to it?' said Hetty, not even trying to veil the excitement she felt.

Stalwart looked at Marsha and Beryl.

'I'll go. You stay here and rest,' he said.

The two women exchanged glances.

'We'll come too. There will be no peace until this is resolved,' said Marsha, standing carefully, one hand pressing against her back, the other leaning weightily on the arm of the chair.

The village hall was heaving. Villagers huddled in groups, chatted in hushed tones. The baker and publican had rustled up more refreshments, although they were charging for their pies and ale this time round.

Michael Stonecutter stood on the stage at the front of the hall. Rigela was positioned on his left and Altair and Deneb on his right. Silas Morte fluttered about, tipping his head forwards and back as he strutted around, looking more like a cross crow than ever. Rigela stepped forwards and raised her hands to hush the chattering crowd.

'We are all tired and upset, so I shall keep this brief. Who are the nominees for the position of judge?' she said, looking around the faces as she spoke.

'I propose Stalwart Woodkeeper. He is known for his honesty and hard work and there are few others who understand this area better,' said Michael.

'Well, let's not be too hasty,' said Silas. 'After all, Stalwart is recovering from a mighty shock. Is there someone more experienced in such matters? Who understands the gravitas of the law perhaps? Someone such as,' he looked towards the floor, his greasy black fringe flopping over his eyes, 'myself.'

There was a moment of silence before laughter rippled around the hall.

'Oh please, Silas. We've had enough catastrophes for one day. Electing you as judge would be the icing on the cake,' said Hetty, to a background of agreement.

'Well, I… I only meant that, well what I mean is…' stumbled Silas, pushing his beak-like nose forwards, and his forelock out of his face.

'Thank you for your kind offer in the hour of need, Mr. Morte,' said Rigela.

She stepped forwards and surveyed the audience, with serious eyes. The laughter and dismissive comments died away and there was silence once more in the hall.

'Will anyone propose Silas Morte?' asked Rigela.

The crowd fidgeted and stared between the floor and the roof rafters. A few of the villagers picked dust off their sleeves, but no one spoke.

'Very well. Will anyone second Michael Stonecutter's proposal of Stalwart Woodkeeper?'

Apart from those on the stage, everyone in the hall raised their hands.

'Well, Stalwart Woodkeeper, are you willing to accept the position of village judge?' continued Rigela.

All eyes searched out Stalwart who was standing at the back of the hall, with Marsha by his side. He gazed into his wife's eyes. She smiled and squeezed his hand.

Looking up, Stalwart said, 'Yes, I accept.'

There was a dignified applause. A few men shook his hand and patted his back and several women kissed Marsha.

'Very well. The Sisters and I approve your appointment. We shall register you upon our return to Skipton,' said Rigela.

'Well, really. You are a ridiculous bunch. What expertise does this man have in the law? I can't work under such conditions. You'll have to find a new usher. I resign,' said Silas and, flapping his black coat tails, he seemed to fly through the hall door.

'He'll calm down. He's more upset about his master than he's letting on,' said Hetty, flattening her lips in a knowing look and folding her arms across her chest.

Stalwart had by now made his way through the crowd and stepped on to the stage.

'My first task will be to attempt a rescue.'

There were a few cheers.

'However, I believe, this will prove futile. Nevertheless, the judge was respected in this village and it is the least we can do for him. It has been a traumatic day. Please go home to your beds and anyone wishing to form a rescue party can meet here at first light with suitable equipment.'

The village people were tired and soon the hall was empty except for the Sisters, Marsha and Stalwart.

The Sisters' horses were waiting outside, each one matching the colour of its riders' hair. They were magnificent beasts and their livery was polished and jewel-encrusted. They snorted and stamped the ground, their hooves sliding on the cobbles, which were now damp from the drizzle. Three burly villagers were holding the reins, their knuckles white as the horses pranced on the spot, keen to be on their way. The pageboy from the trial was waiting by a wooden bench just by the doorway, with three pairs of brown leather boots in a row beside him. The women sat on the benches and pulled off their slippers, each tugging on a pair of boots. The boy collected the discarded footwear and ran and placed each pair in the horses' saddlebags. Deneb was still tugging at her boots.

'Blast! I've snagged a nail,' she said.

Rigela rolled her eyes.

'Please stay the night in the village. It may not be safe to travel and the rain looks set to stay a while,' said Stalwart.

'We can make room for you. It won't be grand but it will be comfortable,' said Marsha.

'Thank you for your kind offer,' Rigela said, 'but my sisters and I have much to do this night. We still have two wands, which will give us more than enough power to ward off any trouble.' Her dark eyes stared into the faces of this good couple.

'May God and Goddess be with you and your offspring,' said Rigela.

Marsha's stomach suddenly rippled and she had to lean on her husband.

'The baby still hasn't settled after the earlier events,' said Marsha, with a forced smile as she tried to mask her discomfort.

'We'll be back the day after tomorrow,' said Rigela, a shadow of concern passing across her face.

Altair and Deneb were already in their saddles and Rigela mounted her ebony stallion with grace. The three horses reared before bounding off, the clatter of their hooves reverberating around the village centre long after those fantastic ladies had disappeared into the night.

CHAPTER 7

SKIPTON CASTLE, MAY 2050
THE DAY AFTER THE TRIAL

The ladies were deeply revered in the region. As well as advising over judicial matters they oversaw many good works and the province, whilst not wealthy, was self-sufficient and the inhabitants healthy and happy.

The case in Ingleset had sent shockwaves throughout the region and beyond, and as the women galloped through the night they knew that when news of the lost wand spread, it would cause disquiet across the whole of Britain.

'Watch out, Rigela,' cried Altair, her words almost lost in the rain, which was now driving hard.

A pack of foolfs was skulking along the path, another example of an endangered species' bid for survival. Wolves that had escaped from a zoo and foxes had interbred, producing a creature the size of a wolf but with the colour and bushy tail of a fox. They menaced sheep and shepherds had to remain on a constant lookout. Their only advantage was they scavenged vermin and kept the rat population at bay. They were vicious and this pack had their teeth bared and saliva flicking from hungry, murderous mouths, but a streak of silver from Rigela's wand sent them howling into the night.

Dawn was breaking when the horses, panting and covered in

white sweat, despite the rain, dashed through the dour gatehouse of Skipton Castle. The horses skidded to a halt on the stone slabs of the yard. Straight away, three pageboys in livery of purple waistcoats and caps appeared and took the reins as the ladies dismounted. Without stopping, the three women strode up the stone steps, across the Tudor courtyard with its towering tree, and through the arched doorway of a round tower. As they ascended a stone spiral staircase, their splendid gowns and long hair flowed behind them, despite being sodden with rain. On the second and highest floor, Rigela, who had led all the way from Ingleset, opened an imposing oak door and the women were welcomed into a circular room by a gently flickering fire in a large stone hearth. The high, flat ceiling was covered with heraldic symbols. Three square windows, with heavy magenta drapes framing them, were set at equal distance around the room. Two of the windows looked out as far as could be seen across the region of Skipton. The third overlooked the courtyard.

The floor was of oak panels but in the centre lay a silk oriental rug, matching the colours of the other furnishings, upon which was placed a low table. Goblets and jugs of water and wine were set upon the table, together with platters of fruits, nuts and cheeses. Leather-bound books sat on oak shelves and three writing desks stood beneath each of the great windows. Cream parchment and quill pens made of the largest white plumes imaginable sat in the ink wells. On the wall opposite the door, and between two of the windows, hung a red damask curtain, suspended from the ceiling by a metal pole, which had the effect of truncating a section of the room. Light was provided by a chandelier of gold descending from the rafters, laden with steadily burning candles. On three oak carved hooks hung simple tunics of red, white and black. The Sisters threw their damp riding cloaks on to an ornate gold coat stand.

'My dress is ruined,' said Deneb, examining her once beautiful gown, now splashed with mud and blood, 'and as for that cat, well if I ever meet it again I'll…' She stepped out of her ceremonial garb and slipped into the clean dry white tunic. There was a soft knock at the door and one of the pageboys from the courtyard entered carrying three pairs of slippers. He placed them by the coat stand.

'If I'd known it was going to be such a long walk up that hill I'd never have worn that dress. And as for my shoes. Useless.'

She held up a once white pair of pearl-studded slippers, now grass-stained, and threw them into a floral-patterned waste bin, before sitting down with a soft thud on the deep crimson cushions of one of three sofas arranged around the low table. Altair poured each of them a goblet of water, which they gulped down noisily. She soaked a pristine cloth in a bowl of water and cleaned the wounds on Deneb's arm before taking a delicate purple glass bottle from a shelf and dabbing a sweet-smelling tincture on the cuts.

'How could she have taken the wand so easily?' said Altair. 'Deneb, you are such a skilled fighter.'

'We knew she had the gift to become one of us,' said Deneb.

'But how did she get the power to use it?' asked Altair.

'Sisters, we deal in logic. I have trained her since she was a baby. She changed. She was exceptional and I have no doubt that she would have become stronger than the three of us put together. I must have underestimated just how talented she was,' said Rigela.

Deneb stared into her goblet as if the answer to her problems lay there. Eventually, with desolation in her eyes, she looked into the concerned faces of her two sisters, who also now wore fresh, dry tunics.

'Our power has been compromised. I am sorry. It is my fault,' said Deneb, rubbing the wound on her arm. 'I can get another dress but not another wand.'

'It is true. Two wands are not as effective, but no matter. Perhaps it is timely. People are putting more hope in these wands than in themselves and the law. They are the remnant of a dark time. It is time to move on,' said Rigela as she refilled the goblets, this time with red wine.

'... although it was a stunning dress.'

'Sister Rigela. I disagree. We must use the ancient law revealed when the meteor landed, to foresee the future. How can we know that Aster has not used strange magic, different to our own? She was adopted by us after she was orphaned by the Global War. We sent her to live in Ingleset. We all knew she would replace one of us, even you, Rigela, the greatest one. I never suspected she was capable of the tiniest lie, let alone such treachery. No, we must fight strange magic with wisdom magic,' said Altair, slamming her goblet down on to the table top, wine slopping over the rim and splashing across Deneb's white tunic.

'Oh! This is a vintage Stella design. Ruined,' said Deneb.

'No, Sisters. There is to be no magic of any kind. These strange days are coming to an end. We must face whatever occurs with our human intellect. I say no.'

Rigela's face flushed as she spoke.

'I agree with Altair. We must consult with the Meteor Table. You cannot refuse two of us,' said Deneb, fixing her blue eyes on Rigela's dark face.

'Very well, but it will not help us,' said Rigela, rising and striding to the damask curtain, which she pushed aside with one easy movement.

In front of her was a circular table, the size of a barrel, but with concave sides. The base was made of a cold, grey metal, tougher than iron. The table top was flat and formed from crystal-clear diamond. This table was made from the same meteor from which were forged the three Wands of Antares.

Around the table's edge were six oval-shaped grooves. The Sisters gathered round and placed the palms of their hands in those settings. Leaning forwards, with their heads nearly touching, they peered into the mirrored surface. At first all that could be seen were their own reflections but slowly, as their gazes intensified, the surface became darker and somehow deeper. A few moments more and bright lights started to twinkle and flash and the reflected images of the Sisters were now absorbed by an infinite blackness.

A light flared out from the table top, filling the chamber with a white glare, caused by a dying star turning supernova at that very moment in a distant galaxy. The women remained steadfast, their eyes now veiled by a fine mist to protect them from the radio-active images. Before them, entire solar systems, black holes and quasars spun in and out of view. Suns and moons swirled past in this weird prism and still they stood, gazing into the void, unmoving, unspeaking, their long hair falling around their faces. This table was a giant receptor that received information from all the cosmos its parent meteor had travelled through, since time itself began, before its journey was completed by its impact with Earth.

As the myriad universes revealed themselves to the Sisters, a scratching could be heard inside the room. The deeper the secrets the Meteor Table revealed, the louder and more urgent the etching became. The feathers of the quills were moving across the parchments, quivering and swishing as invisible hands formed unknown symbols. A draught brushed delicately across the Sisters' faces, stirring their hair. Still the Sisters continued to stare deeper and deeper into the crystal mirror, to the end of every universe and beyond.

After half an hour had passed, Deneb suddenly threw back her head, her white hair unfurling and settling on her back once more. She pulled her hands away from the table top and staggered, blinking, to one of the sofas.

As strangely as they had started, the quills finished their writings, each giving a tap as they placed a final full stop on their parchments. Without a whisper of sound, they returned to their ink pots and resumed their inanimate state. Once again, Rigela stood up to her full height, walked to the table and refilled Deneb's goblet with wine. Altair came and sat down. Rigela pushed Altair's auburn locks from her face. She had been perspiring and Rigela poured her a drink, too. Rigela then refreshed herself and lay down on a sofa, her dark skin tinged with a grey pallor. The eyelids of the three Sisters became heavy and Deneb's bruised arm flopped down, her fingers trailing on the rug, as she, along with her sisters, fell into a deep sleep.

It was early afternoon when the Sisters awoke. They had all slept fitfully, for they had seen things that had first amazed, then confused and finally distressed them to the point where they thought their hearts would break.

Each retired to their private apartments to wash and change, and then at sunset, a full day after Aster had disturbed their world so resoundingly, they met once more in the antechamber to examine the writings on the parchment, echoes from worlds beyond their own.

The three women's eyes were puffy and bloodshot and their foreheads furrowed, evidence of the strain the previous day's events had placed on them, as they met again in the circular room.

Each one went to a desk and picked up several pieces of parchment on which the quills had performed their ghostly dance. The writing was in a different hand from each of the desks. The languages were strange and not spoken anywhere in the realm of humankind.

The three women placed their parchments on the low table in the centre of the room.

'Altair, fetch the meteor dust, please,' said Rigela.

Altair strode over to her desk and removed a drawer, which let out an ancient groan. She withdrew a brown leather pouch, bound shut by a fine gold cord, which she handed to Rigela. Meanwhile, Deneb had set out the parchments across the table and was weighting down their corners with purple stones taken from a shelf, as if to prevent a celestial wind from blowing them away. In the centre of the table was a long blank sheet of parchment, with a piece of doweling attached horizontally at each end.

Rigela took the leather purse and untied it carefully, handing the cord to Altair. She tilted the pouch until a small portion of the contents spilled out across the parchments. Fine silver particles landed with a patter as if several field mice were scampering across the table. These silver filings were left over when the Meteor Table was carved by the hands reborn from folklore, after the impact of the Great Meteor. Those creatures had now faded into myth as humanity edged away from the brink of extinction, but the Sisters never forgot their influence and missed their friendship.

When there was a good number of filaments on the paper, Rigela handed the pouch back to Altair, who resealed it with care before returning it to the drawer, which shut with the same plaintive groan with which it had opened.

Leaning slightly forwards, Rigela slowly moved the palm of her right hand across the silver sand and as she did so the characters of the strange languages began to change shape, expanding and shrinking, glowing and fading and moving about as if they would dance right off the page. Without hurry, the unworldly symbols changed form to what looked like Chinese, then Arabic and finally English. Letters could be seen forming into words until they settled on the page, the ink streaked with silver, so the parchments were now filled with legible writing. The empty parchment remained unmoved in the centre of them all.

Placing her index finger under the first word of the corner parchment, Rigela started to read, moving her hand swiftly across the pages. As she did so, each word flowed right off the page and printed itself on to the plain sheet, each word adjusting its size as the next word landed. The three ladies seemed oblivious to this supernatural phenomena and Rigela continued reading without hesitation. As soon as she uttered the final word from the last page the silver dust dissolved into the air and the ink faded to an obsidian hue.

Rigela stood up and the women frowned.

'I am sorry, Rigela. I should not have asked that we look into the Table,' said Altair, her voice hushed.

'I insisted too, and Rigela was correct. It has served no purpose. There is no comfort from it, only disquiet,' said Deneb, leaning across and taking Rigela's elegant hand in her own. 'Please forgive us.'

Rigela looked at her beloved friends, large tears in her eyes.

'There is nothing to forgive. You were the brave ones. It was the right thing to do.'

'We should have let them be, in the cave. They would have died naturally, may have already been dead, but now we have incited the Meteor Table's intervention they have to *exist* for one hundred years,' said Deneb, staring at the single sheet of parchment.

'My sisters, what is done is done. And there is hope. We must ensure that our actions help the kindred ones long after we are gone. Now we have work to do,' responded Rigela, rising and briskly walking over to her desk. 'First we must secure this text. Then we must give up our wands,' she searched Altair's face for a reaction 'and hide them separately in a location known only to the wand's holder and our chosen successors. Their hiding places must never be traced. This will prevent any single entity gaining the three wands' power and Aster may be defeated.'

'What about the parchment?' asked Deneb.

'That must be sealed and carried by a Sister. It must not be opened until… well the holder will know when that time is. I shall write to the High Council and tell them of our actions,' said Rigela.

Altair and Deneb nodded in agreement. Rigela summoned a pageboy and instructed that their horses be made ready for first light the following morning. At sunrise, all three went galloping back to Ingleset, the early rays tinting their black cloaks with yellow hues, but providing no warmth to the three ladies.

CHAPTER 8

YORK, MAY 2050

FIVE DAYS AFTER THE TRIAL

Mr. Hunter stood in his chamber, a former honeymoon suite in a hotel overlooking Clifford's Tower. He read and re-read Rigela's missive, a frown on his face. He was dismayed that the judge had fallen to a certain death, but relieved that whatever plan Aster had hatched to secure all three wands had failed, and with luck she had fallen to her death. He winced as he held this thought. The Sisters of Antares had not been specific about their plans for the remaining wands. He did not blame them. There were members of the High Council that even he didn't trust. *If only Sir Wesley were still alive, instead of lying cold in his coffin,* thought Mr. Hunter. *At least the Sisters are safe. I should visit them soon.*

He sat in an armchair, shut his eyes and pinched the bridge of his nose with his thumb and forefinger. He was tired of living, but for the sake of the Sisters he must continue. A smile crossed his face as he recalled the first time he had met them.

They had been barely teenagers, orphans of the tribulations. At that time the earth had given up many of its secrets. Creatures of myths and legends had awoken, coming to aid mankind in their plight. The survivors, who had witnessed heartbreaking events, were too shell-shocked to query the appearance of fairies and hobgoblins, giants and mermaids. It was the fairies who had organised the initial settlements. They had brought the girls to Skipton Castle, telling the newly formed High Council that these teenagers possessed special powers and were to be keepers of three wands formed from Moonstone quarried from the Great Meteor. One other child was brought too, Aster, a tiny baby. She was said to be the most special. Rigela, Altair and Deneb had loved Aster. Mr. Hunter recalled visiting the castle over the years, the stone walls and staircases ringing with laughter as the girls played hide-and-seek, chase and hop-scotch with each other, each taking it in turn to tell Aster a bedtime story. It had been Aster who had given him hope and a reason to live. He had failed his own daughter but would not let Aster down. Even though he had been scared of horses before the war, he had taught her to ride her first pony when she was four. Aster had insisted on calling the pony Princess Aurora, which she pronounced with a lisp because her front teeth were missing. He remembered how proud he was when she left the castle to take up the teaching position in Ingleset. Her letters to him were filled with details of the children she taught, the kind neighbours and then of Coran. She had asked Mr. Hunter to walk her down the aisle on her wedding day. His face screwed up, and he crumpled Rigela's letter in his fist, as he remembered that those days were gone.

CHAPTER 9

INGLESET, MAY 2050

SIX DAYS AFTER THE TRIAL

Arriving just after midday, Rigela, Altair and Deneb found the village centre deserted. The sun was now at its zenith and the Sisters discarded their travelling cloaks, revealing long purple tunics and the delicate filigree belts displayed around their hips, Deneb's devoid of its wand. They walked to the court room but there was nobody to be found. Trying the inn, they found it too was deserted. Then they heard a bell tolling from the church tower.

Striding across the cobblestones, they found the church of AFAN full of villagers on their knees in the little wooden pews, or standing at the sides with heads bowed. The gathering, for it was hardly a formal service, was presided over by the new bishop, Bishop Brahmin. He looked up as the Sisters entered and gave them a sad smile of recognition, raising his hand slowly in bleak salutation. The villagers watched in silence as the bishop walked towards the Sisters. He was a short, round Indian gentleman of about sixty years of age, with greying hair and a kindly face.

'My dear ladies. You arrive at a sad time, as if that were even more possible for this already blighted village,' he said with a gentle voice. 'Marsha has given birth to twins but she is not expected to last more than a few hours.' Rigela felt her stomach lurch.

'We must go there now,' she said.

'But there's nothing can be done for her unless,' Bishop Brahmin was now addressing the ladies' backs as they swirled around and walked out of the church, 'you are the answer to our prayers.'

The Sisters rode to Stalwart and Marsha's house on the edge of the wood. As they dismounted, Hetty came out to greet them.

'Oh, mistresses. It is awful. Two of the bonniest babies you could ever wish for but their poor mother, well she is not an age to bear twins and, what with the grief of losing Coran and the beloved judge falling to his doom, well, she is leaving us.'

She started to sob into her apron. Rigela patted Hetty's shoulders, but felt helpless in the face of the grief.

The women entered the humble cottage, which was eerily quiet. The bedroom was to the rear, leading from the spotlessly clean kitchen, where a fire in the hearth was keeping a pot of water bubbling. They entered the chamber without speaking. Stalwart was sitting on the edge of a large bed covered by a pretty patchwork quilt, holding the frail hand of his wife between his two great hands, his eyes shut. When Rigela had last seen Marsha, only a few days before, she had looked weary but full of health and her hair had been glossy. Now she lay limp in her bed, her life ebbing away. Deneb let out a gasp and Stalwart looked up, his eyes swollen and expressionless.

'We must do something,' muttered Deneb to her companions.

'No more magic,' said Rigela, under her breath.

'We are putting the wands away, Sister. One more turn *for the good* will not matter,' hissed Altair, her eyes open wide.

Rigela surveyed the scene.

'Very well and then the wands are gone forever,' she murmured.

'Stalwart, if you trust us, will you please let us be with Marsha in your absence?' asked Rigela.

'But I don't want to leave her. She only has a few more breaths to take.'

Stalwart's voice trailed off as he saw Rigela and Altair draw the wands from their holders. He stood up slowly and kissed his wife on her lips, causing her eye lids to flutter, but there was no other movement. A baby's cry suddenly erupted, hungry and urgent.

'I think Hetty may like some help, Stalwart,' said Altair kindly. 'We shan't be long,' she added, shutting the door behind him.

Five minutes later, when Altair beckoned Stalwart into the room, he came in carrying a black-haired baby boy in one arm and a blond-haired, button-nosed baby girl in the other. He nearly dropped them, for he found Marsha sitting up in bed, a delicate pink hue on her cheeks and a warm smile on her lips, which were changing in colour from the deathly blue to a fulsome red with every passing second. Hetty followed Stalwart.

'Mercy me!' she cried, clasping her hands to her cheeks. 'It surely is a miracle. Praise be! Oh bless you all!'

'Oh the babies are so sweet,' said Deneb, reaching for the little girl.

As she cooed, the infant expelled her first feed over the front of Deneb's tunic, leaving a mealy line running from shoulder to ankle.

'Oh!' said Deneb, handing the baby back to Stalwart, whilst Altair and Rigela stifled grins.

'Stalwart, we haven't much time. We must talk with you and Bishop Brahmin. Can you come with us?' said Rigela.

Stalwart looked at his wife, who nodded her head. He handed his baby boy to Hetty, who was flustering around, and the little girl to his wife.

'Yes, I'll come. And thank you. I'll go on ahead and let everyone know,' Stalwart said.

'Stalwart?' said Rigela.

'Yes? We are both in your debt. Name what you will and we shall do it.'

'There are no thanks to be given. The one thing my sisters and I ask is that you tell no one of what has passed. It is sufficient to say that prayers were answered, which indeed they have been, and that Marsha was on her way to recovery when we got here.'

'But why, Rigela? You should all be honoured.'

'That is how it shall be, Stalwart. People must have faith in the unseen, not the seen. That is all. Your thanks is to do as we ask.'

Stalwart kissed his wife and, though usually known for his reserve and good sense, ran to the church, bursting in through the doors.

'Marsha is going to be all right. She rallied miraculously. I suspect Hetty's broth had something to do with it.'

Everyone laughed at this and then raised their arms in thanks and clapped each other on the back, shook hands and hugged. The Sisters slipped in to the church and whispered to Bishop Brahmin, and together with Stalwart, who extracted himself from his relieved neighbours, the five of them left the church through the rear door.

Nobody took any notice of the flock of crows which had made their nests high up in the trees and roof tops, and which started up an almighty cawing when the officials left the church.

After that meeting, the Sisters parted, Rigela and Altair riding home alone via their own secret routes and when they met again at Skipton Castle, the sheaths which once held their wands were empty.

CHAPTER 10

INGLESET, 2150

THE EVENING OF THE CONCERT

It was approaching nine o'clock by the time the villagers assembled in the hall, which was packed to its capacity of four hundred people. The building was on the same site as the original, in the village centre, but was now built of the local limestone, with a slate-tiled roof, and was much larger. Electric lights, powered by two perpetually spinning wind turbines situated on the roof, hung from the rafters.

Ralph could feel the dampness jostling for space with the smell of fresh sperryberry cakes, prepared by the baker for the party which was usually held at the end of the concert of singing flowers. Steaming mulled wine, provided by the innkeeper, pushed those scents aside before being replaced by the musk of leather and earth, which in turn were overpowered by the strongest odour of them all, the acrid smell of Blowamyte. Ralph would usually have inhaled deeply and felt a sense of satisfaction fill him from his head to toes. Since last year he was allowed a glass of mulled wine, and he and his friends had planned to try to get drunk, but now the smells hung over the hall like a heavy canopy.

At the front of the hall was a large stage on which were seated the six village council members. Ande Milway was amongst them, positioned at the side next to Giena Cygnus. Tara-Zed sat, leaning forwards, murmuring to Ande and Giena, who sat tight-jawed, occasionally glancing at each other, but avoiding eye contact with anyone else.

Tara-Zed's furtiveness was noticed by the gathering crowd and there was an uneasy quiet. She had been appointed to the village only a few months before, but she had already gained the respect and trust of the population. She was unafraid to state her opinion or pass sentence, but she was also compassionate in her dealings with everyday folk. Tara-Zed often spoke in church on all the virtues, which she herself extolled, and clearly enjoyed her regular visits to the school where she taught the children about the laws and history of Britain. The children were in awe of her and made up playground games where Tara-Zed was the heroine saving a villager from the clutches of an evil dragon. This was how the villagers knew her. They had never seen her look nervous before. She had discarded her pantomime costume and was now dressed in loose black trousers and tunic, over which she wore her judge's gown and ceremonial gold filigree belt, which her hand constantly kept touching.

Along from Tara-Zed sat Jasper Corvus, the court usher who was also a councilor because of his position in the village. He was as unpopular as Tara-Zed was popular and was only trusted because Tara-Zed had sent for him from Skipton and valued him highly. Nobody knew quite where he came from, not being a local man. He gave off an air of untrustworthiness and the villagers joked he needed a hooked nose as he was always poking it where it had no business. He waddled over to his mistress and whispered into her ear. Alarm flared in Tara-Zed's eyes and she broke away from Giena and Ande. The two spoke for a few seconds, Tara-Zed leaning towards Jasper, her lips tight and the veins in her neck pulsing. Jasper returned to his seat, arms crossed tightly and a look of grim foreboding across his goblin features.

The next member was Farmer Matthew, an arable farmer who was jovial and hearty. The sixth member was Bishop Guy, a tall middle-aged gentleman, whose hair had turned grey and who had a slight stoop as if he carried the village burdens on his shoulders, which he probably did, though they were usually none too many.

'Friends. I have spoken with Ande, our land manager. What has happened earlier on this evening is unusual...' said Tara-Zed, rising to her feet, her voice clear and steady, though she wore an exceptionally large smile that did not touch her eyes.

'You can say that again,' a villager said from the rear of the hall.

There was nervous laughter, which soon quietened. The judge wasn't the sort of woman who would normally be interrupted.

'Thankfully so, my friend,' continued Tara-Zed, forcing the smile even wider. 'Ande has explained the circumstances to me and I am satisfied that this is nothing more than an unfortunate accident.'

Here, she looked directly at Ralph, who was standing to the left of the stage, sandwiched between his mother and sister. Tara-Zed softened her face and looked kindly at him, her brown eyes brimming with compassion. At that point though, Ralph would rather have been shouted at. The last thing he wanted was people going mushy on him. He'd been an idiot. Why couldn't people just call him that and get it over with? And why did his mother and sister have to stand so close to him? It was probably a feeble attempt to protect him from the stares of the villagers. He stared at a knot in the wooden floor of the hall, which was partially obscured by the fringe which had flopped in front of his face. Rounding his shoulders even more, he bore his hands deeper into his waistcoat pockets, as if he were trying to make his entire body disappear into them. His heart was hammering against his chest and his breath came in shallow pants. The more he tried to control his breathing the clammier his clenched palms and sunken neck became.

Peering out under the now lank strands of his hair, he could see his two best friends, Murgus Bellows and Davyd Baker, standing close by, next to the hall wall. Was it only yesterday he had been swapping wooden Global War action figures with them? *How childish*, thought Ralph. Murgus gave Ralph a surreptitious thumbs up and mouthed the word 'awesome'. Davyd, who had an enormous dopey grin across his freckled face, slowly uncurled his right hand to reveal a little carved 'Derek the Bomber' action figure. Ralph hadn't had enough bartering power to trade for that character, but now here was Davyd whispering loudly, 'All yours, mate. You deserve it.' They had no idea what serious trouble he was in. Adult sort of trouble, not kid's stuff.

Ralph turned his head sharply away from his mates. Needles pricked the back of his eyes and two trails of what felt like molten lava trickled down each cheek. Large splashes appeared on the toecaps of his boots and Ralph half expected the leather to fizz and burn, so sure was he that the liquid was caustic in origin. He shook each boot deftly when he realised that what had fallen were his own humble, salt-filled, tears.

Removing his hands from his pockets, he brushed his eyes and nose with the back of his hand. A line of white mucus attached itself to his left hand. Snot! Would his humiliation never end, he wondered, trying to sniff as discreetly as possible. He felt something soft flutter into his right hand. Looking down, he saw his mother's blue handkerchief resting in his palm. He lifted it to his face and dabbed his eyes and nose. The cotton smelt of home, of his mother, safe and loving. This wasn't helping much, he thought, as he felt a fresh pricking of tears.

Ralph raised his head. He saw that he and his family were in the shadowy recesses of the hall and that all eyes were focused on the stage rather than him, all that is except those of his sister, who stood staring at him with a look of compassion, mixed with fear, across her face. Glowering at her, rather unkindly, he shifted his whole body around so he too could see the council members, leaving his sister with a view of the back of his head and shoulders. Now wasn't the time for her telepathic twaddle.

'I shall provide a thorough report after my investigation, which will start tomorrow. Ande and a team will meet with his chosen working party to ensure the safety of the area. If there are no questions, I suggest we all go home to our beds,' said Tara-Zed.

The villagers looked comforted and shoulders could be seen relaxing and smiles returning to previously sullen mouths. The families with younger children started to make their way to the doors. The council members stood up and Tara-Zed turned, almost hastily, towards Ande and Giena, her arm held out towards the exit.

Then, above the increasing sounds of movement and relief came a rasping voice, like that of an elderly lady.

'What about the writing on the parchment?' said the voice, which seemed to echo – or had it originated? – from the walls.

The effect of the voice stopped everyone from leaving and they turned back towards the stage, an eerie silence now descending.

'Who said that?' asked Lydia Bellows.

'What writing on what parchment?' said the innkeeper directly to the stage, breaking the silence.

'That woman. Where is she?' said Lydia. 'I feel all chilly,' she added and tucked her scarf around her neck.

As she said this, the villagers' breath could be seen suspended in the air and they clasped their hands and stamped their feet with the sudden drop in temperature.

'What's going on? I've had enough excitement for one evening,' said the baker.

'It's dark magic,' cried Lydia.

'Fairytales. Hocus pocus, isn't it now?' said Arfur Sendal, who had been scurrying around the hall trying to locate the old woman but to no avail.

He really didn't want to bother with this mention of magic. He had already pictured his morning's headline: 'Blowamyte Blast: Boy to Blame', and he wasn't prepared to rewrite the story.

'What about the singing flowers? They not magical enough for you, Arfur?' replied the innkeeper.

Tara-Zed exchanged glances with Shelia and Giena, before returning to the centre of the stage, but with the smile gone and her brow now creased. She looked formidable and there was no comfort to be found in her features.

'The woman was correct to mention this matter. The parchment does exist,' said Tara-Zed to a gasp. 'Only three people at any one time know of its existence.'

The audience fidgeted nervously.

'The parchment contains a message written down by the original Sisters of Antares. No one has seen this message, although the events this evening may well be linked to the writings.'

This brought a flurry of voices around the hall as the puzzled neighbours turned to each other, their faces regaining their rosy hue as the temperature in the hall returned to normal.

'If the legend is real, don't you think now would be a good time to share it?' said the baker, to mutters of agreement.

Tara-Zed raised her hands and once more forced a smile.

'After a hundred years, one would not expect any residual magical powers, if that is what they are, to be very strong. The immediate concern is to make sure the area itself is safe.'

'Where is this alleged parchment kept?' asked Arfur Sendal in his weasel voice. 'I've worked in this area all my life and haven't even caught a sniff of its existence and if anyone should know it would be me, wouldn't it now, eh?'

There were snorts from several members of the audience, which Arfur chose to ignore.

Tara-Zed pulled back her robe. Attached to the gold belt was a gilt tube. Everybody had seen her wear it but no one had ever asked what was contained within. The villagers had always assumed that it contained documents of some sort or perhaps it was just a pen and paper holder in case the judge needed to write down a summons or court order when the usher was not to hand, but no one really knew. It occurred to the onlookers that they had never enquired, not because of the awe they often felt for Tara-Zed, but more that when their eyes had settled on the container their thoughts were drawn in an opposite direction. Except apparently two other people did know of its existence, but had never spoken of such things.

The audience watched, spellbound, as Tara-Zed carefully undid a clasp and flicked open a lid at the top end of the cylinder. Using her elegant fingers she withdrew a single sheet of cream-coloured paper.

'This document has not been seen for one hundred years. The message has remained secret in the hope that it would never need to be revealed. The last people to touch this document were the three original Sisters of Antares,' said Tara-Zed.

A ripple of excitement ran round the room.

'So when were you going to reveal these *magic* writings?' said Arfur with a sneer. 'I mean if the old hag… I mean lady hadn't spoken up, would you lot have kept quiet about this, *Your Worshipfulness*, eh now?'

Ande, whose brow had become deeper and jaw set more rigid each time Arfur opened his mouth, stepped forwards.

'Arfur, if you are suggesting there was to be a cover-up, you are wrong and should apologise to Judge Tara-Zed. These matters are serious and even the three who are privileged to know of the parchment's existence do not know what they are handling. Why cause unrest if there is no need? But our dear friend,' he stretched his arm out to indicate the old woman, but could not see her anywhere, 'who has since left us, had every right to raise this and so we shall continue.'

Every villager stood rooted to their spot as Tara-Zed unfurled the parchment and started to read in her clear, strong voice.

Revealed to Deneb

So, on Earth there is a little disturbance, an upsetting time for a few occupants of that strange planet. What of it? An innocent person caught up in an evil snare. Banishment into eternal darkness. There are worse fates, you know. But these are a compassionate people and the order of the Universe needs to reflect charity. So what is to be done for that innocent one, so wrongfully imprisoned, beloved by many?

Revealed to Altair

We shall send a little help to that poor being. The Judge will live on as if sleeping in a sepulchre but, the one they call Witch will also be touched by that power and will live too. The force of the blast has left her imprisoned in a deep cave, her cat for company. She can breathe and hear and see (although what is there to see but eternal night?), but entombed she must be.

Revealed to Rigela Kent

But this is a burden that must remain only for a set time. When daylight enters that deep hollow, then all three of those wretches will regain their physical form and continue in their endeavours for good or for evil. What can stop the evil? There is a truth not for us to reveal, but to be discovered. The Three Wands of Antares will help. All must be hidden – disguised to hide them from prying eyes. If they are brought together once more then their power will be unimaginable. But only those descended from the blood of a victim will have the courage. Otherwise evil will reign. And when shall this happen? Who knows? But one hundred years hence would seem as good a time as any. A ripe time. An opportune time. Let us hope it does not lead to a dark time.

The villagers stood in silence, scratching their chins and blinking with incomprehension.

'Didn't it say that something strange would happen in a hundred years? That's today,' said the innkeeper.

'It's a load of rubbish,' said Arfur Sendal, who was still after his headline blaming Ralph. 'Your Worship, may I see that parchment, eh now?'

'Certainly, Arfur. Join me,' replied Tara-Zed.

The journalist crept up the steps at the side of the stage, mischief on his face. The judge handed him the scroll. Arfur looked at it, blinking through his rodent eyes before the corners of his mouth turned up, in a sickly sneer.

'Pardon me, but there is nothing on this paper is there, eh now?'

He held the parchment up to show his audience, who were at once amazed that anyone should challenge Tara-Zed, yet fascinated to see what would happen next.

'Members of the council – how can this be explained?' said Arfur, excitement in his voice for he was already rewriting this story in his head, trying to work out if 'Judge Lies Over Leaked Letter' was bigger than Ralph and his accident.

This could give him the big break into the national press he felt he deserved.

'Please may I have the document, Arfur?' said Tara-Zed, detaching a small leather pouch from her belt.

Arfur handed back the paper, never taking his eyes from it. From the purse, Tara-Zed tipped what looked like silver sand across the parchment. She handed it back to Arfur. The sneer across his face changed into a look of bewilderment, his mouth opening and closing silently, for the instant he took hold of the paper, strange symbols began dancing across the page, becoming clear and then fading again.

'Please read from the scroll, Arfur,' said the judge.

'You know I can't. It's just a childish trick. It's rubbish. Gobbledygook.' He thrust the document into Tara-Zed's hand.

'Very well. Ande, would you be so kind as to read from the page?' said Tara-Zed.

Ande took the paper in his firm hands and began to read aloud exactly what Tara-Zed had read earlier. The crowd murmured to each other.

'Tell me, Ande, what you see on those pages,' said Tara-Zed.

'Writing, just as you read it. The hand is old-fashioned but very distinct.'

'It's trickery,' spluttered Arfur, 'all I saw was scribble, didn't I now?'

'The only trick is left over from a century ago. The Sisters of Antares encrypted the document. Only those of a pure and noble heart can read from the parchment. Arfur, that does not apparently include you.'

There was sniggering from the crowd.

With this unexpected revelation, Ralph felt the colour rise in his cheeks once more. Not only had he decimated a local landmark but it appeared he had unleashed a century-old curse. *Not bad for an evening's work*, he thought.

His mouth felt as dry as a bone, but he opened it and inhaled and exhaled slowly and deeply, several times. The burning, crimson shroud, which had covered his body since all this began, receded, giving way to a chill that made him shiver. It reminded Ralph of the diagram of an iceberg he had seen in a school book. That's what he felt like, an iceberg, the bulk of his emotions hidden, and just a cool tip piercing the surface. He knew what he must do. If the adults wouldn't listen to him then he would have to sort things out on his own. He wouldn't be waiting for any safety party.

'Ralph? You okay?' said Alba.

Ralph huffed.

'My fellow villagers. It is late and much has happened. At first light we shall investigate all these occurrences and any action that is deemed necessary shall be taken, but I very much doubt that what is written here is of relevance today,' said Ande, who was known for his honesty, so the villagers, as they filed out of the hall, took no comfort from the deep-set frowns and gloomy disposition of the council members who remained on stage.

'Just one thing, Judge, if I may?' said Roger Butcher slowly, as if an idea was forming in his mind as he spoke. 'If only three people at any one time have known of that parchment's existence and you are one of them, then who are the other two?'

'I can answer that, Roger. It is myself,' said Giena, using her walking stick to help her forwards on the stage.

'*You?*' said Arfur, disbelief in his voice.

'The other member of the Sisters wishes to remain anonymous for the time being, but is known to Tara-Zed and myself,' she said, not even glancing at Arfur Sendal.

'Oh, yes, all right, Miss Cygnus, thank you,' said Roger carefully. 'Just one matter more. If only three of you know of this prophecy's existence at any one time, how did that old woman, whoever she was, know about it too?'

A babble arose as everyone turned to each other. Tara-Zed raised her arms to silence the crowd. She frowned as she looked directly at the villagers.

'I honestly do not know. But you have my word that the council members and I will do our best to find out. Please go home and sleep as well as you can.'

The villagers shuffled out, heads tilted towards each other as rumour and gossip began to abound as to the identity of the old crone who had started the talk of a prophecy. No one noticed Jasper Corvus waddle out through the back door and walk towards the woods, neither did anyone take notice of the crows who were flying at night, cawing and swooping low across the newly formed hole in White Scar Hill.

Shelia, Ralph and Alba left the hall by a side door. Ande remained in discussion with the other council members and a few dependable women and men from the village, who would form the morning's working party.

The rain had ceased but a chill hung in the air and Alba walked with her arm linked through her mother's. Ralph marched ahead of them, his head jutting out resolutely, and his mouth tense. Davyd and Murgus rushed out to catch up with their friend, sending several of the villagers staggering out of their way. Davyd was short with black hair and fashionable rectangular spectacles with thick lenses, which made his brown eyes look tiny. Murgus was taller, slightly chubby and had a shock of golden curls which he detested.

'Wait a minute, mate,' said Davyd.

'Yes, tell us all about it. You are a legend, my good fellow,' said Murgus.

Ralph shrugged and continued walking.

'Come on, Ralph. The explosion. What was it like that close?' said Davyd.

'Must have been awesome,' said Murgus.

'Whatever. Sorry. Bit tired. I'll catch up with you sometime,' said Ralph.

His arms swung stiffly by his sides and he kicked stones out of his way as he headed along the path to his cottage.

'Oh, yea all right,' said Murgus, stopping and watching the back of Ralph's head.

'Come on, mate,' said Davyd, tugging Murgus's arm. 'Mum's got some sperryberry cakes left. Race you.'

'All right,' said Murgus, turning away from Ralph, 'but let's walk.'

Alba's head was beginning to ache as she sensed the pressure of guilt and embarrassment that her brother was feeling. There was another emotion present but she couldn't decipher what it was. She heard the familiar creaking of the garden gate as Ralph pushed it open. Rather than going indoors, Ralph walked around the side of the cottage and stood in the garden.

By the light of the moon he picked up his set of horseshoes and started to throw them at the metal marker in the ground some ten metres in front of him. Quoits was a popular sport in the region and Ralph was good at it. He had a keen eye for distance and a feel for the weight of the horseshoe, and with his relaxed throwing technique he was a frequent winner. His father travelled with him to contests in other villages and he was widely thought of as a future champion. Tonight, however, Ralph wasn't concerned with accuracy and the sound of horseshoes ricocheting off the iron stake before landing with a thud on the lawn filled the night.

The cottage had been built by Ande on the site of Shelia's grandparents' cottage. The front door was in the centre of the house and opened into a large hall off which were the kitchen, a lounge, a dining room and a study. The staircase was in the middle of the hall and led to a gallery from which the hall could be overlooked. Oak banisters ran round the edge and the family bedrooms were off this landing. The hall had family portraits on the wall, a vase of red tulips sat on an oak sideboard and a grandfather clock stood silent, like a sentry, opposite the kitchen. It was a family heirloom, thought to be at least seven hundred years old, but had never made so much as one tick-tock despite Ande's best efforts to make it work. The hands were set permanently at six minutes past twelve.

As Shelia made the two children hot honey milk in her spacious kitchen, she could hear the rhythmic clunk as each horseshoe landed, a sound familiar to her from Ralph's hours of practice. She usually chided him for putting quoits ahead of his daily chores. She made a note not to be so hard on him. He was still only a boy, after all.

'Ralph. Come in now. You need to rest.'

She wanted to hug her son but knew this man-in-waiting would not welcome such a gesture. Ralph walked into the kitchen, his face red, tear stains down his cheeks. Before Shelia could change her mind and reach for him, he had taken his mug and went up the stairs, three steps at a time.

Alba kissed her mother goodnight and followed her brother, although her steps were slower.

It was just before midnight, but despite her tiredness, as soon as Alba's head sank into the plump pillow, she was wide awake. She knew this was caused by her brother and she could feel that he was deeply unsettled. Turning from side to side in her bed she tried to get comfortable but in the end gave up and, putting on her dressing gown, with care opened the bedroom door and padded to her brother's room, which was next to her own. She could see the light was still on in the kitchen and she hadn't yet heard her father return home. Tapping with just one knuckle on Ralph's door, Alba didn't wait for a reply before pushing the handle down and creeping in.

Ralph was sitting on the edge of his bed, his shoulders hunched as he concentrated on the pattern on his quilt cover. He had not bothered to put on his light but his room was bright enough, as his curtains were open and the moonlight shone in, giving the room a monochrome quality.

'It was an accident, Ralph. Nobody will think it wasn't,' said Alba, standing in front of her brother.

Ralph did not move, continuing to stare at a square of patchwork.

'I can feel something is not right.'

'Oh yeah. Sorry, sis. I forgot about you and your "feelings".'

Ralph made a speech mark gesture with his index fingers when he said the word 'feelings'. He looked at his sister, his brown eyes staring without expression into her clear blue eyes, one of which had a small tear forming in the corner.

'Ralph, please try not to worry. Just tell me what's wrong. I can help you,' said Alba.

'Tell you what's wrong, sis? Are you stupid? I blow the top off a local landmark. I cause the biggest village meeting ever and now it looks like I've awakened some local curse which might just destroy not only the village but the whole world. Not bad going really for a day's work. I mean White Scar Hill will now be renamed Black Hole Hill and how will I be commemorated? By Village Idiots Day. And then there's you and your "feelings".' He made the gesture in the air again. 'How am I supposed to feel, Alba? Tell me. Happy? Proud? I feel like an idiot *and* I've let Dad down, again.'

After this rant, Ralph's face looked blanched as if the effort of voicing how he felt had exhausted him.

'Ralph, go to sleep and we can sort it out in the morning. Dad will let you go with him, I'm sure. And nobody really believes there's a witch,' said Alba, who sensed her brother was still holding something back. 'What are you planning to do, Ralph?'

Ralph looked up at his sister, his eyes now full of purpose.

'Not your problem, sis. I'll sort it.'

'What do you mean, "sort it"? You're not going to do something stupid?'

'No, I've used up my stupid quota for the day.'

He gave a half-smile.

'Tell me now or I'll go and get Mum and tell her you are planning something.'

Ralph knew his sister would do exactly as she said.

'Okay. But it is a secret. You have to trust me and let me do this.'

'What?'

'I'm going to go down the cave and see if all this talk of witches and curses is true. Then I can tell Dad and all the others there is nothing to worry about.'

'But what if the legend is true? You'll be stuck in a cave system, of which you know nothing, with a witch who is likely to be very angry.'

'Well, I doubt it's true but if it is then at least I'll be in the right place to do something about it.'

'Ralph. That is plain daft. I'm going to tell Mum right now.' But as she said this, a look of anguish crossed her brother's face, which Alba felt in the pit of her stomach.

'Okay, I won't tell. But I'm coming with you. The first rule of caving is never go alone.'

'Alba. Please. Mum and Dad have been really good about the Blowamyte and the hill but if anything happened to you and it was my fault…'

'Either I go with you or I tell Mum and Dad, right now.'

Alba stood with her arms crossed and feet planted in the rug.

'Okay, sis. You win. I was just going to the spare room to get the equipment.'

'Right, we'd better get going then,' said Alba, crossing to the door and opening it a little.

Just as she did, her father arrived home and Alba pressed herself into the shadows on the landing wall. Ande went into the kitchen. Ralph was now beside his sister and they crept on to the landing. The door was open and light from the kitchen spilled into the hall. Weird shadows from the hall furniture loomed across the floor, distorting the sideboard into a large coffin and the silent grandfather clock into a monster. The children started to tip-toe along the landing but then they heard their father's voice talking, the sound rising up to the house rafters despite his hushed tone. What the children heard made them stop in their tracks.

'Tara-Zed believes this prophecy to be true and the endgame is about to unfold. She didn't want to cause panic in the village. We think we've headed that off for the moment,' said Ande.

'How can she be sure?' said Shelia.

'She's been watching the sky and the summer triangle is exactly where it was positioned a hundred years ago with Aster's star right in the middle. And there is something else...'

'I know, Ande. I heard. I am so scared. What if Ralph tries to do something out of his depth? What if something happens to him? I couldn't bear it.'

The unexpected sound of their mother sobbing drifted up to the ears of the children, who were crouching still as statues, by the banister.

'It's okay. Tara-Zed and Giena Cygnus know where their wands are hidden. And of course we've had confirmation tonight where yours is,' said Ande.

The children looked at each other, their eyes as round as orbs and their chins nearly resting on their chests.

'A small group of us are going to work on the cave entrance to block it up whilst Tara-Zed and Giena retrieve their wands. They are then going to meet us at the North Tower. It has a good view of the waterfall. That is the only other way out of the cave and if the witch tries to get out we'll be waiting for her with the two wands.'

Ralph shuddered when he heard his father mention the North Tower, but he wasn't sure why. After all, he had been there dozens of times.

'It all sounds incredibly dangerous. And what about the poor old judge?' said Shelia.

'We'll take care of the witch and then rescue him, although goodness knows what state he'll be in after so long. Apparently he was quite ancient when he got entombed.'

'It's a pity this had to happen, what with the High Council going to the World Reconciliation Meeting soon. It will make us seem very mystical and rustic,' said Shelia.

'The timing is strange. Quite a coincidence. Still, nothing but a big hole in a hill and a bit of magic writing has happened yet,' said Ande.

The sound of a plant pot being knocked off the kitchen windowsill, falling with a thud on to the flower bed below, made them both jump.

'What was that?' asked Shelia.

'Probably a cat. Everything is jittery tonight.'

The children heard the sound of a chair being pushed back. If their parents came out now, they would be caught red-handed, but they heard the water from the kitchen tap and the kettle being refilled. Ralph gave his sister a light shove and pointed to the spare-room door, which they moved silently to. This was the room where the family stored all their equipment for caving, rock climbing, canoeing and skiing.

As soon as the door was shut, Ralph looked at Alba.

'Mum's a Sister of Antares. Can you believe it?' he hissed through clenched teeth.

'Yes I can,' said Alba. 'She's a clever lady and great friends with Miss Cygnus and Tara-Zed.'

'But she makes the dinner and tidies my room.'

'We know the legend is true. You can abandon your plan.'

'No way. Now I have even more reason to sort out the mess I started. We'll just have a look and then report back to Dad and the others. Any information must be of help. It'll be fine.'

But Alba sensed it would be anything but.

Shelia was very neat and everything was stored with care and easy to get hold of. Ande made sure that equipment was in a state of readiness and good repair at all times.

He and several other villagers were the cave and mountain rescue team for the area. Ralph was being trained in this task, although he wouldn't be allowed on a rescue until he was eighteen. The twins carefully took a rucksack each, together with ropes, a harness, a large hand-held torch, a tinder box, a pen knife, their caving hats and a supply of candles. They would take food from the kitchen on the way out. One thing they didn't worry about was water. There was always a supply of fresh, clean spring water in the cave systems around their village.

When satisfied they had all they needed, they sneaked back to their own rooms. They agreed to wait for thirty minutes after their parents went to bed and then meet in the kitchen.

Alba had a feeling of butterflies fluttering around inside her stomach and heart, which was in part from her brother but also from a source unknown to her, yet it was not unfamiliar. From her brother she felt that there was a strong likelihood that either one of them may not return from their expedition, but she knew she had no choice but to follow him. Somewhere from deep within she felt a voice – or could she really hear it? – from long ago calling her to an unknown destiny. Without knowing why, she realised that somehow she and Ralph were part of the prophecy.

Both children had slipped into their beds fully clothed and snuggled deep under their covers. Their leather climbing boots felt like alien intruders on their crisp, white sheets. They knew their parents would check on them before retiring.

Ralph heard the scrape of his bedroom door on the floorboards, before it stopped abruptly. He remembered he had dropped his woolen hat as he had re-entered his bedroom. The hat was wedged between the door and floor. He was certain his dad would hear the pounding of Ralph's heart as he held his breath beneath the covers. The equipment was stashed at the foot of his bed beneath his dressing gown. If his dad noticed it the game would be up. After what seemed like an age, he heard Ande tug the door, releasing it from the encumbrance, and move to his own bedroom. Ralph breathed out and the pounding of his pulse subsided with each beat of his heart. He knew he should feel tired – after all, it had been a hectic day – but he was wide awake, adrenaline coursing through his veins.

Alba heard the door open just enough for her mother to look at what appeared to be the sleeping form of her daughter, no doubt with a little half-smile on her face. Hot tears poured from Alba's cool blue eyes, soaking the pillow. She wanted to reach out for her mother and tell her about the plan, but she knew she must not, could not, for somehow she felt that to not go would bring worse consequences. It all felt so confusing. She heard her mother withdraw from her room, fooled by the ruse that Alba was fast asleep. Alba blinked and blinked as she felt her eye lids grow heavier and sleep overcame her.

She found herself dreamily floating off to two summers before when she and a group of village children had been swimming in the plunge pool of Force Falls, one of many local waterfalls. Whoops of laughter reverberated in her mind and she could almost feel the warmth of the sun on her body, as dappled rays pushed through the leaves of overhanging trees. She saw Ralph, jumping in curled up like a ball, and felt cold droplets of the water splash her, as he met the water. Then she felt herself get ready to jump from one of the ledges. Her foot slipped and she hit her head against the rock as she dove down. Nobody had seen her fall and she plunged into the water semi-conscious, arms flailing to correct herself, but instead she spun round and down. A large apparition of pink flesh loomed in front of her, a soppy grin haloed by white hair. Murgus had rescued her and dragged her to safety, her brother nowhere to be seen. She knew then that Ralph could not read her thoughts or else he would have known she was in trouble.

The thought of her brother made her wake up with a start. Her bed sheets were wrapped around her where she had been reaching out for help. Untangling herself, she shook her head and rubbed her eyes. She knew she had been dreaming, but she still found herself trembling as she slid from beneath the covers.

Not even an owl was hooting when the children crept downstairs and sneaked into the kitchen. Alba took food from their mother's store cupboard. Nuts, seeds, dried fruit and a couple of sperryberry cakes were found homes in corners of their rucksacks. She knew her brother would not have thought of this, but he would become hungry soon enough. Once she was finished, Alba gave her brother a nod and he opened the oak kitchen door an inch at a time, for it was positioned beneath their parents' bedroom window but still made less sound than the front door.

Both children were dressed in light wool trousers, multi-pocketed waistcoats, fleeces and sheepskin jackets. Ralph led the way across the patch of lawn where he had earlier been throwing his quoits. Just by a holly bush alongside the garden fence was positioned an upturned bucket, which he used as a step to climb over the fence. A box was positioned on the other side of the fence, which acted as a step down. Alba gave her brother a quizzical look as she climbed over.

'I wasn't just throwing quoits earlier and it's quieter than the front gate,' he whispered as they set off at a good pace towards White Scar Hill.

Dew had settled on the grass and their boots squeaked, but the moon was still high in the sky, giving the familiar landscape an eerie silver glint. There was a chill in the air and the children were grateful for their jackets to keep them warm. Across the face of the moon, black shapes could be seen darting.

'There are a lot of bats flying tonight,' said Alba.

'They're too big for bats. They look like crows, but they don't usually fly at night,' said Ralph.

'Perhaps something really big disturbed them earlier on this evening,' said Alba.

'Yeah. Those musical flowers do make a racket, don't they,' said Ralph, grinning.

Brother and sister strode out and were soon ascending the hill. The moonlight bounced off the newly scattered white rocks, making them look like shimmering sheep. The children picked their way through these unfamiliar outcrops and by the time they reached the top of the hill were both huffing and puffing.

'We can leave the jackets on the flat stone. The cave systems around here are the same temperature night and day whatever the surface weather. We'll be okay in just our fleeces,' said Ralph, already slipping out of his jacket.

Taking care, both children stepped up to the edge of the new crevice and peered into the blackness. The moon was waning and its beams provided no illumination of what lay within the crater. Nothing moved. Not even a gentle breeze stirred a leaf. All was still and quiet as if nature itself was waiting for the next move to be made by an unseen player in a supernatural chess game.

'I feel cold, Ralph. I'll keep my jacket on,' said Alba.

'At least the crows have settled,' replied her brother. And indeed, the birds that had accompanied them all the way up the hillside had now grown quiet.

The children secured a rope around the base of the flat stone.

'If it withstood the blast, it should withstand our weight. I'll go down first. I'll try abseiling, but if it's too far then I'll come back up. Even I'm not stupid enough to drop into a bottomless pit.'

Ralph took off his woolen hat and put on a hard hat made of

compressed leather. On the front of it was a glass-covered compartment. Behind the glass was a stubby, dull lilac candle, made of wax from local bees who fed on the sperry plants local to that region. The high limestone content in the soil filtered through the wax-making process, mixing with the pollen of the purple fruit, caused the murky colour of the candles. It also meant that they burnt for a good long time. They were also water resistant, thanks to the wax infused wicks, one of Ande's inventions for which Ralph was very proud of his dad. They also gave off a strong beam. Both children had caved before and were amazed that even the darkest hole could be lit up like day by just a single candle and that a passage could be illuminated for up to twenty metres. The glass cover had a little leather shutter, rather like a blind at a window, which could be pulled down if the wearer should need to dim the light.

The candles also had the advantage of not producing wax drips as all the material was burnt off slowly and disappeared into the atmosphere through little vents in the side of the candle holder, which also let oxygen in. These vents could be shut temporarily if the wearer had to be submerged for any length of time. The main disadvantage was that the candles became increasingly hot, so the wearer could become quite uncomfortable, although this was after several hours and the children had never caved for any great length of time before.

'I wish this didn't involve a cave. Why couldn't it have been a pony race or something else?' said Alba.

Ralph smiled as he secured a second rope around the flat stone and then tied the harness around his waist and between his legs. If he fell, this safety device would tighten and hold him secure.

'I've allowed ten metres of rope. If I need any more, feed it through this loop I've made,' said Ralph.

He pulled back the glass shutter on his hard hat and removed the candle. He had taken a tinder box from the family storeroom rather than matches, which were susceptible to damp. He struck the flint deftly against the metal box causing a spark, which caught hold of the candle's wick. A momentary flare lit up the surrounding area until the candle flame settled and Ralph replaced it in its holder.

'Keep talking to me,' said Alba.

'I will, sis. Thanks for coming.'

With that he walked to the edge of the hole and turned so his back was towards the opening. His knuckles turned white as he gripped the rope and then he stepped backwards, so his right leg was pressing against the wall of the crevice just below the surface. Feeling that this part was secure, he moved his left leg back so he was now suspended in the cave entrance, his feet pushing against the wall, the rope tensed as it took Ralph's weight.

The candle light flickered around the cavern, bouncing off walls which had not been seen for a hundred years. Alba moved forwards, getting as close as she could to the edge, and peered into this new world beneath her. Her brother was moving with care down the wall and she could see a firm rock base about ten metres below him. She returned to the safety rope and fed out enough to enable him to land in safety. Returning to her perch she surveyed the weird subterranean landscape being illuminated before her. The walls were formed from a grey rock, much darker than the limestone that was on the surface. Left on its own, the rock surface would have been smooth and shiny, but the earlier blast had made this part, at least, jagged and pitted.

'Ralph, you've got about five metres to go. Are you okay?' shouted Alba.

She was expecting an echo, but her voice fell flat.

'I'm okay. No witches yet,' said Ralph.

Alba continued surveying the scene, which became stranger the deeper Ralph descended. He had quite a bit more room to manoeuvre than expected and Alba soon heard him arrive.

'It's okay, sis. A flat floor and enough room. And still no witches,' said Ralph.

'Okay. I'll pull up the safety rope and send the rucksacks down,' said Alba.

With a gentle swing Alba launched the rucksacks over the cave edge and let out enough rope to allow their descent. The weight of the equipment tugged on her arm sockets. When she felt the rope go loose she once again pulled it up. Ralph had attached the harness, which she climbed into. Checking her hard hat and candle were securely fitted, she walked backwards into the gaping cave mouth.

Close up she could see how beautiful the rock face was and that it was streaked with many different shades of grey from dove white to steely gunmetal. As she looked up, she could see the night sky as if someone were holding a starlit umbrella over her. As she continued into the depths, a few small rocks from the surface became loosened and fell past her, although the ancient flat rock round which the ropes were tied felt solid enough.

'Watch out, Ralph,' she cried, as the debris whistled past her ears.

She heard it land with a patter. Ralph swore.

'Okay, sis?' said Ralph as his sister arrived at his side.

'So far so good,' she replied.

'There's a passage that leads off from this opening. It's the only way to continue. We'll have a look around and if everything is safe, we'll climb back up to the surface and tell Dad the coast is clear of witches.'

As Ralph finished saying this both children shuddered and turned icy cold.

'Well, let's get on with it. This place may be lovely in daylight but at the moment it's giving me the frights,' said Alba.

They slung their rucksacks over their shoulders, Alba looping the spare rope across her body. Ralph led the way, their candles giving the cave an ethereal quality, like a high-domed cathedral.

'I'll just pull the safety rope into the cave a bit further. It might be useful later,' said Alba.

She picked up the end of the rope and held it loosely in her right hand, following her brother into the gloom of the unknown cave system. The passage curved subtly until their entry point to the cave, together with the reassuring canopy of stars, was hidden from the twins' view. A few steps later, Alba stopped abruptly.

'Ralph, the safety rope. It's gone taut.'

'It must be the end. Just leave it.'

'No, there should be at least another twenty metres of give in it.'

Alba started to agitate the rope, but it moved no more than a lightly vibrating guitar string.

'It must be snagged on something,' said Ralph, continuing along the path.

'No, it can't be. There wasn't anything to get in its way.'

Holding the rope with both hands, Alba gave it a hard tug. Nothing. The cable remained tight. She yanked at the rope again, this time grunting loudly with effort, the sound bouncing around the cave walls as if a herd of swine was hidden in the stony labyrinth.

Her brother stopped and spun round, just in time to see Alba pulled forwards with great force as the rope was snatched from her hand by an unseen presence. Her left shoulder hit the side of the wall and she crumpled to the floor. A low rumbling followed and then, for the second time that night, the ground vibrated and the children were deafened by an enormous boom. Ralph crouched by his sister, both children covering their ears with their hands, huddling together as billows of dust and rock fragments covered them. The bend in the passageway afforded some protection from the full force of whatever had caused this mighty commotion, which seemed to the twins to last hours but was over in less than a minute. However, as the dust settled and the cave returned to its noiseless state, the silence felt eerier than ever.

'What was that, Ralph?'

'Thank goodness you're okay,' said Ralph, helping his sister to her feet.

Alba rubbed her shoulder.

'My jacket took most of the force. I just ache a bit.'

They shook the debris from their clothes and checked their safety helmets and candles.

Despite his apparent calmness, Alba could sense panic rising within her brother as he carefully retraced his steps along the passageway, his boots crunching on the freshly formed layer of gravel, the lamplight picking out glints of rock fragments strewn across the floor.

'No!' said Ralph as he rounded the bend.

'Nooooo,' came the cave's reply, as if mocking him.

Alba gingerly followed her brother and stood alongside him as she viewed the source of the disturbance. The space where they had stood just a few moments earlier was filled by the flat rock that had hung over the lip of the cave – the same rock that had protected Ralph and his father only a few hours before, and from which the children had secured their ropes in order to enter the chasm. The same rock that had been placed on the hillside tens of thousands of years ago by the relentless force of glaciation and which was so unyielding. The same rock that had been upended by a sharp pull on a rope by a teenage girl, completely blocking the only certain way in or out of the cave.

'What have I got you into, sis?'

'Nothing, Ralph. You got me into nothing. I insisted on coming. We're in this together. Right. Let's get the guide twine out.'

'What? You're not planning on walking through the caves, are you? Dad will come and get us out. Somehow.'

'Ralph. It's still a few hours before Dad finds out we are missing, and then works out we just happened to jump into a cave. Next, remember, Dad said there was another way out, through the waterfall on the east side. Okay, it's a bit high up but we've still got another rope. There is only one waterfall, so we'll follow the water sources and that's where we'll end up. It beats sitting here for hours. And if it all goes wrong we'll just follow the twine back and wait for Dad.'

'Okay,' said Ralph, after a brief pause, 'but the first sign of any danger, we turn around, come back and wait here.'

'Ralph, the only danger will be from rock falls. Let's face it, nothing could live down here for one hundred years. The only living things are us.'

A chink in the rocks framed the night sky, giving the children a last glimpse of the outside world. With their way illuminated by the candles on their helmets, the brother and sister entered the myriad tunnels and passages that made the cave system of White Scar.

'I can hear running water,' said Ralph.

'Follow that sound. The cave floor is okay to walk on,' said Alba.

'Water continually running into the hillside then freezing and melting over the centuries will have formed these passages and made them smooth,' said Ralph.

They could feel they were descending and as they did so the rushing of the unseen water grew louder and more urgent. At the start of their journey into the cave, the walls were formed of cold granite, but as they continued further, strange formations began to emerge around them. Glistening deposits of minerals had solidified on to the walls making them appear bulbous and slimy, like a family of giant slugs squeezed together. Alba tried to poke her finger into the surface, certain that it would be like pushing a sponge, but the shapes were cold and hard to the touch. A clammy deposit stuck to her fingertips, which felt gritty when she rubbed her fingers together. The walls were a mixture of colours, some the colour of straw, some a reddish hue whilst others were charcoal grey.

'These are so weird.' Alba had to shout so as to be heard above the increasingly loud noise of the water.

'They're caused by rain seeping through the soil above and reacting with chemicals in the soil and limestone. They solidify when they hit the air in the cave. The yellow and red show that iron is present and the blackish formations are due to carbon and manganese in the deposits,' said Ralph.

'I didn't know you knew all this stuff. I thought you were daydreaming in lessons. Miss Cygnus will be pleased,' said Alba, smiling.

'I've seen this type of thing in other cave systems around here when I've been down with Dad.' Ralph went quiet.

As they walked, Alba had been letting out the twine they would use to trace their way back to the entrance, if need be. Every twenty metres or so, she secured the cord by twisting it around little crystalline formations jutting out from the walls. There were an increasing number of stalagmites perched on these rock ledges, reaching up to their parent stalactites who drip-fed their protégées below. Eventually they would join up, and the parental job of nurturing the growing pile of minerals beneath it would be done and a new pillar formed. There were different types of these continually forming rocky families. Some were long and pointed, others curved and shapely like tall-stemmed flowers.

'Stalac-'tights' go down,' said Alba. 'That's how I remember.'

'What?' said Ralph.

This new subterranean home was full of unseen beauty and strangeness and Alba sensed that there were still more wonders to behold. She shivered. Perhaps she had been hasty in thinking that she and her brother were the only forms of life down there.

They walked past one extra-distinctive stalagmite and both children used their helmet candle lights to illuminate it.

'It looks like a rather podgy judge,' said Alba, staring closely at the formation.

'Look, there's the wig, and little glasses. How funny.'

The children continued, peering around corners with caution and keeping an eye on their footing. Passages of all sizes led from the main path to the left and right.

'We'll stick to this main passage. It looks like it once had a river flowing along it,' said Ralph.

'How do you know this stuff?' said Alba.

'Like you said, I must have been paying attention in class. Plus, the swirl pattern on the exposed part of the ceiling. These side passages would have been rivulets.'

'Glad we cleared that up,' said Alba.

The clothes they wore protected them from the pervading dampness, but Ralph had been correct when he said the cave complex would maintain the same temperature whatever the surface heat, and neither of them felt uncomfortable.

'Is it me or does the sound of water seem more distant now?' said Ralph.

'You're right, but I don't fancy the look of the other passages. We'll have to keep going. I wonder what the time is. It feels like we've been down here for hours. I'm glad we brought extra candles and food with us,' said Alba.

They walked past more strange stalagmites and their suspended partners. They came round a sharp bend where their passage ended in a rocky wall with a slit in it just big enough for them both to fit through. Passing through the gap, they found their rocky path joined a rusting, crumpled metal walkway, with metal handrails, which ran over the underground river. The lamps illuminated plastic coverlets on the wall, which would once have been an electric lighting system.

'This must be the old tourist route,' said Ralph.

'What were tourists?' said Alba.

'People who took trips away from their homes for pleasure. Apparently it was big business a hundred and fifty years ago.'

'Imagine being able to travel further than York,' said Alba.

'Well, you're a tourist now,' said Ralph, stepping on to the metal grill of the walkway. 'It feels quite safe.' And with that, there was a loud creak and he disappeared.

'Ralph!' said Alba, looking at a gap in the walkway where her brother had just stood. She fell to her knees.

Ralph was clutching the grill, which was hanging by its hinges. His feet were in the water, being dragged along by the current. His fingers were being cut by the metal, as Alba reached forwards, grabbed the rucksack on his back and heaved. This gave Ralph the momentum he needed to grab hold of the metal poles, which acted as the handrails, and haul himself on to the walkway, Alba pulling him by his arms.

'You were saying?' she said.

'Yeah, might have to watch our footing,' said Ralph, with a grin.

They took a large stride over the gap and continued.

One of the stalactites looked like a beautiful lily, similar to the ones that emerged for the concert of the singing flowers. Another looked like a sabre used in eastern lands, which Alba had read about in adventure books. The tunnel started to climb upwards.

'This passage would have been made by an earthquake millions of years ago. I'll go first. It gets a bit narrow,' said Ralph.

'Show off,' said Alba.

As abruptly as the tunnel had risen, it started to drop down and the children had to soften their knees and lean backwards to prevent themselves from falling. The passage became narrower and it felt, to Alba, colder, the walls a dark granite. They rounded a sharp corner. Ralph stopped without warning.

'Watch out, Ralph,' said Alba as she bumped into her brother's back. 'Wow!'

The children found themselves at the far end of a great cavern, the size of a football pitch and three times the height of the village hall.

'Get the hand-held torch, from my rucksack,' said Ralph, turning his back to his sister.

'Please?' said Alba, but she reached into the bag and, after a little rummaging, found what she was looking for.

The hand-held torch was also lit by a candle and worked in exactly the same way as the head-mounted version, but it had a wider front so the beam could penetrate further into the gloom. Alba opened the glass door in front of Ralph's flame, using this to light the torch. She shone it around the vast cavern. Ralph swallowed hard.

A walkway elevated them above the floor of the cave. Metal scaffold poles supported wooden boards, some of which were now missing.

'We'll have to go easy. The wood is probably decayed,' said Ralph.

'This must have been where the tourists viewed the cave,' said Alba. 'All those boulders on the cave floor. It looks like giants have been playing marbles.'

'Look at all those stalactites on the ceiling,' said Ralph pointing the torch upwards. 'There's thousands of them.'

And sure enough there were a myriad of the stalactites dangling from the roof like so many strings of spaghetti. Alba continued to shine the torch, resting it on a point on the cavern floor where the surface met the cave wall, beyond where the boulders petered out. What looked like a smooth, brown, solidified pond stretched across the ground.

'Look, sis. Prehistoric mud pools.'

'I was hoping you'd say it was an underground supply of chocolate,' said Alba.

'I don't think it'd taste too good. It's probably about half a million years old and contains dinosaur poo.'

'Great,' said Alba. 'So it won't even help us find the way out.'

'Sis, this is exciting.'

'Sorry, Ralph, but I'll celebrate when we get out.'

'Okay, Alba. It's just, well, these caves could tell us so much about our past.'

'More worried about the future, at the moment. Now let's go and find some running water.'

Alba started to walk towards the end of the walkway. She stopped suddenly, her heart missing a beat. Ralph had not said a word, but she had felt a cry of anguish emit from his mind. She spun round.

'What is it, Ralph? Why are you scared?'

Ralph was staring at a point on the longest cave wall, the light from his head lamp dancing off it. His jaw was rigid and even in the artificial light Alba could tell he was a ghostly white. She shone the torch at the point where her brother was looking.

'Ralph, it's just a random pattern on the wall. The white will be pure calcium and the brown bits must mean there's iron. It would have taken thousands of years to form. See, I was listening to you. Now come on.'

But Ralph just stood there.

'Can't you taste it? The cave. It tastes like blood,' he said in a distant voice.

'It's just the iron in the atmosphere down here,' said Alba.

'Don't you see her? She was here all along,' said Ralph.

'Ralph. What are you on about? You're scaring me. Is there such a thing as cave fever? What do you mean "she was here"…oh my goodness, Ralph. Is it her?'

Alba clutched her brother's arm. She wasn't sure if the rising panic she felt was hers alone, Ralph's or a combination of the two, for there, imprinted on the wall, was a face. It was that of a woman and had deep-set eyes, a long nose, cruel lips and a jutting chin. Helictites, unusual formations growing out sideways from a rock, protruded from the face like warts and red-tinted stalactites gave the appearance of unkempt hair. The rock surface on which it was displayed was uneven and the undulations caused shadows, which added definition to the face. The image was far larger than that of a real person, as if it had been magnified several times over.

'That's not all, sis,' said Ralph, placing his hand on Alba's and lowering the torch beam. 'She brought her cat, just like in the story, just like in my dream.'

And there, sure enough, outlined just below the effigy, was the shape of a cat, standing on the tips of its paws, its tail erect and back arched.

'Ralph,' said Alba, trying to keep calm, 'it's not possible. It's just a weird composition of rock and minerals dripping down over the years. It's like a cloud formation where you see a picture in the sky, or like one of those faces we imagine we see in the bark of an old tree. It's just a mirage.'

'There is one more thing, Alba.'

'What, Ralph?' said Alba.

'I just saw her move.'

Ande and Shelia were both exhausted from the events of the previous day. The alarm candle had been set for five o'clock that morning. It was a crude but effective device. A candle was cut for the hours of sleep wanted, one centimetre equalling one hour, and then placed in the bottom of a blackened jar, shaped like an upturned bell. It was lit using a taper. Next to the candle in the base was a sharp needle, pointing upwards. A little balloon made of dried tree sap was inflated with air and placed in the jar. The hot air from the candle made it hover until, when the candle burnt out, it dropped to the base of the jar and burst with a pop.

It was this sound that woke Ande from a deep slumber. For a few moments his brain struggled to remember why he was up quite so early after only a few hours' sleep. Then the fuzziness cleared from his mind and he swung his legs over the edge of the bed. Despite being early summer, it felt cold. He went to the cast iron burner which stood on a large tile and, using a tinderbox, quickly lit some wood that was already in the heater. The flame illuminated the room and soon the wood was spitting and crackling as the warmth began to unfold.

Shelia sat up and yawned, stretching her arms above her head.

'Morning, love. I slept all right, just not enough of it. How about you?' she said.

'Surprisingly well. You stay in bed. I'll see myself out.'

'Be quiet. The children need to sleep, especially Ralph. He'll want to join you but I'll hold him back as long as I can,' she said, returning to beneath her quilt.

Ande smiled as he pulled on his clothes. He couldn't blame Shelia for wanting to keep the day at bay for a few moments longer. He crept out of the room. A floorboard creaked as he tiptoed past Ralph's room. *Why did things always sound so much louder when you didn't want them to?* He had packed his rucksack the night before and left it by the door, not noticing that items were already missing from the storeroom. Ande took some bread, cheese and pie left over from the picnic. He splashed his face in the sink and then opened the front door carefully, using a scarf to muffle the creak of the door latch, but still the noise reverberated around the hall.

He was the first of the party to arrive at the meeting place, which was along the path at the foot of the hill. Although the sun was hinting at its appearance over White Scar Hill, it was still dark and a veil of mist hovered just above the ground. From the ether he heard the steady plod of hooves from two horses padding over the grass, the sound of them clearing their nostrils muted by the mist. A few moments later two pale apparitions appeared, soon changing to flesh and blood creatures as they drew closer to Ande. A powerful black stallion was being led by Tara-Zed. Giena Cygnus was in her carriage. Both ladies wore black trousers and tunic tops and leather riding boots. Long black hooded capes were draped over their shoulders. The only colour was given by the intricate gold belts both ladies wore on their hips, together with a sheath in which to place the recovered wands.

Not far behind them came Farmer Matthew and his son Barry, a strapping lad. Roger Butcher, Simon Beer the innkeeper and Sam Bellows appeared too. Matthew was leading two ponies pulling a cart laden with pick-axes, shovels and ropes and a barrel containing Blowamyte.

'Morning,' said Ande, setting off up the hill at a pace.

'Giena and I will come and assess the damage with you and see what, if anything, happens at sunrise. Then we shall retrieve our wands,' said Tara-Zed.

From behind them came the sound of wheezing. The group continued their ascent, until they saw who was making the commotion.

'Arfur Sendal! Who invited you?' said Ande.

'Just taking an early morning stroll, aren't I now? Good morning to you all,' replied Arfur, mopping his brow with a dirty handkerchief for, despite the chilly morning, he was perspiring with the effort of keeping up.

'Please leave us at once. We cannot take responsibility if anything happens to you,' said Tara-Zed.

'Like I say, ma'am, just out for a walk. It's good for my constitution,' said Arfur, coughing phlegm into the hankie. 'I'm not interrupting anything, am I now?'

'Arfur, you weasel. If you write anything in your grubby little column about this before a full report for the village has been prepared, I shall personally shove you in the cave and fill in the hole myself. With pleasure!' said Ande.

The group arrived at the cave mouth just before dawn, the first of the sun's rays teasing the horizon.

'What has happened here?' said Matthew.

'Something's missing,' said Simon.

'The flat stone. It's gone,' said Ande, standing on the spot where it had been only a few hours before.

'Where?' asked Matthew.

'Down there,' said Tara-Zed, pointing into the chasm.

'Judging by the look of these markings in the mud, it looks like it's been dragged,' said Giena, who had disembarked from her cart and was examining the earth with her walking stick.

As the sun finally peeped over the horizon and the first rays gingerly touched the hillside, Ande let out a cry.

'It's not the only thing that has been dragged down there,' he said, picking up a sheepskin jacket. 'This belongs to Ralph. I think he's in the cave.'

As he said this, the newly risen sunbeams shone into the hole through the small crack in the cave entrance, penetrating the gloom for the first time in five hundred years.

'You must be mistaken, Ralph. It's just a trick of the light. Rock can't move,' said Alba, trying to keep a note of panic from her voice.

'Yeah, right. Torchlight. Of course,' replied Ralph, still directing the beam at the unusual shape.

From the darkness of the passage by which the twins had just entered this great cavern came an almost invisible shaft of sunlight. These rays had squeezed through the tiny opening left after the rock fall, as if they had been sucked into the cave. They had sped along the passage ways, bouncing off the walls, ricocheting around corners until, like a volley of bullets, they stopped, their journey interrupted by the cave wall. The beams showed up for a split second as pinpricks of light settling on what looked like the cheek bone of the effigy, before they extinguished themselves. Alba had not had the torched angled on that area and both children gasped when they spotted the tiny flickers.

'What was that?' whispered Alba.

'Beams of daylight,' replied her brother, his mouth barely opening.

Without warning, the face of the woman slowly peeled itself away from the wall until, instead of being one dimensional, it turned and stared at the children with cruel, orange eyes. The creature's form began to contract and it became less part of the wall and more part of the living world. As its head shrunk, the shape of a torso and limbs began to emerge on the cave wall, adjusting and readjusting itself like an image in a funfair mirror, at first round and curvaceous, and then pinched and spindly. The foul being opened its spiteful mouth and let out a rasping cackle, which turned into a screech like someone running their fingernails down a chalk board. The cackle echoed around the giant chamber and filled the pathways of the cave system. The twins, who had stood transfixed at this terrifying scene, in unison shouted 'run' as they fled back along the passage from which they had just come.

'What was that noise?' asked Simon Beer.

Procyrion's ears pricked up, his nostrils flared, and he gave a half rear. Stardust stamped and whinnied.

The rescue party froze, looks of bewilderment on their faces, except for Arfur Sendal, who was now quivering behind a bush. The sound seemed to have come from the very centre of the earth and had emerged through the partially blocked chasm like a caustic belch.

'If I am not mistaken, dear friends, that was the cackle of a witch who has just awoken from a hundred-year coma and is very unhappy. We have no time to lose. The stories of what she did to her victims are quite gruesome and if Ralph is down there, well, I don't want to think about the consequences,' said Tara-Zed as she mounted her horse, Procyrion. Giena took up Stardust's reins and began to turn her carriage round, the pony treading with care on the damp grass.

'We must act with haste. We shall retrieve the wands from the places known only to ourselves. That will be the only way to contain the witch if she possesses the third wand,' said Giena.

'Ande,' said Tara-Zed, fixing her brown eyes on this good man. 'You must seal this hole. We cannot risk the crone getting out. If she has the wand she can use the daylight to increase her power and she would be able to wreak havoc on the village. Giena and I will not make it back in time. We must meet you at the North Tower. It overlooks the waterfall, which is the only other escape route, and will be quicker for us to get to.'

'Do you know what this means? Ralph will be trapped. You can't ask me to do that. Let us work on removing the stone and rescuing him. I can't seal him in.'

Ande stared at Tara-Zed, giant teardrops coursing down his face.

The sound of hooves made them look up. Shelia, mounted on her chestnut mare, Sunbeam, was cantering up the hill.

'The children's beds were empty and they've taken caving equipment. I thought I'd better come up and see what was happening,' she said.

Her face became grim as she saw the looks of fear staring back at her. 'What's happened?'

'Not Alba as well? It can't be. Are you sure Alba isn't at home?' said Ande, colour draining from his face.

'Of course I am,' said Shelia, her voice trembling.

Ande stepped forwards and placed his hand on Sunbeam's reins, the steam from the beast's nostrils warming his face.

'The children are in the cave. There's been a rock fall and we don't know how to get them out.'

'Well, why aren't you down there digging, instead of just standing here like plumpberries?' said Shelia, as she leapt off her horse.

'Shelia, I'm sorry,' said Giena, 'but the witch has woken. We have to seal this exit route and flush her out through the waterfall on the north side.'

At this news, Shelia stumbled backwards, pushing away Ande's helping hand. Her body seemed to buckle and she crouched on her haunches, arms locked around her knees, swaying gently. She placed a clench fist in her mouth as if trying to plug a primeval scream. The others exchanged awkward glances, not knowing what to say or do. After a few moments, she wiped her face with a sleeve.

'You can't leave them. You must do something. I won't let you just… bury them. They're our children,' said Shelia, her jaw clenched.

'I'm sorry, love. We have to seal up the hole. It would take us days to get in the cave this way, but it could take the witch only a few moments to get out,' said Ande, glancing at Tara-Zed as he talked.

'We need to get going,' said Tara-Zed. 'Leave Simon, Roger and Farmer Matthews here to block the hole up. If the children do make contact, they can be told to go to the waterfall. The underground water table will lead them to it. We must contain the witch at all costs. We can rescue the children later, but if we don't stop her then there will be no afterwards for any of us.'

'Shelia. Ande. I love those children too,' said Giena, 'but there is a possibility that the witch may already have… well, we know her reputation and you must prepare yourselves for…'

'No!' screamed Shelia. 'They are alive. Seal up the damned hole if you must, but never forget they are alive.'

There was a moment of stunned silence. Tara-Zed spoke first. Her voice was soft but contained an undercurrent of her natural authority.

'It is imperative we seal this entrance as much as possible. It would take a lot of force for one wand to break through so much stone. We have to flush her out through the waterfall. Make your way to the North Tower and watch what happens from there. I have a feeling that that was always going to be the meeting place. We'll get there as soon as possible. If there were any other way, Shelia, I would do it, but I feel something is playing out that started a century ago and Ralph and Alba are central to it. I am truly sorry.'

'I know. I am part of the Sisters. It just doesn't make it any easier. God's speed to you both,' said Shelia, through sobs.

With that, Tara-Zed and Giena Cygnus pushed their horses on, Procyrion easily cantering ahead of Stardust and the cart. The ladies' cloaks billowed behind them, the newly risen sun glistening off the gold sheaths, soon to fulfil the purpose for which they were fashioned, to be home to the wands.

'Okay, Ande, we must go too. I have to remain strong for the children. I need to return home first. You go back to the village and raise more help for our friends here. There is something which I cannot put off any longer.'

Shelia jumped on to Sunbeam's back and urged the mare forwards. Ande muttered his farewells and left the three villagers to lower themselves into the chasm to secure the exit route. Conversation was limited to the task in hand, for none of the would-be rescuers liked the feeling that they were sealing a tomb for the living.

Ralph led the way, trying not to trip over the twine which Alba was rewinding, but for which they were moving too fast, so it kept getting tangled. They ran back along the slimy corridors, their candle flames highlighting nooks and crannies that appeared like bulbous faces leering at their maniacal progress. They passed the stalactite shaped like an arum lily and rounded a corner. Alba fell behind as the rope wrapped across her body started to weigh her down. She felt the metal walkway vibrate as Ralph pounded ahead of her, flakes of rust bouncing in the beams of light. She was still trying to rewind the twine, which had become a tangled clump in her hand. Ralph's torchlight disappeared into the narrow passage, which seemed even smaller than before, but Alba pushed through, expecting to see Ralph's light bouncing ahead of her along the path.

'Ouch!' she said, for Ralph had stopped running and was standing quite still as she banged her chin on his rucksack.

Ralph ignored her and pointed a finger ahead, his eyes wide. The stalagmite formation, which they had joked about because it resembled a judge, was cracking, rather like a chick hatching from an egg. The stony shell crumbled and a white-wigged head emerged. A pair of dumpy arms suddenly stretched out, brushing the debris away and a short man, dressed in judges' garb, stood upon the ledge, pushed his pince-nez up his nose and promptly banged his head on the cave ceiling.

'Ahem. Oh for goodness' sake. Who put that wretched roof there?'

These were the first words spoken for a hundred years by the judicious man, who now stood rubbing his head. His voice reminded Ralph of a frog croaking.

'Can we help you down, sir?' asked Alba.

'Who spoke? Where am I? Ahem,' said the judge, clearing his throat and removing a red spotted handkerchief from his pocket, which he now used to clean his glasses. He then dusted off the black ring he wore.

'It's just too weird,' said Ralph.

A loud cackle echoed around them. The judge looked through narrowed eyes, a quizzical look upon his face.

'Ahem. Is that, is that, I mean to say, is that...?' stammered the judge, his voice a squeak.

'Yes, it's the witch,' said Alba.

Shaking himself back to reality, Ralph reached up and grabbed the judge by his arms, lowering his frame to the floor. The judge was extremely short, only just reaching the twins' waists.

'Follow us,' said Ralph.

The two children sprinted off but drew up after a few paces when they realised the judge was not following them.

'We'll have to go back for him. He is over a hundred years old. I expect he's a little stiff,' said Alba, turning round.

They found the strange man huffing and puffing along the passage.

'Sorry. We didn't mean to leave you,' said Ralph, as he and his sister stood on either side of the judge. 'On three, sis,' he said, nodding at Alba. 'One. Two. *Three.*'

As he said this, they each grabbed an arm and hoisted the judge up. He dangled between them, his legs making a walking motion as the children broke into a jog, following Alba's trail of twine. Behind them, they could hear a fiendish croaking and the rustling of clothes. They rounded the corner that brought them back to the cave entrance.

'Let's hope Dad's started the rescue attempt,' said Alba, but her words trailed off as they faced the solid stone wall once more.

The corner where the sky could once be glimpsed was now packed with rocks and stones. A sudden low boom, nowhere near as big as the explosion the previous evening, but enough to make Ralph's stomach churn, shook the cave, and from beyond the stone wall they heard the sound of falling rubble. The children looked at each other. Ralph knew that Alba could feel his own heart sinking. The sadness in her eyes –

no, more than that, desolation – made him want to cry. They placed the judge down, releasing their grip on his arms.

'Ahem. I must protest. This is really no way to treat a man of the law. Am I now to believe that we are stuck in this tunnel? My rescuers needing to be rescued? Pah!'

The sound of slow footsteps came from behind them, about the pace that a foolf would stalk its prey before the final leap for its victim.

'We need to take one of the side tunnels, but which one?' whispered Alba, moving back down the passage, hoping the witch was further away than her footfall suggested.

'This one,' said Ralph. 'It's quite wide,' he added, glancing at the judge.

'I'll leave the twine. It's not going to help us,' said Alba, dropping it at the foot of the rock fall.

Ralph led the way with Alba behind him and the judge to the rear. Ralph moved a lot more slowly to allow for the judge. The sides of the pathway began to narrow until they reached a section where the rock on one wall had become rounded with solidified calcium deposits and looked like a bloated stomach pushing towards the facing wall, which looked like a stomach breathing in.

'We'll never get through,' said Alba, glancing back at the judge, who was only just managing to keep up.

'Of course we will. At least I can't hear the witch. Now we've been around a few bends she won't be able to follow our lights, and with a bit of luck she'll choose a different passage,' said Ralph.

A low chuckle came from behind them.

'Ralph, she's already found us. Hurry,' said Alba.

Ralph felt his sister shove him in the back. She tugged at the judge's arm, who started to protest, but before he could say a word he was pushed into the slit behind Ralph.

'It's okay if you breathe in. And I can hear running water,' hissed Ralph.

'Well, I appear to be stuck. May I have it recorded that this was a singularly ridiculous idea and that I would not endorse such a plan if my life depended on it. Ahem.'

Ralph felt anger bubble up within him.

'Keep calm, Ralph,' said Alba.

She always seemed to know what he was feeling. He could see her face through the gap, above the bulbous body of the judge. She was frowning, her eyes narrowed as they did when she was worried. He grabbed the judge's arms and started to heave, placing one foot on the cave wall to add leverage. He could feel his face strain with effort. Alba pushed the little man, her neck muscles straining, and Ralph could see her face contort with distaste as she put her shoulder against the judge's squashy backside, but he would not budge. The cankerous rasping of the witch was getting nearer and Ralph was sure his sister would be trapped at any second.

'Ralph. You must go on,' she whispered.

'And leave us here? I think not. I'll have something to...' said the judge out loud.

The sound of breathing in the passage behind Alba stopped, as if the breath were being held in suspense. The witch was listening. After a few moments there was a wheeze as if the air were being pushed through crumpled bellows, before it recommenced with more vigour than ever.

'Pull, Ralph, pull,' cried Alba, her panic almost tangible.

The lamplight from the twins' helmets glistened against the wall. Ralph blinked as he saw the walls ripple, as if they were coming alive. From the rock, little translucent arms, like tentacles, appeared, oozing from the porridge-like walls. The arms then wrapped themselves around the ensnared judge.

'Ralph, do you see what I see?' hissed Alba.

'Yes, sis.'

'What foul work is happening now?' cried the judge, but then stifled a giggle. 'Stop tickling me.'

The diaphanous arms were squeezing between the judge's torso and the walls between which he was wedged. They then tightened around his body, but in a soft way, so his bulk moulded into the contours of the cave.

'I think those things are trying to help,' said Ralph. 'Keep pushing, Alba.'

Ralph pressed his foot against the wall and pulled even harder on the judge's arms. As the children exerted themselves, the jelly-like arms, which by now had cocooned the judge's body, contracted. He gasped and, with a pop, was propelled through the gap, pushing Ralph to the ground where he broke the judge's fall. As quickly as the amoebic creatures had appeared, they vanished, melting into the wall. Alba eased her slender frame through the now vacant gap.

'The water sounds really loud here. Run towards it,' said Ralph, pulling himself and the judge to their feet.

'Well I never. This is most unpleasant. I…' said the judge.

He did not get a chance to continue as, without a word, Ralph picked the judge up by his armpits and ran down the new passage way, with Alba following. They sprinted into a cavern, tiny in comparison to the one in which they had found the witch. Alba once again bumped into Ralph's back as he stopped, right on the edge of a pool, and for a moment it looked as if he might drop the judge into the water, but he managed to stagger backwards and place him on the floor. The roar of water, which filled the cavern, made it seem enormous. A waterfall, in the shape of a horseshoe, cascaded from an overhanging ledge into the pool, the sound of it relentless and eternal. In turn, the pool then flowed into a small river. The floor was damp where water from the pool splashed over its edges. Ralph could see no way out of the cave except the way they had come or by jumping into the river.

'Oh! There's something tugging on my hand,' said Alba, but her words were lost in the spray of the waterfall.

Looking down, she saw her lamplight reflected off a limpid arm.

'I think they want us to follow them,' she said. 'It's squeezing my hand.'

Ralph shrugged, unable to make out Alba's words. He watched as she moved to the side of the cave adjacent to the waterfall, her right hand extended as if she were being led.

He watched with curiosity as his sister seemed to climb up the side of the cave on thin air. His lamplight just picked out the silver glimmer of a liquid hand. Training his lamp towards her feet, he could see she was climbing steps formed by different layers of rock, which led behind the waterfall to a ledge just beneath the lip where the water cascaded into the pool. The various strata had created an optical illusion so the steps blended into the wall and were unnoticeable if one didn't know they were there.

Ralph nudged the judge towards the wall. Before he helped him on to the rock steps, he saw one of the tentacles from earlier on reach into the pocket of the judge's gown and remove the handkerchief. The arm then extended into the pool and placed the handkerchief so it appeared snared on a jagged rock at the mouth of the river, floating like a red lily pad being tugged by a current.

Ralph saw the judge's mouth crinkle, no doubt about to moan about the loss of his handkerchief. He shoved the judge up the steps. The noise of the waterfall seemed to fill his entire body. Ralph could see Alba's lamplight ahead of him. The reflection from the beams of light made the waterfall look like shooting stars falling down, ever down. Still pushing the judge forwards, he edged around the ledge, which, to his relief, was wide enough to fit the judge. Ralph had to crouch. The ledge emerged into a little grotto, the water gushing in front of them. He crouched next to Alba, leaving the judge standing. He wasn't that bothered if the strange little man fell into the waterfall. As soon as he had that thought, he saw Alba glare at him sideways.

He felt the soft tentacles reach up and stroke his face, before moving up to the head lamp, on which they started to tap. He could see Alba was experiencing the same thing, as she touched her cheek and smiled. Realising what their invisible friends were suggesting, Ralph pulled the leather cover over his light. Alba did the same, which plunged the three of them into pitch black. The waterfall thundered before them, but it was invisible now. Ralph felt he existed only in the elements of darkness, noise and water spray, as if he were suspended in a void. The little creatures stroked his face as if to soothe him, and he did not try to brush them away, as he would if it were his mother's hand. The thought of his mother made the pit of his stomach lurch. He felt Alba's hand touch his and he held on to her, glad she could not see his few tears which had joined the spray from the waterfall. He shook himself. The judge had not moved. Ralph suspected that the tentacles might be formed into some sort of manacles around the judge, to stop him tugging at Ralph in complaint.

Just then the comforting arms tensed. He squeezed Alba's hand tighter, feeling her hand tense too. Ralph looked in the direction of the plunging water and in the blackness saw two fierce orange eyes burning through the darkness. The witch was here. Ralph felt Alba gasp, but the sound was lost in the roar of the water. The ochre eyes, like flaming orbs, danced around in the blackness. Another pair of eyes, much lower and emerald green, flickered around like fireflies. Her cat was with her. Both sets of eyes stared hard into the depths of the waterfall and the children felt that they must surely be seen, but the eyes averted. The orange eyes and the green eyes moved toward the wall that the twins had climbed up moments before. Would they pick out the steps? Ralph felt Alba's hand tighten in his. He held his breath, his pulse racing. The eyes stared and then bobbed away, looking towards the flow of the river. After concentrating on that area for what, to Ralph, seemed liked hours, the green and amber orbs disappeared, as the witch and her cat turned their backs on the waterfall and disappeared into the inky darkness.

Ralph breathed out and realised he was sweating. After a few moments, the little creatures stopped their stroking and tapped on the children's heads once more. The children exposed their lights again. He felt a tugging on his hand and saw that he was being pulled to an exit from the ledge into yet another passage. Alba was ahead of him. He felt tired. The rucksack was beginning to weigh on his back, but he was determined not to give up and strode out, before remembering the judge and slowing to an amble. He rounded a corner and found himself in another little grotto, this time with a smaller pool of water fed by a stream, an overflow of the main river which was somewhere above them. It was quieter now and Ralph felt that for the moment they were safe from the witch.

'That was close. She must have thought we'd gone into the water,' said Ralph.

'Those creatures saved us again,' said Alba.

'But what about my handkerchief? It is quite disgraceful,' said the judge.

Ralph and Alba took the rucksacks from their backs and sat down on the stone floor, which was covered in dents shaped like cereal bowls. Pits, like pockmarks, lined the inside of these abrasions. Ralph traced his finger around one of the dents, and then looked upwards, the light from his candle spluttering as he tipped his head back.

'The same indentations are on the ceiling,' he said.

'Are you hungry?' said Alba.

'This caved must have once been filled with water which swirled around at great pressure and carved out all these ruts. I've seen similar when I've been caving with Dad, but not this distinctive. Amazing,' said Ralph.

'I'm hungry,' said Alba, opening her rucksack. 'By the way, Judge, I am Alba Milway and this is my brother, Ralph. An accident has brought us into this cave system, but we know who you are from your legend and we are here to rescue you.'

'Ahem. Well, never mind all that. Have you any food? I haven't eaten for…well, I am famished,' said the judge.

'Certainly,' said Alba, through gritted teeth, and she handed the judge a slice of her mother's fruit cake.

Alba took out the nuts, seeds and fruit she had packed.

'We'd better ration our provisions. Just in case,' said Ralph.

He knelt by the pool and, using his hands, scooped up some water to drink. Alba knelt down beside him and did the same, but stopped and stared hard into the depths, without drinking the water which drained through her fingers.

'Look, Ralph. Little green lights.'

Below the surface were delicate fluorescent points floating around in the pool. When the lamps shone upon them the carefree movements ceased and became more deliberate.

'They're waving to us,' said Alba, waving back.

'They're like some primitive amphibious creature,' said Ralph.

'Ralph, they're not that primitive. They've saved us twice, and they can communicate. I'd call that quite intelligent. They certainly have better conversational skills than Murgus Bellows.'

Ralph scooped up some water and took a gulp. It was cool and refreshing and tasted of minerals and ice. He turned towards the judge, whose cheeks were bulging like a squirrel's on a particularly successful nut hunt. A few crumbs were scattered down his black gown. He looked away from the Ralph towards a helictite on a far wall.

'He's eaten all the food, the greedy pig,' said Ralph.

'Shush, Ralph, don't be rude,' said Alba.

'May I suggest that on your next venture you carry a better selection of morsels and more of it,' said the judge, wiping his mouth with the back of his hand.

'Well, might I suggest that in future you don't allow yourself to be dragged down into a cave by a witch,' said Ralph.

'Well, I really expect you to treat your elder and better with more respect,' said the judge.

'We're trying to rescue you,' said Ralph, jumping to his feet, his arms rigid by his side, his fists clenched.

Ralph felt Alba grip his arm.

'What my brother means is we don't know how long we'll be down here and some spare food would have been handy. Still, it's less to carry, huh, Ralph?' said Alba, forcing a smile. 'Our aim has got to be to find the wand before the witch does. Do you remember, Ralph, we saw a formation like an arum lily?'

'Yes,' said Ralph.

'Well, the wands in the concert are represented by arum lilies,' said Alba.

'That means we've got to go back,' said Ralph.

'It'll be all right,' said Alba.

The judge struggled to his feet, as Ralph fiddled with a flap on the rucksack, pretending not to notice. Alba picked up the rope. They set off along a path that ran beside the small river. The water was flowing steadily and the sound was familiar and comforting, like the stream near to their home, where they paddled and swam. Their momentary feeling of relief was, however, shattered as the water coursed around a bend. A familiar cackle boomed out from the tunnel system behind them.

'How did she find us?' said Alba.

'I don't know but I'm not stopping to ask. Come on, Alba,' said Ralph, picking up the judge and dashing into the darkness.

CHAPTER 11

THE WELSH LAGOONS

Fingers, with skin stretched so tight across the knuckles it was almost transparent, moved crab-like on the wooden arm of the chair, as if playing an invisible piano. Wispy white hair sprouted from a skeletal skull. Lady Anna's eyes were shut. Blue veins fluttered beneath the thin eyelids, so she looked as if she had a map covering each eye. Her chest rose and fell as if fluttering, her breathing shallow.

She was not asleep. Just waiting, listening to the waves lapping against the base of the tower where she had been exiled all those years ago. The castle, of which her tower formed just a small corner, had at one time been a stronghold to quell Welsh rebellions against the English king; over the years it had become a tourist attraction and now was its own kingdom again, surrounded by seas; Lady Anna's prison.

Whatever the season, a fire always burnt in the ancient hearth. Presently, a guard would bring her lunch. The tins had run out years ago. It would probably be some form of mutated fish netted from the seas. And, of course, carrots and potatoes. The boat bringing fresh supplies would not be here for another fortnight.

A flapping at an open window caused her to open her eyes. She smiled to herself. Nobody had expected her to live this long. She had outlasted them all. She stroked the ruby in the wooden cross she still wore around her neck, the symbol which had led to her undoing. A crow flapped into the room and settled on the round table next to her

111

chair. She raised a hand and stroked the bird's chest with the back of her index finger.

'Well, Scavard. What titbit have you for me today?' Her voice was still strong. The crow responded with a series of clicks from the back of its throat. Lady Anna tilted her head towards the creature as it responded to her.

'I knew there were no more fairies for you to bring me. They disappeared years ago. But now you tell me there are no more tainted toadstools. Then I shall die. And soon.' Lady Anna sank back in her chair, her fingers once again drumming a silent tune. The tainted toadstools were those left from fairy rings, where some of the magic had seeped into the fungi, infusing them with mystical properties.

Scavard, however, hopped from one foot to the other and clicked out a frantic message. Lady Anna's eyes grew wide and she clutched her wooden cross so that it left an impression in her palm.

'The cave is open? The three wands will be brought together. I *must* have them, Scavard. I could restore everything. *Everything*! You have served me well. Now go and engage help. My bloodling who has been in that cave will need help to defeat our enemies. Those humans who refused to use the magic available to them will suffer for their weakness.'

Lady Anna turned to the cheese dish set on the table next to her. She slowly lifted the lid from the dish. A twitching, whiskered nose emerged from beneath the lid. As Lady Anna raised the lid higher, two shiny eyes and two pink ears poked out. Before the mouse could run for freedom, Scavard snapped it up so only a long, pink, thrashing tail emerged from the bird's beak. The bird flapped out the window by which it had entered. Lady Anna replaced the lid.

Next to the cheese dish was a photo frame. The glass was cracked but the young graduate still smiled back. By the frame was a small, black urn with a gold lid. Lady Anna, with the stiffness of age, rotated her body in the chair, and placed a hand on the vessel.

'Anthony. We shall all be restored soon, my son. And then we can govern the planet.' She sank back into her chair to await her boiled fish and carrots.

CHAPTER 12

Arfur Sendal was still hiding behind a large gorse bush. He had watched Ande, Shelia, Tara-Zed and Giena Cygnus go their separate ways. He reached into a pocket of his jacket and pulled out a tatty notebook and a well-chewed pencil. On a page in the pad, which had the puckered stain of a mug on it, he started scratching notes from the conversation he had overheard, a grin across his pointy face.

The front page would be his for at least a week. That would shut his fellow journalists up. However, for the time being, 'Brats Buried Alive by Barmy Parents' and 'Witch of White Scar Wakes' would have to wait. He paused, screwing the pencil tip into the pad, his forehead screwed up with concentration. *Now, Arfur, where shall you go? Wouldn't you just love to know where those wands are hidden, eh now? I can't believe that Miss Smarty-Pants Cygnus is a Sister of Antares. But they are on horseback so I'd never keep up, even with the cripple.* He chewed the end of his pencil. *Yes, that's what I'll do. I'll go to the North Tower and conceal myself. I don't have to get involved. I'm a journalist, not an adventurer, aren't I now?*

Twigs and leaves were stuck to his clothes and he brushed off as much as he could with his wiry hands, but the gorse was sharp and its needle-like thorns pricked his fingers. Arfur dropped his notebook and pencil. He bent over to pick them up.

'What was that?' He cried out, as he felt a sudden draught across his neck. Standing upright he looked around but saw nothing. Placing the notepad back in his pocket, he continued to pick at the irritating foliage. A swishing sensation passed right over the top of his head.

'Who's there?' He raised his arms and rubbed his fingers through his greasy hair.

Just then, Arfur was enveloped by a flock of oily feathers beating around him, ebony beaks pecking at his arms and legs. The shiny jet eyes of several crows hovered in front of his face, before rushing off and diving at him again. Arfur crouched down, covering his head with his arms.

'Oh! Mummy!' he whimpered.

Crow by crow, the attack receded until just five birds, one almost the size of a raven, continued to pester him. The remainder of the crows circled overhead, their harsh cries resonating through the hillside. Arfur rubbed the tops of his arms and thighs where he had been jabbed by the stout beaks.

Feeling braver, he began to shoo the five birds away, but with a loud caw the entire flock plunged down once more from the sky. Arfur covered his head and fell cowering on his knees, but the birds passed right over him, leaving just the five birds tugging his trousers and jacket sleeves.

It occurred to Arfur that the remaining birds were not going away. His plan had been to skirt around the hill and head north, so, with great trepidation, he rose to his feet and moved in that direction. This brought more furious pecking from his winged companions, forcing him to halt. The birds were tugging him down the hill to the west.

'All right, I'll go with you, won't I? You're only stupid birds and I'll soon get rid of you, won't I?'

So Arfur was pecked and pulled by his feathered escort down the hill towards the woods at the edge of the village.

Ralph and Alba darted through the labyrinthine passages as best they could with the cumbersome figure of the judge being dragged along, the sound of his grumbling filling the narrow space. The lights from the head lamps flickered up and down with each stride, picking out peculiar shapes on the walls. It reminded Ralph of lumpy porridge that had boiled down the side of a pan. The passageway divided in two ahead of them.

'Left or right?' said Ralph.

'I don't know. Left,' said Alba.

Ralph veered off along the path, which soon bent back to the right and sloped steeply downwards.

'Great choice, sis,' said Ralph.

The path became so steep it was impossible to stand up and both children were soon on their bottoms with their feet flexed against the passage walls to act as brakes.

'Judge, you'd better come here,' said Ralph, turning his body and reaching out with his arms.

'Oh me, oh my. Most undignified. I'll have something to say about this later,' said the judge.

Alba shoved the man towards her brother and Ralph wedged him between his legs, gripping the judge's robes with both hands, inching forwards down the slope.

Behind him Ralph could feel Alba mimic his actions. The cold of the floor penetrated his clothes.

'Ouch,' said Alba. 'This rock is like sandpaper.'

'It's getting steeper,' said Ralph.

A loud cackle ricocheted around the confined space.

'There's no way back,' he said. 'Alba, I think this is what is called an aven. It's a hole made by torrents of water filled with rock and stone. Like an upside-down whirlpool.'

'And…?' said Alba.

'If I'm right we should eventually get to a hole,' he said.

'Great. We can get out,' said Alba.

'Well, assuming it's big enough for us all to fit through, there is just one problem. It will be in a cave ceiling.'

'Okay. We've got a rope. Let's just keep edging forward. At least the side of the walls are getting smoother,' said Alba.

'Oh cripes!' said Ralph.

Before Alba could ask what was wrong, Ralph, still with the judge perched between his legs, slid forwards, as if he were sledging down the side of an icy hill. He heard his sister shout his name, but it was soon lost behind him. The judge held on to his wig as if it were life itself. By instinct Ralph lay back, keeping his head just off the floor. As he gained momentum his shoulders rubbed alternately from the top of one side of the passage to the other. At any other time such a chute would have been great fun, especially if he were going to land on Davyd Baker's head in a pool of clear blue water on a sunny day. It seemed more likely that he was going to plunge to his death, as he weaved from side to side. The lamp gave the illusion that the walls were moving too, trying to keep up with him. The air in the narrow chute was cold against his skin as it whooshed past. Goose bumps pimpled his body. Suddenly, Ralph's light picked out a break in the passageway.

'This is it, sis, watch out,' he yelled.

He hoped Alba was still behind him, but before he had time to think any further, he and the judge, who appeared to have been silenced by terror, plunged through a hole at the end of the tunnel.

'Aaaaahhhh,' cried Ralph as he shot through the opening.

'Ouch,' came a muffled cry.

He found himself staring at the ceiling, the beam from his lamp picking out Alba's form as she fell through the air, so the scene reminded him of a faltering black and white film he had watched last summer in the village hall. His candle spluttered, and when it revived, it showed that she had landed on the judge. Ralph couldn't help laughing, the sound strangely muted in this peculiar cave.

'Ralph, it's not funny. You were terrified. I could feel it,' said Alba.

'Sorry, sis. You looked really funny landing on the judge.'

'How come you're not hurt?' said Alba, standing up and checking herself for any damage.

'Our little friends helped out again. I was expecting to land on rock. Probably would have broken every bone in my body, but they'd piled themselves up on the floor and it was like landing in a bowl of jelly. Then they just slithered away,' he said.

'Ahem. Disgraceful,' said the judge, as Alba bent forwards to help him to his feet.

'We're all in one piece, so we must be thankful for that. Those little cave dwellers are quite remarkable,' said Alba.

Looking around, Ralph saw that their latest stopping place was another small, circular cave. The stone of the wall was more like granite than the limestone porridge they were used to. Ralph walked up to the wall and touched it.

'This is harder rock, more resistant to flood water. That's why there's an aven up there. Like a pressure reliever. I never thought I'd fall through one though,' he said.

Ralph and Alba moved their lights around the cave and both beams settled on something smooth and shiny, like a spillage of oil, in front of them. They edged forwards and saw that it was a small lake that seemed to stop at the opposite cave wall, about twenty metres away. It appeared that the cave they now stood in had no means of escape, other than the way they had just entered. The children looked at each other, their faces contorted with worry, Ralph's moment of euphoria dispelled.

'I'll take a dip, sis. See if there's another way out,' said Ralph. 'I'll wear a rope just in case you need to pull me in. The lamps are waterproof, for a short spell at least.' He pulled down the shutters over the helmet's vents.

Ralph was already unbuckling his rucksack and pulling off his boots, socks and jumper. He took the rope from Alba and knotted it around his waist.

'I'll give one tug if I'm in trouble and need hauling in and two tugs if I reach the other side safely.' And before Alba could argue, he had slid into the black pool and was edging forwards, one foot feeling the way, before the next followed.

He looked over his shoulder at Alba.

'The floor of the pool ends here. There's nothing after, so I'm going to have to swim for it,' he said.

'Be careful,' said Alba, holding the rope.

It was a relief to have taken the coil off her back and for the moment her body felt as light as a feather, although her mood was as heavy as lead. She and the judge watched as Ralph's light danced across the gloom, going deeper into the cavern, the reflections of the pool making the roof seem as if it were shifting above them in rippling movements. Gentle splashing sounds filled the void as Ralph pushed his way through the underground tarn with strong, confident strokes. The beam from his lamp expanded as it touched the overhanging rock and then, without warning, it plunged beneath the surface, turning the black water a blue-green before disappearing, seemingly straight into the rock. Alba gasped but continued to feed the rope through her fingers, which, despite the steady climate of the cave, were clammy with perspiration.

After a few minutes Alba began to panic. She couldn't sense her brother and he had been gone too long under the water. She nearly fainted with panic when she felt one tug on the rope.

'Oh goodness, he's in trouble,' cried Alba, but before she could tighten her grip and start to pull, another tug followed.

Alba choked back tears of relief as moments later she saw Ralph's light emerge from beneath the rocky lintel and soon he was back on the stone shore.

'There is a way out of here, but it's under that wall, which is really a big rock hanging down into the water. You only need to hold your breath for about ten seconds, no more.'

Ralph looked at the judge.

'Oh dear. Ahem. I can't swim and even if I could I'm not sure I could hold my breath for all that time. You'll have to find another way out for me, or leave me here.'

The man sat down and exhaled a long sigh, his shoulders hunching over. Alba stared at Ralph, a pleading look in her eyes.

'There is no question of us leaving you here,' said Alba, touched by this ancient creature's uncharacteristic show of emotion, 'is there, Ralph?'

'No, of course not,' he said, hands in pockets and scuffing the floor with his foot.

'Ralph? Can you swim the rucksacks over and then come back for the judge? I'll wait here with him.'

'Okay,' said Ralph. 'Watch out as you go in. It's about ten paces to where the floor runs out and then there's a sheer drop.'

'Judge, it would be helpful if you could take off your robe. Is that possible?' said Alba.

The judge glared at Alba as if she were the witch herself, and Alba's earlier bout of sympathy began to evaporate.

'Certainly not. These are ceremonial robes, suited to my office. Removal is out of the question,' said the judge.

'So?' said Ralph.

'I'm sure Ralph will manage, won't you?' said Alba as patiently as possible.

She removed her own shoes and socks and folded them in one of the rucksacks, together with Ralph's garments.

Placing one rucksack over each shoulder, Ralph entered the pool again, this time plunging forwards, making a large splash which covered the judge.

'I say. How careless of him. How rude. Does he know…?'

'It was an accident,' said Alba, 'and you are about to get a lot wetter.'

'I'll drown. I've been holding my breath for so long, I can't do it for another minute.' And, as if to reinforce this point, the judge breathed in with a wheeze and immediately started coughing and spluttering.

'We really don't have any choice, Your Worship,' said Alba.

She placed her arm on the tiny man's shoulder.

'Please try. Ralph's a strong swimmer. You will be okay. We really want you to get out of here. To see the world again and, well, we're not sure if we can defeat the witch without you, especially if she gets hold of one of the three wands.'

'Three wands?' said the judge, sitting up straight once more.

'Yes,' said Alba. 'Our present judge, Tara-Zed…'

'Does she have a wand?' said the judge.

'Yes. Tara-Zed and the teacher Giena Cygnus know the location of the other two wands and are going to use them to defeat the witch. If the witch gets hold of the wand that is somewhere down here, your knowledge of that creature could make all the difference. Please try to get across.'

'I saw firsthand what Aster was capable of. I'll make the crossing.'

They peered into the silent blackness, Alba's own light picking out eerie shapes and rock formations never before seen by human eyes. She shivered. There was a moment when she felt alarm followed by a feeling of consternation. Was this her brother's or her own feelings? She couldn't tell. Two sharp tugs on the rope reassured her that Ralph had reached the opposite shore safely and before long, unencumbered by the weight of the rucksacks, his lamp light appeared once more from under the rock and broke the surface of the water.

'What kept you?' said Alba.

'Bad news. I lost one of the backpacks. The one with the spare candles. It snagged on a bit of rock and just disappeared. Sorry, sis.'

'Ralph. You're okay. That's all that matters. Now let's get the judge across and find a way out of here.'

'I'm going to swim on my back and hold you under the chin, like lifesaving,' said Ralph, looking at the judge, 'but you must relax and not struggle. If I let you go, you will sink like a stone dressed in those robes. I couldn't see any bottom to this pool.'

With that he reached up and gently took the judge by his hands and, with Alba guiding, they entered the water. Ralph had gathered the rope up and coiled it so it was wrapped over his right shoulder. With his left arm he held the judge across the chest and, sliding back into the water, he began to paddle with his right arm.

Leaving her jacket in the cave, Alba entered the pool, catching her breath. It was like standing in a bath filled with ice. The water quickly saturated her wool trousers, and as she waded further in, her clothing became heavier. It felt as if the subterranean lagoon were soaking her up.

How many paces had she gone? At least eight, she thought. Nearly at the shelf. A wave of panic rose up within her and she hesitated before she used her legs to push herself forwards. She submerged her shoulders beneath the surface, only her head above water. She pulled herself through the water after her brother. Alba afforded herself a grin as the cave filled with the sound of the judge's voice.

'Oh mercy me. I am over a hundred years old. Oh good heavens,' he exclaimed, the echo making it sound like one long, sonorous howl.

Alba saw Ralph stop just before the overhang and heard the reassuring tone of his voice, calming the judge and hushing the echoes. She wanted to cry out like a wild animal in pain as she watched her beloved brother disappear beneath the surface with his human cargo, leaving her paddling alone in this watery nightmare. The ripples she made looked like black eels slithering about her.

The beam from her lamp picked out the point where the rocky obstruction dipped into the water like a lead ball. She paused for a moment. She had nearly drowned once before. Why did this have to be the only other way out of the cave? Alba wasn't sure if she would rather take her chances against the witch.

Treading water, she touched her safety helmet to make sure it was firmly in place, the candle momentarily warming her hand, igniting a little spark of courage within her. Taking a deep breath, Alba let the dank air expand her lungs to their capacity before she dipped beneath the surface and started to pull herself downwards, the water numbing her face. No more than ten seconds Ralph had said, and she was a strong swimmer so it should be less than that. The candle held firm, but the light barely penetrated that dense gloom, simply picking out the strange swirling patterns from the rocky ceiling above her, as she forced her way through the water.

One crocodile, two crocodiles, three crocodiles, thought Alba, a childish game to make the seconds pass more quickly. *Four crocodiles, five crocodiles, six...*

Alba felt something stroke her face. She wanted to gasp but checked herself. It was probably one of those strange little cave dwellers trying to help. There it was again only this time it felt like a thin cord cutting into her forehead. Now treading water, she brushed her hand up and a fine wire wrapped around her fingers. As she tried to untangle herself, a section of the thread caught under the safety helmet and dislodged it. Alba grabbed for the helmet, but her hands were still tied up in a bizarre game of cat's cradle, and she watched it spin away from her. The candlelight appeared to flicker on and off as it spiraled down and down into the black emptiness.

She managed to disentangle herself from the twine and at once dived after the helmet, a rush of bubbles rumpling her cheeks as her air-starved lungs vented their meagre contents. But it was too late. The light became just a pinprick before the darkness extinguished it and Alba was left suspended in a freezing black solitude.

The blackness enveloped her like a blanket used to smother a fire. She wanted to scream and she *had* to breathe. Her body cried out for air. Unable to resist the urge, Alba opened her mouth, but instead of oxygen, she gulped down a cold, metallic liquid, which rushed along her windpipe, filling her chest to bursting. Her heart pumped madly as she tried to expunge the vile water from her body, but it would not leave.

She moved her arms and legs around trying to find anything that she could use to guide her, for she could see nothing but the obsidian darkness and feel only a consuming wetness. Alba couldn't even tell if she was sinking or rising. She wasn't cold anymore but now there was a pain that was crushing her chest.

Then out of the gloom Alba saw her mother swimming lazily towards her, a big smile on her beautiful face, her golden hair floating around her like a halo. She would make all this better. Trying to ignore the pressure on her torso, Alba reached out her arms and attempted to propel herself forwards, but before she could move, her mother's image floated away into the void. *How strange*, thought Alba.

All at once, Alba was struck with the urge to claw at her throat, fear rising in her like a wave before it crashes on to a shore. She would be late for school. What would she tell Miss Cygnus when she arrived sodden and shivering, leaving a large puddle on the classroom floor?

The fear ebbed away and she felt a calming warmth run through her, like that from the lamplight. She saw a light moving towards her, or was she moving towards the light? She couldn't tell. Isn't that what people saw when they were dying, an ethereal light sent to guide them to a better place? And then Alba realised, without any sense of panic, she was drowning. The pain in her chest had subsided along with the fear, which, as she floated weightlessly in the atmosphere of water, was replaced with a deep melancholy. What a horrible place to die. She would never be found by her heartbroken family.

The light got closer and became so bright Alba tried to look away, but found she couldn't move, being now suspended like one of the pickled frogs in the jars at the apothecary's shop, her hair waving around her like tendrils from a sea-anemone.

A pressure tightened across her chest, but Alba, just a few strained heartbeats from death, could do nothing. Her lumpen body was moving, being pulled, possibly upwards, towards that divine light. This was it. The point where she crossed an unknown threshold into death itself.

Alba felt something unfamiliar, and yet so familiar, touch her skin, but before she could think about this strange reception into Heaven, her arms were yanked over her head and she felt her back being scraped across a hard, cold surface as she was dragged by her wrists on to a hard shore. Someone was talking quietly, desperately. Fear, but not her own, filled her heart.

'Come on, sis. Be all right. Just breathe. Don't die!'

An unseen force roughly raised her body and then she felt something grip her torso. She felt a jolt as something pressed into her stomach and a sharp pain wracked the space behind her ribcage. Then water spewed from her mouth. She spluttered and gasped as cold air invaded her body, burning her windpipe and searing her lungs. Finding she could now move for herself, she rolled on to her side and coughed and wretched again. More liquid spewed from what felt like her very soul. She collapsed, panting, on to the unforgiving floor, her heart pummelling her chest as it sought to pump the precious oxygen around her body.

Alba felt herself being tucked up against something soft, a light warmth touching her skin. Relief flooded into her from this source as she was gently rocked.

'Thank God,' said a murmuring voice, before she was lowered back to the floor with great care.

As her heart beat steadied, Alba looked up and saw her brother kneeling beside her, the light on his head hurting her eyes. Of course! The light she had seen was her brother's head lamp. The final pressure she had felt was his strong arms pulling her to the surface. The desperate voice, his own. She wasn't dead after all. She sat up and grabbed her brother round the neck, squeezing him in an embrace.

'Watch out, sis. You might crack my ribs,' he said, with slight embarrassment in his voice.

Alba pulled away from him, wiping tears from her eyes.

'Oh, Ralph. You saved my life. I was drowning. How did you know?'

Ralph looked at the floor, his earlier well of emotion once again buried within him.

'I *felt* you drowning, sis,' he said.

'What do you mean, you felt me?'

'I've always been able to feel what you are feeling. I just never admitted it, even to myself.'

'But I nearly drowned before, at the Force Falls, two summers ago. Why didn't you save me then? Don't you remember?'

'Of course I remember. I just suggested Murgus dive at that exact spot. I told him there was a bag of Global War figures down there.

He saved you. I just didn't want all the fuss that being different would mean.'

'Thank you,' said Alba, hugging her brother once more.

'What happened down there, sis?'

'I don't know. Something tangled around me and I knocked my hat off.'

Alba inspected her hands and touched her wrists. A yellow thread was still attached to one of them.

'It's the safety cord I used when we first got here. What was that doing in the water?'

A jowly splutter made both children turn to the judge. Ralph moved closer to him and peered round the side of the diminutive creature. A tiny piece of yellow thread, showing up easily against the dark material, protruded from a pocket in the judge's robe. Ralph grabbed it and a small coil of the cord fell on to the cave's floor.

'It was much bigger than that when I last used it,' said Alba, staring at the judge through narrowed eyes, as she rose to her feet.

'Have you been using it to leave a trail? Is that how the witch found us?' said Ralph, his teeth clenched.

The judge shuffled from side to side, twisting the ring on his finger, and looked up at the children, a doleful expression peeping above his little half-glasses.

'Yes. It's true. I have been leaving a trail, but only so we didn't get lost. You have to understand. I've been down here so long. I just want to see sunlight one more time before I die,' said the judge, with a loud sob. 'I know there's nothing to live for on the surface. All my friends are long gone. I probably won't even recognise Ingleset. But the thought of being trapped down here any longer... well, it made me selfish. I wouldn't blame you for just abandoning me.'

The judge took another deep breath and sighed.

'Now don't be silly, Your Worshipfulness. We're all going to get out of here and stop the witch. Just think before you act in future,' said Alba.

She dropped to her knees and gave the little man a hug. Surprisingly to Alba, he felt quite dry and firm, unlike her and Ralph, whose trousers were clinging to each respective set of legs and whose hair was stuck to their heads.

'Let's get out of here. We're all starting to freeze and need to get moving,' said Ralph.

'What supplies have we got left?' asked Alba, who was now shivering and wrapping her arms around herself.

Ralph opened the remaining rucksack. Thankfully the shoes, socks and jumpers were still dry and the children pulled them on.

'Not much,' he said. 'A tinder box, which is still dry, but no candles. A pen knife. And I still have this rope. It's really heavy now it's sodden.'

'Well, we'd better find our way out of here pretty quick then. I think we must forget about the wand,' said Alba.

Her teeth chattered as she walked off along the passage before remembering she wasn't wearing a light anymore and she was soon engulfed by the total darkness. 'You'd better lead the way, Ralph. I can't see.'

'Here, sis. You wear the safety helmet,' said Ralph, reaching up to his head.

'No, you wear it. If I hear a clunk, I'll know to duck. Plus, I can blame you if we get lost again.'

Ralph looked at Alba and smiled. She had taken the judge by the hand. *She really is very kind*, he thought. He moved into yet another unknown passage, the darkness closing in behind them.

CHAPTER 13

The floor was smooth, but ancient rock-filled whirlpools had gouged out potholes, so in parts it was cratered like the surface of the moon. Ralph led them along the passage with as much speed as he dared. The walls in this part showed the centuries of layering and rock formation through the different coloured strata: ochre, light grey, granite. He let his fingers drift along the wall, the thrill of touching stone hundreds of thousands of years old abating some of his anxiety. Alba stumbled in one of the potholes.

'Oh flip!' she said but carried on.

Ralph concentrated again. To twist an ankle now could mean the witch caught them, and he didn't want to think what could happen then.

Their route became narrower and steeper. The judge rocked from side to side as he panted on the incline, pulling on Alba's hand for support. The beam from Ralph's light grew bigger as it reflected off the face of the cave.

'Not another dead end,' said Alba.

'No, look. I've been watching the strata and these layers of rock end here and a new set of weaker rock starts. The ice flows will have pushed upwards. There is a way through. We might need to climb upwards, but we can do it,' said Ralph.

He shone his lamp and sure enough there was an opening, which the light just penetrated. He took off the rucksack and stood on it for extra height. He felt around, his fingers gripping on to a ledge.

He heaved himself up, his head disappearing through the fissure, leaving his legs dangling in mid-air. Finally he pulled his feet through the hole, all the time conscious he was leaving Alba and the judge in pitch black. A moment later, Ralph stuck his head back through the opening, filling the gloom where his sister stood with a welcome light.

'It brings us back in to that giant cave where we first saw the witch. We can get to the passage where we saw the formation that looks like an arum lily. We can still get the wand. This opening looks quite fragile. Stand back as I've got to make it wider to, err, make it easier for the judge.'

He vanished again, leaving Alba and the judge with their backs pressing into the hard wall.

Hurry up, Ralph, thought Alba.

The blackness had a physicality of its own and weighed down on her. Suddenly, the sound of falling rubble pattered against the cave wall, like a rainstorm. Above her, Ralph had found a small boulder and was smashing it against the edge of the opening.

'Oh deary me. I shall never see the light of day again,' whimpered the judge.

'Of course you will,' said Alba, 'and you'll be made to feel most welcome and at home again.'

Alba had been brought up not to tell lies and she hoped what she had just said was the truth, as her mouth filled with dust particles.

Light flooded into the passage as Ralph's head dangled down once more, revealing a pile of rocks and grit covering the rucksack, which none of them had thought to move before Ralph started his excavations. Alba scrabbled around in the rocky debris to drag it out.

'It's completely flattened,' she said undoing the buckle. 'The spare torch is crushed. Even the candle in it is ruined. The firelighter is in pieces. Everything is broken.'

She sat down on her haunches, her head hanging down, tears splashing into the dust.

'Okay, sis. I'm sensing you now, and it's not great,' said Ralph. 'We are going to get out of here. Come on, help lift the judge up and we'll be on our way. We really have no time to lose.'

Alba looked up at her brother without blinking. She turned towards the judge and held out her hand, which he grasped. Alba winced, as it was the one that had been grazed, but she led him to the spot beneath the opening. Ralph stretched out his arms. Alba picked the judge up by the waist and thrust him upwards. A wave of nausea swept over her and she stumbled backwards, still holding the judge, for he felt heavy in her tired arms.

'Ahem. Excuse me. Watch what you are doing, you clumsy girl.'

As she steadied herself, Ralph grabbed the judge's arms very tightly, and hauled him up. Even Alba in her state of despondency had to smile as the judge's short legs dangled for a moment above her, before disappearing, but her reverie was short lived as she stood alone in the darkness, wondering if she should have just stayed in the bottomless pool.

'None of those thoughts, sis,' said Ralph, as the cave lit up once more.

Alba smiled. Perhaps it had been easier when Ralph hadn't admitted to picking up on her feelings. She stood on the pile of rock and stretched towards the ledge, heaving herself upwards, emerging in the centre of the grand cavern. Ralph's light hardly penetrated the depths of it. The trio moved towards the passage where they had originally entered the cave.

A white flash illuminated the gigantic cavity, making the party lose their sense of direction.

'What was that?' said Ralph.

In response, the hollow cackle of the witch echoed around them. Before they had time to gather their wits, a crash nearby made the ground shake beneath them. Ralph sent his light in the direction of the quake and saw that a large boulder lay on the surface.

'How the...?' But before he could complete his sentence another blinding flash lit the cavern. Silhouetted on a rocky shelf high above them, at the farthest end of the cave, the witch, with arm outstretched, held a startling silver wand.

'She's got it. We need to make a run for it,' said Ralph, but the witch pointed the flashing silver rod in the direction of the cave roof and another boulder crashed down.

'We'll never make it,' said Alba, as yet another rock hit the floor.

The group edged towards the cave wall and cowered against it.

The witch got into the stride of her onslaught and boulders and rocks rained down continuously from on high, littering the once flat cave floor with debris. Dust swirled in the air, but by some miracle the children had positioned themselves beneath an outcrop of rock. They were standing next to the ancient mud pools that only a little while before Alba had wished were chocolate.

The three of them covered their ears to blot out some of the noise, but their very teeth shook in their heads with the vibrations of the continual bombardment. Their eyes ached from the icy flashes of the wand as it unleashed its power, pent up from a century of disuse.

'She's cracked the mud pools,' said Ralph.

'What is it with you and those mud pools?' said Alba.

'Ahem! I'm not sure if my bones can take this shaking. I am over one hundred years old, you know.'

'Of course, Your Worship,' said Alba, looking at her brother. 'We can't stay here forever, Ralph. The candlelight will be running out soon.'

As she spoke, Alba felt the strange little touches of the peculiar cave-dwelling creatures stroke her face and hands. Ralph looked at her.

'Can you feel them, sis?'

'Yes. They must be here to help, again.'

'Be careful.' Ralph touched his face and moved his hands up to the light on his head.

'I think they want me to cover the light up.'

'That would make sense. It does give our position away,' said Alba, 'and they haven't let us down yet.'

Just then the rumbling of the rocky attack stopped. The cave floor was strewn with boulders of every shape and size. The ceiling above the witch's head was higher and hollower than ever before, having been sacked of its stone.

Clinging to another part of the ceiling, further into the cave, were thin stalactites suspended like pieces of straw in a topsy-turvy field. Ralph had noticed them earlier, fascinated by the way they were formed hollow, but he didn't have time to contemplate their beauty for the witch launched a second onslaught with her wand.

'Aaahhhh!' she screeched, making the blood in Ralph's veins run cold.

Under the direction of the wand, the thin sticks became waves of arrows whistling to the ground, landing dangerously close to the inadequate hiding place. They splintered into shards as sharp as glass. The travellers hid their faces as particles powdered their bodies.

'Ralph, put out the light and let the creatures guide us. We have no choice,' cried Alba, as the missiles hurtled down in their tens of thousands.

Ralph pulled the cover down over his light, plunging them into darkness save for the strobe flashing of the witch's wand. Alba grabbed the judge's arm as she felt the soft, silent fronds tighten around hers.

'I'm on the move, sis,' said Ralph, his voice seeming to trail off into the darkness, which was now saturated with the hissing and smashing of the stalactites.

Alba felt herself pulled forwards and she allowed herself to relax as much as possible and be guided by these kind beings. They tugged on her legs when she needed to lift them over the numerous obstacles. Whenever she staggered, which was quite often, a little pad of gel was there to cushion her fall. This didn't seem to apply to the judge though, who she could hear complaining as she dragged him over the boulders.

The flashes of white showed Ralph that he was edging to the end of the cave opposite to the witch, who, realising that her quarry was escaping, ceased her bombardment, making the cave eerily calm after the awesome upheaval. With the aid of the cave dwellers, he felt weightless, as if he were walking through outer space, like those famous astronauts from the history books.

Alba was led out of the cave by the pliable arms of the cave dwellers. As soon as a bobbing beam of light ahead of her indicated Ralph's location, as quickly as they had arrived, the little cave dwellers slunk away.

A strong torrent of water was gushing past them. The passage they now found themselves in had walls that looked like bulbous masses of melted wax, the hue of pink flesh. The walls looked as if they were about to ooze out and absorb the travellers beneath their clammy surface. Alba surveyed the scene and shuddered.

'We must follow that water. It will lead us to the only way out. Can you hurry up, Your Worship? The witch will need to cross those boulders, but it won't take her long to catch up,' said Ralph.

'Ahem, well yes of course I will, but you make it sound as if I'm going slowly on purpose. I am not blessed with your strident attributes, young man, and I am over one hundred years old. One can't help…'

'My brother didn't mean to sound rude, did you, Ralph?' said Alba, glaring at her brother. 'Of course you are doing your best, sir. So shall we get going? Our only candle is wearing down.'

They made to set off down the new passageway when, without warning, a furry black blur tore past their legs. Ahead of them, with its back arched and fur raised, the witch's cat stood spitting and hissing. It turned towards a malevolent-looking rock formation, suspended from the ceiling, split into three prongs like a dark pink fork or devil's tongue. From the cat's mouth a line of silver-blue spittle shot out and touched the shape. In front of their eyes the deposit lost its solidity and began to curl and uncurl as if it were a real tongue. Then the three prongs of the tongue sprang forwards, restrained only by their attachment to the wall. The tongue filled the passageway, nearly touching the children, before it recoiled.

'We're trapped,' said Ralph. 'Behind us is the witch and in front of us is a tongue-lashing far worse than even Mum could give us.'

The tongue spat out again, this time catching Ralph on the arm and tearing his sleeve, which solidified against his arm. Alba gasped and pulled Ralph away from the tongue. The cat hissed and tried to shoot past the travellers. Ralph lunged at the cat with his foot, catching the bewitched creature on its underbelly. The cat screeched and as it did so the last of the enchanted saliva escaped from its mouth, landing on a sabre-shaped stalactite. The cat raced off to its mistress, none the worse for the encounter with Ralph's boot.

Ralph reached up to the stalactite and snapped it away from the ceiling in one sharp movement. The stalactite transformed into a silver sabre, and the roughness of the rock transformed into cold, smooth steel in his hands. A smile crossed his face as he sliced through the air with it several times, testing the weight of the weapon. The disturbed air whooshed in response.

'Crucial,' he said.

'That sword looks dangerous,' said Alba.

'Good,' said Ralph.

The teenage boy faced the demonic tongue, which was flexing and contracting its newly formed muscles, licking the air in a gluttonous manner, the calcium deposits dripping from it like avaricious drool. In some diabolical way it must have sensed Ralph's approach, for it ceased its aimless movement and became taut, recoiling as if waiting to attack. The tongue's strike came faster than lightning and Ralph only just managed to duck out of the way.

'Watch out!' cried Alba, who was having difficulty moving, as the judge had clung to her legs in terror and wasn't about to release his grip.

The awful tongue recoiled once more, as if preparing to pounce. Ralph used the time to position himself just out of its range, but then he leant towards it waving the sabre and prodding the air just in front of the monstrosity. The goading paid off and the tongue spat forwards again. This time, Ralph caught the tip of one of the prongs and sliced his sword into it. The blade was so fine that it was as easy as cutting through a piece of paper. The prong of the tongue, now severed from the host limb, slithered to the floor with a stomach-churning splat and immediately returned to stone, harmless and inert.

The remaining two prongs of the tongue drew back, but this time seemed to take on a new level of ferocity. More calcium-filled saliva dripped on to the growing spittoon on the floor. The tongue moved restlessly, as if in pain. It struck out again with renewed malice, as if trying to break away from the very wall itself. The speed of the attack caused the wall to creak.

A sound of rubble and rocks being disturbed came from the cavern behind them. A low mutter of a crone's voice could be discerned.

'Revenge,' the voice rasped.

'She's on her way. Hurry up,' hissed Alba.

'Oh me! Oh my! She'll kill me,' said the judge, squirming around Alba's legs.

The tongue lashed out towards the judge's voice in a manic way. Alba flinched, but she managed to pull her stomach in just as the tongue swept past.

Ralph removed his sweater and lowered himself to the floor. Carefully, he lay on his back, his head closest to the wall. He placed his sweater alongside him. With care, he placed the sabre on his sweater. Slowly he pushed himself towards the wall, pulling the sweater alongside him, the garment silencing the otherwise inevitable scrape of metal on stone. He came to the very point where the tongue protruded from the wall, so he was looking up at it. Alba could hardly bring herself to watch, confused by Ralph's action. The tongue flicked the air, searching for its quarry. It dipped down and Ralph had to hollow his stomach, so the tongue tip just missed him. He couldn't make a sound or further movement, for if he did, the monstrous tongue would close in on him without mercy. He had risked moving there and now he needed to take one more risk. He shut his eyes and concentrated. Without speaking a word, he thought, *Trust me, Alba. Move towards the tongue.*

Alba, still with the limpet-like judge clinging to her, looked at her brother. She had watched with alarm as he manoeuvred into his precarious position and now she thought she could hear him speaking, but his lips weren't moving. The word 'What?' silently formed on her lips.

Move towards the tongue.

Ralph lay there with a grin on his face, despite the peril he was in.

Okay, Ralph, whatever you think.

She gently prised the judge's hands from around her legs, pressing a finger to her lips to keep him quiet. Alba then jumped at the tongue, crying, 'Over here, Squelchy!' In an instant, the tongue jerked with violence towards the noise. As it did so, Ralph thrust his sword upwards into the very base of the tongue, where it met the stone. The tongue almost reached Alba's stomach and she expected to be split right through, but then it seized up mid-attack. Ralph had driven the sword in as far as he could to the hard flesh of the tongue and then, rising to his knees, sliced the tongue clean off the wall so it landed with a thud next to him. The tongue quivered in one final effort to cling to its short life, and then returned to stone. Ralph tried to remove the sabre, but it too was set solid. The cave had reclaimed its property and the sword and tongue would eventually be engulfed by the chemical process once more.

'Ralph. Are you all right?'

'Fine, sis. I just think fighting a tongue and using telepathy for the first time has rather taken it out of me. By the way, who's *Squelchy?*'

Behind them, the clatter of movement over rocks could be heard coming ever closer, although the echoes of the cave system made it impossible to gauge the distance.

'We'd better get going.' But as she said this, Alba felt a sudden flatness and, looking at her brother, saw that he had fainted.

After leaving the hill, Shelia had dug her heels into the mare's sides and urged her back towards their home.

'Come on, Sunbeam. Quick as you can. I have a date with destiny. I'm just not sure whose,' whispered Shelia.

Sunbeam's ears pricked up and her gait quickened. The sun was rising high across the hill, warming the ground and causing the dew to evaporate, so a fine spray swirled around the bay's fetlocks as she cantered on. By the time Shelia arrived back at her home, she and her pony were both panting.

'It's going to be a warm day, Sunbeam,' said Shelia, as she dismounted and tied the reins round a garden fence post. 'For those of us above ground.' She choked back a sob.

Her horse purred and nudged Shelia gently as she loosened the girth, trying to comfort her mistress in its animal way. She kissed the mare's velvet muzzle, smelt the oaty warmth of the breath, and felt a little calmer.

Shelia ran around the side of the cottage to the outside water pump to fetch Sunbeam a bucket of water. With the morning sun casting shadows across the garden, she noticed the barrel positioned by the fence.

So that's how they got away without disturbing us, she thought with a half-smile, hoping that sort of resourcefulness would help her children deal with whatever dangers they would face in their subterranean adventure. Gulping back tears once more, she shook her head, concentrating on raising water for her thirsty mount. Once Sunbeam was tended to, Shelia pushed open the heavy oak door, the familiar creak jarring on her nerves. *Why hadn't Ande fixed it? He was always doing jobs for others. Why couldn't he do this one thing for us?*

Ande's features, captured in charcoal, stared down from a portrait hanging from the hall wall. She stared back at it, for a moment losing herself in the strong, kind gaze. She felt guilty for thinking bad of him. This was what the bad magic did. Ate away at you. Nothing significant or so it seemed, just dripping like a tap, until a flood was caused. She could have fixed the door herself, but it was never a problem; in fact, they all loved the familiar creak. It was part of their home. She must be careful to remain focused on the good and not be distracted by the negative. Something else was different in the hall. Then she heard it: a steady clack-click, clack-click. She stood in front of the grandfather clock. Its faded face said eleven forty. Shelia reached out and carefully turned the brass key in the body of the clock and prised the door back. The ancient pendulum moved back and forth hypnotically, the backdrop of chains and weights swaying in rhythm. *How strange,* she thought as she looked the case. *It must have been in tune with the movements of the earth.*

Shelia continued into the study at the back of the house. Once more she fought back tears as she saw a pile of books Ralph had dumped on the floor, along with a couple of broken quoits. She had nagged him to clear the mess up. The room itself was well lit, but the sun hadn't come round far enough to penetrate the window, which filled half the outer wall, so the room was still chilly. A large, oak desk was positioned beneath the window, covered in neat piles of letters and books belonging to all four members of the family. Pens and pencils, rulers and rubbers were scattered across the desk top. A wooden chair was tucked into the desk and in the corner of the room was a rocking chair, with dark green cushions. A deep red silk rug covered the floorboards.

Shelia pulled the rocking chair into the centre of the room, her arms straining with the effort. She sank to her knees and pulled back the corner of the rug. For all the untidiness of the family, Shelia insisted that the home be kept clean, so the revealed floorboards were shiny and polished. Disturbed dust was a dead giveaway for a hiding place.

The floorboards ran the length of the room using one continuous plank of wood for each, except for the third one from the wall, where two barely discernible lines marked out a separate segment. This was about thirty centimetres long and lay nearest the wall where the rocking chair usually sat. The break in the plank would not have been spotted at a quick glance, but Shelia had known exactly where to look and now she placed her thumb on a knot in the wood and pressed down, making her thumbnail turn white. A light click told her she could release the pressure. The plank lifted up, revealing a compartment beneath the floor. Shelia reached both hands into the gap, her face tensing.

With great care she withdrew her hands, manoeuvring a package through the narrow gap. Shelia laid the parcel, which was wrapped in faded soft leather and tied up with a leather lace, on the floor. It was the same length as its hiding place and about the width of a hand. Shelia ran her fingers across the leather and, taking a deep breath, tugged at the knot, undoing it easily. She gasped as she unfolded the leather covering. The glittering beauty of the filigree gold belt never failed to take her breath away. She picked it up. It looked so delicate and yet was surprisingly heavy. The sheath in which her Wand of Antares should rest was also lying in the wrapping. Shelia held it in front of her, admiring it like it was a newborn baby.

A sudden whinny from Sunbeam made her start and she quickly attached the wand sheath to the belt, before placing it around her hips and tightening the golden buckle. She replaced the floorboard and rug and moved the furniture back into place before leaving the cottage. Ande was coming down the path. Shelia glanced at the ticking clock. It said eleven thirty. Ande came into the hall. He stopped when he saw Shelia and stared at the belt around her waist.

'I hoped it wouldn't come to this,' he said.

'So did I, for the twins' sake, but there's no going back. We must face this as a family. The clock's started,' said Shelia.

'One less job to do,' said Ande, running a hand through his hair.

'It's ticking backwards,' said Shelia.

'Ralph will always be late for school then,' said Ande.

He moved towards Shelia, his arms open. She ignored him.

'There'll be time to hug later. Hurry up and get your horse ready. The children are in trouble.'

Ande moved swiftly to the stables at the back of the house. Shelia was right, of course, but she was never sharp with any of them. The dark magic seemed to be seeping out from the side of the hill already. Ande saddled and bridled his horse, Polaris, a large, heavyset black animal. The beast's hooves were the size of Ande's hand but it still picked its knees up and arched its neck as it strode proudly towards Shelia and its stable companion, Sunbeam. A slight clicking came from the nearside hoof.

'You've got a loose shoe, haven't you, old man?' said Ande to his steed. 'I haven't got time to mend it now, but it should last the journey.'

'Sorry,' said Shelia, leaning across and squeezing Ande's hand. 'It's just...'

'I know. Nothing to be sorry for,' he said, pointing Polaris in the direction of the valley. 'What the blazes is that?' he said, standing in his stirrups and shielding his eyes with his hand against the morning sunlight. Shelia looked up, squinting.

'It looks like a black swarm of... crows. Isn't that Arfur Sendal in the middle of them?' said Shelia.

'You're right. I don't like the look of that. Come on. The sooner we get to the North Tower the better,' said Ande, pushing his horse into a trot followed by Shelia and Sunbeam, who cantered to keep up.

The gilt belt shone brilliantly from her side, the empty holster moving in time with the motion of Shelia's thigh, as if expecting soon to be weighted down with the item it was always intended to carry, a magical wand.

Tara-Zed had galloped straight to Skipton Castle, completing the journey in half the usual time. Although she preferred to live in the village she served, the castle had been entrusted to her by a surrogate uncle, before his death. It was used as a centre for learning, but she still kept private chambers in the West Tower, which had once been home to the members of the Order of Antares. She left Procyrion with a pageboy in the courtyard, with instructions to make him ready for a further journey, even though the creature was panting heavily.

Tara-Zed almost knocked the solid door off its hinges as she strode into the tower. Gathering up her cloak, she ran up the spiral stairs, searching for her chamber door key from a bunch held around her waist. Finding a big brass key, she fumbled with it in the lock before the latch gave and she strode into the room.

The room was decorated in a similar, ornate style as that of the original Sisters of Antares. The low table in the centre of the room and the desks were those used by those revered ladies, but Tara-Zed was in no mood to ponder on antiquities. She marched over to one of the windows. A table cloth embroidered with delicate summer flowers, a gift from a well-meaning villager, covered a table of sorts, on top of which was a large floral arrangement of purple peonies and pink anemones. With one sweep of her hand, Tara-Zed sent this arrangement crashing to the floor, throwing the cloth after it.

'Mistress, are you well? Let me clear up for you.'

A male servant had appeared in the doorway, a look of anxiety across his face. Tara-Zed spun round.

'Leave me, Nigel. And shut the door behind you,' shouted Tara-Zed, more beautiful than ever in her anger.

The servant stood open-mouthed in the doorway for a moment, before retreating, closing the door behind him as quietly as he could.

Tara-Zed placed her hands in one set of the three pairs of grooves positioned around the stone table and peered into the crystal surface, seeing only the reflection of her strong features.

'Rigela, my sister, I call to you from beyond time. The prophecy has been ignited and your wand is needed to defeat the evil we face.'

Slowly, her reflection began to mist over and lights flashed before her. The table top took on a liquidity and depth. The cosmos flashed before Tara-Zed's eyes. Then, from what could have been a million miles away, she spotted a pinhead of white light travelling towards her at unimaginable speed. Galaxies shuddered for a split second, as the object hurtled through them on its unstoppable journey, growing closer to Tara-Zed by the millisecond. Her fingers were now curled up and her palms pressed harder into the stone of the table edge. The pinprick took on more definition. It looked like a silver javelin launched by some Olympian hero on the edge of the universe.

Beads of perspiration formed on her brow. She yearned to look away, for what she saw was so amazing and yet so awful. The object was aimed right for the centre of her forehead. She concentrated harder than ever, for to break eye contact would see this object fall back into space. She was a homing beacon. The missile charged on, rippling its way through the universe. Tara-Zed's eyes grew ever wider. The tendons in her neck were strained. Blood pumped deafeningly in her ears.

The dart-like wand pierced the surface of the table and shot into the room. Tara-Zed twisted her head away just in time, as it swept past her. Drops of black water, like liquid night, pattered on to her face, dripping on to the floor. But she ignored this as she grabbed at the wand for all she was worth. It felt freezing in her palm, and it pulled her right off the floor towards the ceiling, but she held tight, not wanting to let go lest it shoot out of the window, or worse, drop back into the void from which it had come. She felt the wand quiver in her hand and then it seemed to relax. As it did, she floated back to the floor, but not before she noticed some cobwebs behind the drapes of the curtain.

She strode back to the Meteor Table. The surface began to lose its fluidity and took on an icy sheen once more, but not before Tara-Zed had leant forwards and whispered into it, 'Thank you, my sweet sister.'

Tara-Zed walked into the centre of the room and held the silver wand before her. It was as magnificent as the day it had been refined, still cold in her hand, from its hiding place in the depths of time. She placed it in her golden holster and departed the room. Nigel was standing on the stairwell, looking bewildered. Tara-Zed placed her hand on his shoulder.

'Nigel, I am sorry for my harsh words. I would be very grateful if you could restore my room. Oh and perhaps take a long duster to the top of the curtains, when you have time.'

'Certainly, mistress,' said the loyal servant with a nod. He smiled with relief and went on his way as Tara-Zed returned to the courtyard for her journey to the North Tower.

Giena Cygnus had not needed to take such a long journey as Tara-Zed. To the north-west of the village, beyond the woods, were the ruins of an abbey, nestling in a remote valley. In the time of the good judge, Ingleset Abbey had been a thriving community of godly men and women, many of whom were seeking refuge and solace after the dreadful years of the Global War. The abbey itself had been built around the ruins of a medieval monastery, which had been sacked and vandalised during the English Reformation. Its splendour had been recreated in part, by the use of stones, glass and artefacts rescued from churches before they were lost to the environment or the war, and for several years it had been a place of peace and restoration for the war-damaged occupants. But after the death of Bishop Roland and the banishment of the witch, a murder of crows had built their nests in the abbey roof. They made life miserable for the inhabitants, pecking at the stained-glass windows, stealing the seed and pestering the workers in the fields, but the most awful thing was the unrelenting cacophony of cawing.

Gradually the abbey's occupants moved away to neighbouring villages. The church had officially closed the abbey forty years ago and removed what valuables and furniture hadn't already been placed in storage in the local people's homes for safekeeping. It had been decided that nature should be allowed to claim the main building, but that the little chapel housing the crypt should be maintained and a crypt keeper appointed.

Giena often came here to pray and afterwards take tea with the crypt keeper, so as she approached the square, limestone chapel, a short man of about seventy years (although nobody knew his exact age) appeared from a small, plain cottage adjacent to the church. A large black hound walked by his side.

'Ah was 'specting you, Miss Cygnus, after t'commotion up t'hill last night,' said the man, nodding his head towards White Scar, patting the dog who was now sitting with ears pricked, tail wagging and a look of excitement in his eyes.

'Good morning, Leo Gammacom. And to you too, Canis, my hairy friend,' said Giena, moving towards the back of her cart in order to step down.

At the sound of his name, Canis moved forwards and stood with both his front paws on the side of the cart so Giena could hold on to the scruff of his neck and alight more easily. The dog then walked closely by her side as she approached Leo.

Stardust stood patiently, not worried by the dog who his mistress was now making a fuss of, rubbing him behind the ears as he bounced up and down.

'Can ah make you some tea? The kettle's always on, as you know,' said Leo, pointing back to his cottage where a plume of smoke could be seen curling from the chimney.

'Not today, my dear friend. I have work to do. Please look after Stardust. I'm sure she would welcome some water.'

The pony looked around and snorted.

'Very well, miss. C'mon, Canis. Miss is busy today. Seems she's the one we've been guarding the crypt for all these years,' said the old man, turning slowly towards his cottage.

Giena moved as briskly as she could towards the oak chapel door, although she put her full weight on her walking stick, as the paving slabs that led the way were uneven. A gargoyle poked its stone tongue at her from above the doorway. Usually Giena would poke her tongue right back at the vile caricature, but she had no time today. As she entered the little church it felt as if she had passed into another dimension. The morning sun had not yet warmed the thick walls or passed through the thin arched windows. Her eyes blinked as they adjusted to the darkness. Several large candles were planted on tall, brass holders, their waxy entrails forming grotesque shapes as the candlelight barely touched the gloom. A silver cross stood on the simple altar, casting a long shadow down the nave. Two candles on silver holders burnt slowly on either side of the cross. Stale incense saturated the air. Despite the solemnity, Giena felt at home here. She felt connected with the past, her history. This time, however, she ignored her favourite pew and continued to the far end of the chapel, beyond the altar, to a doorway hidden in the shadows.

From the headband of her hat she pulled out a chain on which were suspended two brass keys. She used one of the keys to unlock the door, pushing it hard with her shoulder as she did so. The door stuck fast. She shoved harder, using her free palm as well, nearly losing her balance as the door edged open. Giena put her shoulder to it once more, this time leaning on her walking stick so as not to topple forwards. A loud creak filled the chapel and, righting herself, Giena saw that the door had scraped open. Nearly a century of dust and cobwebs greeted her. The musk of decay filled her nostrils. She heard the sound of scuttling feet, presumably those of spiders, rats and mice who were not used to disturbance. She shuddered.

Taking hold of a silver candle stick from the altar, she held it ahead of her and brushed away the veils of grimy webs with her walking stick. The candle barely illuminated a flight of ten stone steps descending into the dusty blackness. Coughing, Giena edged forwards. The stairs were steep and uneven. There was nothing else for it. She lowered herself, until her bottom was perched on the top step, and bumped her way down, moving the candle one step at a time.

Very elegant, Giena. You certainly know how to make an entrance, she thought.

At the base she pulled herself to her feet and found herself in the crypt, a large rectangular room with four recesses along each long wall and two at the shorter ends. Eight of these spaces contained stone coffins, but Giena could see that the remaining spaces had once held wooden ones, which had now disintegrated, revealing piles of bones and decaying fabric.

In the centre of the vault were two large sarcophagi standing side by side, which Giena approached without hesitation. Michael Stonecutter, the original mason, had fashioned these. Four ornate wooden candle holders were placed at each corner of the tombs, their contents long ago burned out. She placed her own candle on one of the stands. Strange shadows danced around her as the deathly objects reacted to the first touches of light they had felt in many years. Giena ignored these and concentrated on swiftly dusting the surface of the tomb she was closest to with her sleeve. It was a difficult task as Giena was short and she had to stretch as far as her spine would let her, whilst trying not to inhale the corpse-laden dust. At last the carved outline of a man's reposing body was revealed, his stone features kindly and tranquil, his carved hands pressed together in eternal prayer. She worked at clearing the tomb's side and although the carving was old she could clearly make out the words 'Here lyeth the body of Bishop Roland.'

Bishop Roland had been murdered well into the twenty-first century and Giena had been fascinated that following the Global War many survivors had chosen a more old-fashioned manner of speech. It was as if they were attempting to erase the modernity that had caused their apocalypse. She smiled as she thought of her dear friend Tara-Zed who spoke in old-fashioned English, despite having studied the language of Text Speak. Giena hoped that Tara-Zed's wand was more accessible than her own.

Giena looked across at the tomb by the bishop's side. She could just make out the dust-clouded features of a serene lady. She knew it was where the body of Beryl, the bishop's wife, lay. She had lived only one more year after the murder of her husband and died, according to local history, of a broken heart. Beryl was thought of as the witch's fifth victim.

The second key was now held firmly in Giena's hand. Made of crude iron, it was the length of a pen, and rather than the usual grooves of a key, it had a thick flat end which she now twisted. It lost its flatness as a section unfolded. A further twist produced a final edge, which protruded out so the key looked like part of a complex puzzle.

Across the reposing bishop's chest was an emblem of a cross with a crescent moon behind it. A stone lamb sat meekly at the foot of the cross. Giena placed the key on the emblem where the foot of the cross met the bottom point of the moon and the lamb's head. She pressed hard, twisting the key as she did so. The crypt filled with a sudden hiss of air as if the dead were releasing the one last breath they had been holding on to for posterity. She did not flinch as the lid of the sarcophagus began to sink, supported by a rolling mechanism. She shuddered as she felt an exodus of furry creatures brush past her hands and feet, hurrying to escape the unwelcome intrusion into their home. The lid dropped half a metre and then stopped. There was no sign of the bishop, Giena was relieved to see. A small shelf was revealed containing a slender, faded red box. She leant in and picked it up, snapping the lid open as she did so. A length of silver metal shone back at her.

'I'll take that, if I may, Miss Smarty-Pants Cygnus,' said a nasally voice behind her.

'Arfur Sendal,' said Giena, not bothering to look at the reporter, her eyes still transfixed by the wand. 'And what if I don't want to give it to you?'

'Oh, you will. Otherwise I'll get my new friends to peck dear old Leo the Lion to death. Just imagine, a lion murdered by a murder of crows.'

Arfur began to splutter through his nose at his joke.

Giena fixed her gaze upon this odious man who was standing half way down the staircase.

'Arfur, I think you are a low-life rat who brings your profession into disrepute on a daily basis, but a murderer you are not. The dark magic which has been disturbed is twisting you. Resist it and do what you know to be true and right.'

'Very noble of you. Always so prim and proper. Doing the right thing all the time despite your, your...' He looked at her walking stick with disdain. 'You make me sick. Sticking your hoity-toity nose up at me all the time. Now give me that wand and don't even think about using it, or your friend and his dog will die before you could even crawl up these stairs, won't they now?'

With that, the chapel above filled with the noise of cawing and flapping. The piercing scream of an old man was followed by the pitiful yelping of a dog. Giena never took long over decisions and held out the wand.

'You'd better not harm my friends any further, Arfur, or so help me I will track you down and make you pay,' said Giena, her jaw clenched so tightly that her lips hardly parted as she spoke.

'Noble sentiments, but it will be rather difficult for you. Unfortunately my winged friends and I haven't time to linger, but who knows, we could be back to finish the job. It depends what our noble leader bids, doesn't it eh, now?' said Arfur, as he picked his way down the steps and reached out his bony hand, grabbing the wand.

With that Arfur, waving the wand above his head, ran up the stairs and slammed the crypt door behind him. The lock clicked and Giena saw from the dim candlelight that there was no lock on the inside. A scuttling came from behind her and the black legs of several spiders protruded out from beneath the ancient coffins.

Great, thought Giena. *If there's one thing I hate more than Arfur Sendal, it's spiders.* But look as she might she already knew there was no way out other than through the locked door. She was trapped.

CHAPTER 14

'Ralph, speak to me,' said Alba, shaking his shoulders.

A cackle from the cave behind them made her shake Ralph harder.

'Do something, do something,' said the judge, hopping from one foot to the other, his hands clasped into his chest.

Alba looked around, searching for anything to help her, when once more, the tender touch of those weird creatures crossed her hands, guiding them to Ralph's head.

'Of course,' she said. 'How stupid of me. The lamp must have got too hot and he passed out with the heat.'

She placed her hands on either side of the hat and pulled it off. Beads of sweat trickled down her brother's face, as if he were in a rain shower. He groaned. Alba put the helmet upon her head, but not before she noticed how low the candle had burnt.

'We only have another two hours of light, at the most,' she muttered.

'What, what was that? Two hours before I'm plunged into darkness again for who knows how long, with nothing but those slimy creatures and a mad witch for company. Dreadful,' said the judge.

'There is nothing wrong with your century-old hearing,' said Alba crossly, 'and don't forget my brother and I are in the same boat, so kindly be quiet.'

Alba was beginning to wonder how this little man had earned the titles of 'good' and 'kind'. She had made allowances for his lengthy interment, but even so he seemed quite horrid to her.

'I couldn't agree more with you on that one, sis,' said Ralph, struggling to sit up.

'Ralph, you're okay,' said Alba, hugging her brother.

'Bit of a headache, but I'll survive,' he said, rubbing his forehead.

Above his head was a shelf, the size of a wash basin. It contained water. Alba scooped some up. It felt cold and heavy with minerals as it rested in her cupped hands. She allowed her brother to drink it, before using another scoopful to mop his head.

'Can you move, Ralph?' she asked, already pulling him to his feet. 'She's not far behind us. And we only have a couple of hours of light left.'

Ralph got to his feet, rubbing his head. Alba led the way, once more taking the judge by his arm as if he were a sulky toddler, to make him keep up.

They moved along the passage, the walls bulging with minerals in their glistening array of hues, a river running next to them on their left. A couple of times Alba slipped on the floor and had to steady herself on the bulbous walls.

'Watch out, Alba. At times of high rain or snow the passage we're in would be full of water. Look, you can spot the high-water line above our heads.'

'Thank you, Ralph. You are such a comfort. Let's hope the weather is fine on the surface, then.'

Alba stopped and her brother, who had been admiring the way the water had carved out its river bed, piled into her.

'What now?' he said.

'Well, the judge will be all right, but we've got a problem.'

Ahead of them the cave roof sloped down until it was only one metre off the ground. The lamplight penetrated the low tunnel, but Alba could see no end. She crouched down, her hands nearly touching the floor. The judge bent slightly and followed her. Finally Ralph followed, sticking out his bottom and making gorilla noises, recalling what he had read about the magnificent creatures.

'Ooo ooo ooo,' he said.

'Ralph, don't be silly,' said Alba. 'We have to get away.'

'Ooo ooo ooo,' aped her brother again.

'Ralph, please be quiet,' said Alba.

'Ooo ooo ooo.'

'Ralph. That's enough.'

'Sis. That time it wasn't me. Hurry!'

Ralph pushed the judge so the little man's legs scurried from side to side in a rocking motion. Their hands grazed the sides of the wall, and his hair brushed against the low ceiling.

Ralph could feel the fear rising in his sister. It mirrored his own feelings. The ceiling seemed as if it would press down on them at any moment. The roaring of the water was now deafening and the spray splashed over them like a ghostly mist. Ahead of him the lack of space diminished the spread of the lamp's beam, and he trod on the judge several times in the dimness.

'I can see the end. Ouch!' said Alba, banging her head on the ceiling.

At last she found herself able to straighten up again, and she found herself in front of a waterfall, which was pouring straight out of a hole in the cavern's roof. She grabbed the judge's arm, whom Ralph had seconds before shoved out of the tunnel, and dragged him through the cascade. The lamplight spluttered but continued to glow, and they found themselves in a cave, the ceiling barely above the twins' heads, with the waterfall gushing into the river, which continued on its tumultuous way to the left of the cave. Another passage to the right led into darkness.

'Where can we hide?' cried Alba.

'Quick. Cover the light and go down the passage without the water. Feel your way,' hissed Ralph. 'All link hands.'

Alba hid the flame and with the judge firmly grasped between them, she gingerly led the way into the thick blackness, the thunder of the water quietening the further along she went.

When Alba felt they were deep enough into the stony corridor, she stopped and waited, holding her breath. Flickers of light appeared at the entrance to the passage as the wand sparked and flashed. At one point all three held their breath as the silver light seemed to move towards them, but then they heard a low grunt and the light receded. The trio stood frozen to the spot for what seemed like an eternity until Alba whispered, 'Do you think it's okay to let the light shine?'

'We have to risk it,' said Ralph.

Alba uncovered the lamp and as she did so she knelt in front of the judge.

'I'm very sorry I was harsh earlier. Just spending a few minutes suspended in darkness was awful. A hundred years must have been dreadful.'

'Well, it was quite ghastly, but your apology is accepted. Although a little overdue and I must speak to the modern parents about manners in children, if you two are a typical example,' said the judge.

'Well, if you're going to be...'

'Sis. Let's just get out of here. The witch will be ahead of us if we follow the river, but this passage curves around and starts to descend. I bet it's an overflow route in times of flooding and leads to the outside too. Look, you can see the marks left by the water,' said Ralph.

'I'm definitely going to recommend you for an A-plus in geography. At least the witch doesn't have a broomstick. That could have been a problem,' said Alba.

The party walked as quickly as their tired legs and sodden clothes would allow them, along the passage way which seemed to have rather more twists and turns than Ralph had been expecting. It was difficult to get any idea of their bearings, as the cave walls all looked the same in this part of the system and the drips of water and weird echoes served to disorientate them. Alba's legs were beginning to drag and the judge frequently stumbled. Hunger pangs were cramping the children's stomachs. At one time Ralph's belly rumbled so loudly it echoed off the walls, adding to the ghostliness of their subterranean world. They trudged on for what seemed like hours, Alba feeling more and more anxious with each step, which seemed to take them closer than ever to nowhere. The candle light grew weaker, hardly penetrating the gloom.

'Ralph. I think this is it. The candle has only got a few more minutes, and then we're in darkness. I'm really scared.'

'I know, sis, so am I. But you probably felt that already.'

Alba stopped walking and turned to her brother, a grin forced on her face.

'There's no point walking anymore. Just let me look at you until the light goes out. It may be for the last time.'

'Still, at least the last thing you'll ever see is my handsome face. It could have been worse. You could have Dean Dimwater down here. You'd have his fuzzy black mono-brow imprinted in your mind forever,' said Ralph, with a wink.

'Oh, Ralph, don't be so awful,' said Alba, wiping her eyes.

'Ahem. Fine rescuers you turned out to be. At least before I was in a state of suspension. Here I'm lost and cold and likely to die. Useless. Absolutely useless,' said the judge, sitting down and glaring through his beady eyes at the twins.

'Oh please shut up. You've been quite horrid to us. We only wanted to help and all you've done is eaten our food and moan,' cried Alba.

'Well really, this is most intolerable,' said the judge.

'My sister is right. You have been a pain. Now be quiet,' said Ralph.

He turned back to his sister. They wrapped their arms around each other's waists and squeezed.

'Do you really want my ugly mug to be the last thing you see, sis?'

'Oh, Ralph. You dope,' said his sister through her tears.

With that, the candle spluttered, flaring up with one last gasp to cling to life. Then, with a final hiss, it went out.

The children stood very still, clinging to each other, waiting for the blackness to envelop them like a velvet shroud.

'Ralph. I can still see you.'

'And I can see you, too.'

Both children stared at where the judge was sitting sulking.

'He's still there,' said Alba.

And it was true. The passage where they stood had a grey tinge to its walls.

'There must be light ahead. We're safe. We're going to be all right,' cried Alba, dancing around in her brother's arms.

She leant over and dragged the judge to his feet, hugging him between her and Ralph and continuing her jig.

'It's great, but you need to calm down. There's a witch ahead, too. And she's really not happy,' said Ralph, quenching his own excitement with the thought of an angry witch.

'I know. But at least if we die, it'll be in daylight.'

'I'm not sure if you made that sound like a good thing, but come on, let's get going.'

With that, Ralph strode out along the tunnel, followed by a still grinning Alba and a judge who was, for the moment, silenced.

Rounding a bend, they were met by a breeze which blew Alba's hair behind her and sent Ralph's black mop flapping ecstatically around his face. The judge's gown billowed and he used his chubby hands to keep the robe from flying above his head. A torrent of noise overwhelmed them as they rejoined the surging underground river, fully filled by all the channels and waterfalls of the cave. As they approached the river the spray dampened their hair and garments, and they placed their hands over their ears against the noise.

They edged forwards, following the course of the river, their path running almost level with the water's surface, so occasionally it lapped over and doused their feet. The judge walked even more slowly as the hem of his gown became sodden with water. The tunnel wall curved gently. They each shielded their faces as a bright white light touched the very backs of their eyes. Their pupils, used only to the artificial candlelight in the sepulchral gloom, ached from the sudden exposure. Slowly, they lowered their arms.

'Daylight,' cried Alba, 'beautiful daylight!'

They found themselves facing an archway in the stone, as if they were on the inside of a gaping mouth, the river pouring out like a silver tongue. Beyond that was a sight none of them had dared hope they might see again: a cloudless, blue sky.

They edged as close to the opening as they dared and stood transfixed. They were high up and seemed level with the vast sky. On either side were the cliffs of Malham Cove, curving like a horseshoe. Below them was a valley of shining pea-green grass, the limestone outcrops smoothed by years of weathering. A river meandered across the valley floor, fed by the very torrent they were standing beside. In the distance, on an opposite escarpment, stood the North Tower. Ralph gave a half-smile, but looked anxious, as they edged forwards. He kept glancing behind to see if there was any sight of the witch or her feline companion.

Maybe she's already out, thought Alba.

Ralph shrugged and looked doubtful.

The judge spoke first, straining his thin voice above the noise.

'Oh me. Oh my. I'd forgotten how lovely it is. Quite lovely.'

'Come on. We've still got problems,' shouted Ralph, inching forwards. 'This is Malham Waterfall. It's at least a hundred metres above ground level. If the witch has left the cave then she must have brought her own flying machine with her. In fact, it would be handy if she could lend it to us, because I haven't got a clue how we're going to get down.'

He had to yell as the noise of the river was now accompanied by the thunder of the waterfall.

Both children glared at the judge, whose lips were already parted as if to make some sort of complaint, but upon seeing the children's faces he thought better of it.

'It's noon. The sun's behind us,' said Alba, pointing at the crescent-shaped shadow of the escarpment they were standing in.

Ralph unravelled the rope he was still carrying.

'It's only fifty metres long. I could lower it to one of the ledges in the cliff wall below, but we'd be stuck. Perhaps all we can do is hope that Mum and Dad will find us.'

All three continued surveying the inviting scenery. They had doubted that they would ever see daylight again, and yet their initial elation at reaching the cave mouth had subsided and the faces wore forlorn expressions, their shoulders hunched in despondency.

Alba looked up. The water seemed to be talking to her, or at least carrying a message; it seemed to be saying 'revenge'. She shuddered.

'What did you say, Ralph?'

'Nothing,' he yelled.

The twins' eyes locked and they both felt each other's hearts miss a beat. Slowly they turned back towards the depths. They both let out a cry, for standing not twenty metres from them was the witch of White Scar Cave.

Up close she was even more ghastly than the children could have imagined. Her skin seemed to have turned into the calcified rock on which her image had been frozen. She was stooped and her hate-filled orange eyes leered at them from beneath a fringe of matted, crusty ringlets. Large warts, like dripping stalactites, hung from her nose and cheeks. Her hands were gnarled, the long bony fingers of her right hand gripping the solid moon-silver wand tightly as it spat icy flames, which dropped to the floor and froze on the damp ground, so it looked as if a trove of diamonds had been spilled at her feet. Around her wizened frame hung the rags she had worn on the day of her judgment, which were now in shreds. The cord belt, which held the garments around her thin waist, was frayed like a cat o' nine tails. Her putrid scent of decay was borne by the droplets of spray and made the children's noses sting.

Pusskin wove in and out of her mistress's wrinkled legs, padding carefully over the shoeless, leathered feet. The cat's black and white ears twitched and its emerald eyes glowed.

The witch reached out her hand and grabbed a stalactite hanging near to her head. She snapped it off with one swift movement, as if it were a dry twig being broken from a tree. Never once did the ochre eyes cease staring at the judge, who was hiding behind Ralph's legs screeching, 'Oh somebody save me. Oh me. Oh my.'

The witch raised her wand and the children shrunk back, preparing themselves for the lightning bolt that would see them turned to a pile of crushed ice. Instead, she touched the stalactite with the wand. A blinding flash made the twins turn away, but when they looked up, amazed that they were still alive, the witch was now clasping a solid silver broomstick.

'We're for it now! What can we do?' said Alba.

'I have an idea. I think it's the judge she's after,' said Ralph.

Above him was a rocky outcrop. It looked like a hardy layer of granite which had remained more or less in tact whilst the softer stone around it had been worn away by the elements. Alba had been following her brother's gaze and spotted the protruding rock. She touched his arm to let him know she knew what he was thinking. Ralph glanced back at the witch and saw her place the broomstick horizontally between her two contorted hands. Whilst the witch was momentarily distracted, Ralph flung the rope over the ledge above him, so one end of the rope dangled either side of it. He turned to the quivering judge and tied the rope securely about the stout man's waist, leaving a length still free. The judge, who had been mesmerised by the witch's gaze, now looked up at Ralph, fear masking his face.

'You've got to stop her. She intends to kill me. The look on her face. It is exactly as it was all those years ago. I was only doing my job, but she hates me,' said the judge, shrieking against the noise of the water.

'Trust me,' mouthed Ralph.

Alba stood next to her brother. They both grasped the loose end of the rope that was hanging over the ledge. The twins stood very still, pressed as close to the cave wall as possible.

'What's happening? This doesn't look like much of a rescue plan. I mean, she'll just blast us with the wand. I demand you do something more robust,' cried the judge.

'Great,' said Ralph to Alba, 'he's moaning again. And just when I was feeling sorry for him.'

The witch was now astride her broomstick, hovering above the gushing river, so that the spray caught the ragged hem of her clothes. Pusskin was balancing on the end, her claws sunk deep in to the silver twigs that acted as the brush. The judge, having for a moment lost his tongue, was once again cowering against the rock face.

Gazing at the judge, the witch suddenly let out a terrifying screech, the cat arched its back and dug its claws in deeper, and the broomstick lurched forwards. It gathered speed as it hurtled along the path of the river, causing the water's surface to part and froth in its wake, spilling on to the adjacent pathway. She raised her right arm, aiming the wand directly at the browbeaten judge. Just at the moment she twitched her wrist to unleash the wand's power, Ralph shouted, 'Now!'

Both he and his sister hauled with all their might on the loose end of the rope, elevating the stunned judge from the rock floor so he dangled in mid-air. A silver bolt spurted past the children and smashed into the wall where the judge had stood only a second before, causing the rock to freeze as hard as iron.

The witch tore onwards to the cave mouth, gaining more and more speed.

'Hold on,' cried Alba as the velocity of the witch's passage dragged the twins after her. The suspended judge acted as an anchor, but it was insufficient to stop the children from being lifted off their feet and sucked towards the opening. A burning pain seared through their shoulders as they felt their arms nearly pulled from their sockets.

Just as they reached the cave edge, where the sheer, watery drop awaited them, the suction was broken. As the witch raced away along the valley, the children crashed to the floor. Without a second's delay they used their tired and aching legs to push themselves back from the lip of the cave, until they lay panting side by side. With care, they unwound the rope from their sore arms.

'I wonder why she didn't come after us, Ralph.'

'We'd have been goners if she had, sis.'

'Ahem. When you two have finished playing around like toddlers, perhaps you would like to assist me,' said the irate voice of the judge.

The children rolled their eyes and looked towards the man who was now wedged between the spur of rock and the cave ceiling. He had acted like a stopper and prevented the force of the witch's flight from dragging them over the edge.

'Perhaps it's just as well he did eat all our food. He might not have been large enough to act like a plug otherwise,' said Alba.

Ralph looked at his sister and both dissolved into laughter born of relief, at the judge's dilemma. They laughed until it hurt, until tears had stopped rolling down their face, until all their fear and worry had left their bodies.

'Ahem. Really. You two are quite a disgrace. I demand you get me down,' cried the judge.

'We really had better get him down, Ralph.'

'I know, tempting as it is to leave him.'

Ralph stood beneath the granite shelf and took hold of the end of the rope dangling in front of judge. Alba took up the slack from the rope behind him.

I'm fed up with his backside, she thought, and saw Ralph smile.

'On three, Alba, pull as hard as you can. One. Two. Three.'

Alba yanked the rope and, with a loud yell, heard above the noise of the rushing water, the judge came falling towards her. Ralph braced his legs against the base of the cave wall. He steadied the judge's descent with his end of the rope; his arms felt like they were burning as they slowed the momentum of the judge's fall. Ralph fed the rope centimetre by centimetre through his hands, until the judge landed safely on the ground.

'Well really. This is the limit,' spluttered the judge.

I should have just dropped him, thought Ralph. Alba giggled.

'The witch has gone, for the moment. But I am sure she will be back, and we still have to get out of here,' said Ralph.

Just then, the children felt the familiar tickling around their faces as their translucent friends emerged along the passageway. Ralph looked down and could just catch glimpses of light reflecting off what looked like sacks of water. What he did notice for the first time was little patches of mud left behind where the creatures had moved. He bent down and picked some up in his fingers.

'I think they're from the prehistoric mud pools,' said Ralph.

'They are amazing,' said Alba, who had picked one up and was cradling what looked like a blob of clear jelly in her arms. 'I can just make out a beating heart. They have no bones, and I can't see any ears, nose or mouth. They feel soft, yet like they could be made of stone. How is that possible?'

Ralph shrugged.

'They're certainly kinder and more intelligent than some people I could name,' said Alba, glancing towards the judge.

A movement in the cave caught the corner of both their eyes. The cave floor seemed to be alive.

'There's loads of them,' said Ralph.

As he said that, the one Alba had been cradling slid from her arms. The twins felt themselves once more led by the imperceptible arms, which extended from the globular bodies. They were guided towards the cave mouth. Alba grabbed the judge and held him close.

They were standing on the very brink of the cave, the unstoppable water right next to them plummeting to the plunge pool far below. Foam and mist sprayed across them, but the children were not getting wet, for they were being covered by their diaphanous friends until they both felt as if they were wrapped in a bubble.

'What is going on? What is all this stickiness around me?' cried the judge, until a nearly invisible hand slithered across his mouth.

Can you hear me, Alba? said Ralph without moving his lips.

Alba opened her eyes wide and stared sideways at her brother.

Yes. I can, thought Alba.

Do you think this is heading the way I think this is heading?

With that, both the children, together with the bemused judge, felt themselves being propelled over the edge, falling down with the tumbling water, down past the weather-beaten rock face, down, down to the river below. Yet they did not crash into the cliff face or get pummelled by the surging waterfall. They were cushioned, their descent controlled, for the cave dwellers had wrapped the twins in a membrane made up of themselves and were now gently unfurling. Upon reaching the surface of the water, they halted, and the gel-filled limbs reached out and attached themselves to the river bank, finally unrolling Ralph, Alba and the judge on to dry land with nothing more than a gentle bump. The creatures then gave final light brushes to the children's faces before rolling themselves back up to their cavernous home in one gentle, seamless action.

Ralph and Alba sat gaping at the opening where the water emerged high above, and where moments before they had been standing. They caught glimpses of the cave dwellers as, on the return to the cave, sprays of water cast rainbow shadows across them. Finally they were gone.

'They were so friendly,' said Alba.

'Revolting, disgusting,' said the judge, ignoring the twins and trying to rub imaginary slime from his skin.

'I wonder why she didn't kill us in the cave. We were like sitting harebits for her and the wand,' said Ralph.

'Ralph. I feel so tired and hungry. It's sunny, but I'm cold,' said Alba, who had turned quite pale and was only now removing the safety helmet.

'Me too, sis. We'll have to go on. Warn people that the witch has escaped, if they don't already know,' replied Ralph, who had taken off the rucksack and was rotating his shoulders.

'I don't think I can go on. I need to sleep,' said Alba, shivering and curling up on the grass.

'Come on, Alba. We have to move. We're too exposed here. The witch could turn up at any moment. She may not be so nice to us next time we meet.'

With that, the sound of galloping hooves echoed around the horseshoe-shaped cliff walls.

CHAPTER 15

Tara-Zed had been keen to depart Skipton Castle, but her loyal servant Nigel, still recovering from the shock of hearing his mistress speaking harshly, had nevertheless insisted that she eat. He provided her with fruit and honey bread, and a glass of fresh spring water. She had been impatient to continue her journey but saw the sense in what her kind servant had advised, and she was now grateful that she had taken a moment in the castle court yard to take the proffered sustenance, aware of the glances her abnormal behaviour was attracting from the students and workers alike. It was not every day they saw their most revered and respected tutor and judge perched on the side of a water trough, tearing bread roughly with her hands and feeding chunks of apple to her horse.

She smiled as she rode Procyrion at a canter towards the valley that would take them northwards to the tower. If only those spectators had been aware of the enormity of her mission. It had taken little under two hours to retrieve one of the most powerful instruments ever revealed to mankind. For one hundred years, the wand had hovered on the very edges of the universe, unnoticed amongst the galaxies, like a tiny needle in a celestial haystack. Now it moved gently on her thigh in time with Procyrion's rhythmic stride. Tara-Zed's black cloak barely moved in the breeze and her long, ebony hair flopped lazily in a ponytail against her back. It was a warm day and she could feel the sun's rays against her skin. For a moment she forgot the urgency of her mission, and shaking her head to dispel the daydream, she encouraged Procyrion to quicken his pace.

She wondered how her two fellow Sisters were faring. All had received strict and lengthy instruction by the women who had passed the knowledge of the wands' power to each of them. They had been tutored in the responsibilities of this revered and mystical Order. In time, Tara-Zed herself would need to choose a successor and one girl stood out to her, as long as that child could survive the ordeal.

The teaching concerning the use of the wands had, until now, been theoretical, for since that fateful event a century ago, no one had seen the wands let alone used them. A previous Sister had even questioned their very existence, although thankfully she had been rigorous in passing on their knowledge should the wands prove to be real.

Lady Eta Carinae, an august woman whom Tara-Zed loved as a mother, had been her mentor and revealed the Wand of Lightning's stellar hiding place. She had taught Tara-Zed how to call the wand home and harness its unimaginable power.

Tara-Zed thought of Giena, and wondered where she might be. Neither woman had ever revealed their own wand's hiding place although each member held a parchment sealed on the day the wands were hidden. This parchment revealed the location of each wand and the seal was only to be broken on either document if the Sister died before choosing a successor. The seals had never been broken and now their task was obsolete as two of the wands were back in the hands of the Sisterhood. The third wand was another matter.

Procyrion covered the ground easily, despite his earlier exertions. When he approached the many dry-stone walls that crisscrossed the landscape, his mistress did not stop to open the gates, but pushed this mighty beast on, to leap over the obstacles effortlessly. He splashed through streams, never breaking his stride. The harebits scampered out of his way as best they could as they fell over their ears. Several times on the journey, he disturbed some nesting pheasants or wandering geese and they flew up squawking and flapping their feathers in his face, but Procyrion was not about to be spooked by a few stupid birds, and he cantered on unfalteringly.

The horse felt the tension in his mouth as Tara-Zed's hands tightened on the reins several times during the ride when she spotted a large flock of crows in the sky ahead. They wheeled around and flew away again as if monitoring the horse and rider's progress.

Tara-Zed checked the surroundings and knew she was not far from the North Tower. She guided Procyrion to the right and headed up the long slope of the valley, lengthening the reins so Procyrion could adjust his stride to prepare himself for the ascent. The trusty beast pressed on, never hesitating, despite an increase in the limestone rocks and the ground becoming more uneven. The tower would then be approached from the rear and Tara-Zed hoped that Ande, Shelia and Giena would already be there, making preparations should the witch have escaped the cave.

The pair made unwavering progress to the summit of the hill, when the crows suddenly appeared over the top. The birds were in a chevron formation giving them the appearance of a spearhead, as they flew towards the horse and rider. Instinct drove Tara-Zed's next actions. She quickly knotted the reins and left them resting on Procyrion's neck. At the same time she dug her heels in, leant forwards and said into her horse's ears, now pressed flat on his head, 'Fly like the wind, boy.'

Despite the incline, Procyrion stretched out his neck and lengthened into a full gallop, sending stones spinning off, the little flopsy harebits falling over themselves to escape the flying hooves. With her left hand, Tara-Zed held on to a clump of Procyrion's silky mane, and with one fluid move of her right hand, she withdrew the wand from its golden holster. She extended her right arm, leaning forwards so that horse and rider looked as if they were one being.

The birds were now descending at full speed down the hill towards Tara-Zed and Procyrion. They were so close to the flock that Tara-Zed was sure she could see her and Procyrion's reflection in the dispassionate, coal eyes of the birds.

When the birds were about twenty paces from Procyrion, they dove down into their final attack, beaks pointed like daggers at the eyes and limbs of Tara-Zed and her horse, but despite this the noble creature strode unflinchingly on, faster than ever.

Just at the point of collision, Tara-Zed centred her thoughts solely on the attacking crows and gave the tiniest flick of her right wrist. A jagged line of lightning spurted out from the wand's tip; Tara-Zed's arm jarred from the power. Instantly the trajectory of the birds was torn apart as the creatures panicked. They seemed to hover in mid-air, pecking at each other. Tara-Zed could feel their bony wings beating against her face and smell their oily bodies before Procyrion galloped through the maelstrom.

The more fortunate birds flapped away cawing and fretting, but those who had been in the direct line of the wand's emission fell like stones to the hillside, the very life struck from their feathered bodies.

They were about three-quarters of the way up the hillside when on seeing the flock separate and fly off in every direction, Tara-Zed drew Procyrion to a halt. He stood panting and shaking.

'Easy does it, boy,' said Tara-Zed, dismounting, placing the wand back in its sheath. Apart from a few scratches, Tara-Zed had not been injured. She patted Procyrion lightly on his glistening neck. Her hand felt clammy, and when she looked at her palm, she saw a red substance covering it.

'You poor boy. They did get you,' said Tara-Zed, examining the horse's side, sinking her finger into an open wound about the size of a large plum. Procyrion shuddered and let out a low neigh.

'Okay, boy, we're nearly at the North Tower. I'll walk from here,' she said.

She placed her hand around the reins near the bridle and started to lead Procyrion up the hill.

A loud cawing, far to her left, drew Tara-Zed's gaze to the skyline along the valley. The birds, like a swarm of black locusts, were speeding up the valley. Tara-Zed withdrew the wand again and crouched down, with her right knee on the ground, the left foot extended in front of her, providing balance, her cape draped lightly round her body, her head bowed. The wand, held in her right hand, rested across her bent leg. Procyrion, despite the pain from his shoulder, stood behind his mistress, his neck arched, his right hoof pawing the turf.

The birds were soon above them and started to circle the pair like a macabre, feathery wreath, their shrieks cruelly taunting their prey.

'Be prepared, boy. And stand firm. I need to gather a well of concentration if I am to repel an attack. It may take time,' said Tara-

Zed. Procyrion neighed loudly as if in acknowledgement of his mistress, whilst at the same time extending a challenge to the circling crows.

At the sound of the horse, the flock turned their beaks inwards and attacked without mercy. Tara-Zed and the horse held firm as the beaks pecked, tore and ripped at their bodies. She felt a pair of scabby claws entangled in her hair. She winced as the bird tried to free itself from the snare, flapping its wings manically and using its nib to pull on her scalp. Eventually, it freed itself by pulling so hard it took a clump of Tara-Zed's hair with it, bound around its feet, but she knelt with her head bowed, harnessing the power of the wand to help them. Still the onslaught continued. Wave upon wave of crows thrashing around, getting in each other's way, all trying to take a bite at either of their quarry. Tara-Zed's cloak afforded her some protection, but Procyrion felt the full force of the venom being exuded by these evil birds, yet he never faltered, for his mistress had told him to stand firm.

A sharp caw from the largest of the birds instructed the flock to withdraw their attack and once more they began their circling of the duo, their wings beating more rapidly as they prepared for a second offensive. Another loud cry indicated the next attack and the birds dove down.

This time, however, Tara-Zed extended her wand arm and gave a stronger flick of her wrist. A silver bolt flashed out but this time the thin line of lightning cascaded outwards and formed a shimmering canopy like an umbrella, over the pair. The birds leading the attack flew straight into this force field, which sent them crashing to the ground, stunned or dead. Those behind the lead file shied away but not before the lightning shield gave them a nasty shock, singeing their wings, so the air filled with an acrid smell like burning oil. The birds flew off in all directions shrieking and fretting, but it was only when Tara-Zed saw the last bird disappear in the distance that she released her grip on the wand and the shield was broken.

She stood up and turned to her horse, who had sunk to the ground, his breathing shallow. She knelt beside him and surveyed his once glorious skin. During the second attack, great clumps of hair and flesh had been torn from every part of his body. His left eye was a pulp of pink flesh. Blood oozed from a deep wound on his belly, so the grass on which he lay was stained a vile crimson. Her horse had suffered a mortal attack, and his very life was seeping away.

Without hesitation, she placed the tip of the wand on Procyrion's limp lower lip and squeezed gently. Little silver droplets, like crystals, emerged from the tip of the wand and trickled into the dying horse's mouth. Withdrawing the wand, Tara-Zed gasped as she saw the progress of its power through the great beast's body. Each time the silver particles encountered a wound, a little puff of silver dust would break through the skin and when it came to settle, the flesh would be healed. This unflappable woman watched in wide-eyed amazement, as the power erupted in wafts of silver even in places where there was no discernible injury. After a short time, the healing process was completed and Procyrion lay still, his newly repaired eyes shut, his breathing relaxed. Tara-Zed touched a section of his hide where there had previously been a gruesome flesh wound. The new skin was hairless and shiny, so Procyrion looked like he had been randomly shaved. Tara-Zed smiled and as she did so Procyrion opened his eyes, raised his head and sneezed. Silver dust was propelled from his nostrils, adhering itself to Tara-Zed's black cloak by the mucus it was transported in.

'Is that all the thanks I get, boy?' she said, as Procyrion scrambled to his feet.

Tara-Zed took hold of his reins and once again started up the hill, but Procyrion stood firm.

'What is it, boy?' she said.

The beast looked at her with his large eyes and turned his face to the saddle.

'If you are sure,' said Tara-Zed, mounting lithely.

As she sat down and took up the reins, Procyrion let out a loud whinny, gave a half rear and shot off at a lively canter.

'Show off,' shouted Tara-Zed.

As they reached the summit, Tara-Zed pulled the horse to a halt and wheeled round.

'I wonder what's been happening to the others?' she muttered quietly. 'And who is controlling those crows?'

A movement in the corner of her eye made her stare back along the valley. Rounding a corner, below her sight line she saw a small, dark flying object. Her jaw dropped as she realised exactly what she was looking at.

'It's the witch. On a broomstick.'

As she said this, the flock of crows rounded the valley corner, following the flying hag. Without warning, an evil cackle bounced off the sides of the valley and a dash of pure white spurted out from the witch's person, hitting a boulder further up the valley, shattering it into a million glistening particles of ice.

'She's got the missing wand, Procyrion, and the crows are on her side. On to the North Tower as fast as you like. We have to tell the others. This is as bad as it could get.'

Lady Anna held the wooden cross in front of her face. Through the ruby in the centre she could see through Scavard's eyes. She had laughed as he had pestered that ridiculous man.

'He's weak willed and easily controlled,' she had said to the photo of her son, as if to explain why that particular man had been chosen.

She gasped as she saw the power of the lightning wand unleashed skywards.

'Just wait until I have all three wands in my possession. There will be nothing I cannot do. Not one thing I cannot control,' she whispered, for she had heard a guard moving outside her door.

She chuckled as she watched the birds tearing chunks from the black horse's flesh as it stupidly tried to defend its mistress. But her lips turned hard and her eyes like steel as she saw the lightning canopy flare up and her precious crows fall like rain drops from the sky.

'No matter,' she rasped. 'It is only a minor setback. My bloodling will soon have all three wands and then...' She turned to the photo, set next to the urn of ashes, and smiled.

CHAPTER 16

The soft earth on which the children were sitting vibrated as the pounding of hooves grew closer. Centuries before, farmers had terraced the earth to help with crop growth. The twins hid on one of these ridges, sheltered by a pile of rocks from all that was left from a derelict farm building.

'There are two horses, one ahead of the other,' said Alba.

'Oh deary me. It's the witch coming to finish us off,' said the judge, tugging on the ring on his podgy finger.

'I hardly think she'd jump off her broomstick and go by horse. Broomsticks are actually quite crucial. I wonder if it's only witches that get to use them,' said Ralph.

'You really are rude. Wait until I meet your parents,' said the judge, who was turning his head from side to side as if searching for something.

'You won't have long,' said Alba, jumping to her feet and waving her arms, forgetting the exhaustion she had felt only seconds earlier. 'Look. It's Dad on Polaris. And Mum's following on Sunbeam.'

Ralph leapt to his feet and joined in with the frenetic waving until the features on their father's face were clearly visible.

Before Polaris had even slowed to a walk, Ande had sprung from his horse's back and caught the twins in his arms. Both children clung to him, sinking their faces into his chest, inhaling that familiar smell of leather and wood that made them feel protected and loved.

Shelia caught up and as Sunbeam staggered to a halt, she

bounded forwards to her children, who, loosening their grip on their father, rushed to their mother's side. By now, tears were flowing as fast as a waterfall down all four faces, as they hugged and kissed each other.

'Oh, Mum. Dad. We thought we'd never see you again,' said Alba.

'It's all right, love. You're safe now,' said Shelia.

'That's just it. We're not. None of us are. The witch. She got out. On a broomstick. And she's got a wand,' said Alba, who had begun to feel quite tired and sick again.

Ande, seeing that the colour was draining from his daughter's face, caught hold of her and with great tenderness lowered her on to a moss-covered stone. Shelia, wiping away tears with the back of her hand, attended to practical matters. She opened her saddle bags and withdrew two clean, dry sweaters for the children. Ralph and Alba looked at them as if they were the most precious gifts ever, feeling the softness of the fabric between their fingers whilst remembering the hardness of the cave walls, catching a waft of the delicate lavender scent of the washing soap instead of the dank smell of rock and calcite.

After the twins had changed clothing, Shelia handed out sperryberry cakes and flasks of warm honey milk. The children savoured every crumb and sipped the drink as if it were as precious as nectar, allowing the heat to pervade their bodies and the sweet smell to calm them.

After he had eaten, Ralph looked up at Ande.

'Dad, I'm sorry. All this, it's my fault, I…'

'Ralph. It's all right. I'm proud of you,' said Ande, placing a hand on his son's shoulder.

They had all but forgotten the judge, who had spotted a hiding place and was crouching behind a clump of tall reeds, having not believed Ralph's opinion that the witch was unlikely to approach on horseback. He now struggled on to his short legs and, adjusting his tattered robes with a pompous flourish, stepped out towards Ande.

'Ahem,' he said.

Ralph and Alba looked up.

'Oh. Sorry. We forgot to introduce you,' Ralph said.

'Yet another example of your rudeness,' said the judge.

'Good heavens, Your Worship. You're alive. How pleased we are to meet you,' said Ande, stepping forwards, his arm outstretched in greeting.

'Yes, Your Honour. We never dared hope you would have survived all this time. But here you are. Delighted. Here, have some food,' said Shelia.

'Well, it's in no way thanks to these two,' said the judge, glaring at the twins. 'I hope you take them to task. They are, without exception, the rudest children I have ever met.'

Ande and Shelia stood for a moment with their mouths hanging open, staring first at the judge and then back at their children, who by now had adopted expressions of indifference. Suddenly, Ande let out a chuckle.

'You had us there. A hundred years evidently hasn't stunted your fabled sense of humour. Very good,' said Ande.

'He's not joking, Dad,' said Ralph.

'I can assure you there is nothing humorous about my complaint, although perhaps your reaction goes a long way in explaining their behaviour. They are indolent and have no sense of respect for authority,' said the judge.

'That's rubbish. He's the one that's rude. And greedy. And he nearly led the witch right to us at the beginning,' said Ralph.

'That's right, Dad. And I nearly drowned and he did nothing. I think he wanted me to,' cried Alba.

Upon hearing this news, Shelia rushed to her daughter and hugged her. She then stood up, returned to her saddle bag and took out some more provisions.

'Your Worship. Please have this to eat and drink. We shall address these issues later, as there are more pressing matters to attend to, such as how to stop the witch. We are relying on your knowledge to help us. Can you think of any weaknesses, or things she strongly dislikes? I can assure you that our children have been brought up to be polite and respectful. You have been exposed to dark magic for such a long time, I'm sure it must have a negative effect on your temperament,' said Shelia.

'Negative effect. What piffle,' said the judge, who was now busy tucking into mulberry wine and hog pies. 'There is no excuse for rudeness, and these two…'

'Would you like a change of clothes? I have a spare pullover,' said Shelia.

The judge stopped chewing for a moment, and glowered at Shelia through beady eyes, as if she were a fly that had irritated him, before he looked away and shovelled more pie crust into his mouth.

'We'd better get going to the North Tower. It's not far. You can see it in the distance,' cut in Ande, who had grown quite red in the face at the judge's criticism of the twins. 'Your Worship can sit on Sunbeam and you two,' he said, looking at Ralph and Alba, 'can both ride on Polaris. Your mother and I will walk.'

'Am I to think you expect me to ride on that beast?' said the judge, looking disdainfully at Sunbeam who was tearing up clumps of grass.

'You can walk, if you prefer,' said Ande through clenched teeth, as he helped Alba on to Polaris's back before giving Ralph a leg up to sit behind his sister. 'After all, Sunbeam is good enough for a Sister of Antares to ride on.'

The judge's mouth fell open, a half-eaten hog pie visible on his tongue. Everyone looked at Shelia, who pulled back her long waistcoat, revealing the gold filigree belt and empty holster.

'Mum. It is true, then?' Alba was the first to speak.

'We overheard you and Dad talking in the kitchen' said Ralph.

'Sorry for eavesdropping,' said Alba.

'Don't worry. I was going to tell you when you both turned sixteen. It hasn't meant much really, until now. You see, the witch is riding around with the wand I am responsible for, and I really need to get it back,' said Shelia.

'Well, this does change things, it really does. Come on then, someone help me on this noble creature. We have a rendezvous at the North Tower. Does it still have all that ivy growing around it?' said the judge, scurrying to Sunbeam's side and looking expectantly at Ande.

'No, Your Worship, it doesn't,' said Ande, lifting the small man, none too gently, into the mare's saddle. 'The walls are quite bare,' he said as he took the horse by its bit and led her back up the valley.

The sun was still high in the sky as the party approached the hill on which the North Tower stood. The sides of the hill, which like all the scenery in the area had been forged by glaciation over thousands of years and then softened and refined in the many intervening centuries, ran into the valley.

No one knew who had built the tower. Excavation indicated that it was once part of a much larger structure, such as an abbey, thought to have covered the plain behind the tower, but now this solitary building was all that remained. There were references to it in local documents, but no architect or owner was ever mentioned; it was always simply referred to as the North Tower.

It was a strange construction, about the height of a lighthouse but with four straight sides and a turreted roof. There was one heavy wooden arched door at the base of the tower facing north across the valley. There were fifteen windows set in threes, over five levels, but the first level was above ground floor height so a curious person could not simply peer in. Many had taken ladders and ropes up that hill, but the ladders had always slipped just at the point where the person was about to reach the window. This happened every time. Attempts had been made to scale the walls by securing ropes over the turrets, but the ropes had mysteriously broken and the would-be voyeurs had been unceremoniously dumped on the ground. The door was also a great mystery. There was no lock and attempts to force it had been met with bent crow bars, or battering rams left fit only for match wood. But on some days, any passersby would swear they had heard voices and footsteps from within the tower and, from time to time at night, lights had been seen flickering from the windows. As such, the tower had earned a reputation for being haunted and people nowadays tended to ignore it or use it as a landmark, keeping well away from it.

The walk to the tower had taken just over an hour and the afternoon shadows were beginning to lengthen. Nobody talked. The children had been dozing on the broad back of Polaris as he plodded on, waking themselves up with a start when they felt themselves lean too heavily to one side. Nobody wanted to talk to the judge.

As they approached the tower, Shelia, who had been tight-lipped as she led Sunbeam, softened her features and said in a gentle voice to the judge, 'Does the countryside look familiar to you?'

'Yes of course it does. It's my home,' he said.

'Can you tell us about the North Tower? Nobody has any idea who built it or why,' continued Shelia.

'I can tell you nothing. Except I signed an authorisation to have it demolished and the stupid workmen came back with some idiotic story that their sledgehammers and shovels had broken when they took their first blows. Bone idle. Needless to say they didn't get a penny in payment.'

'Oh,' said Shelia 'Why did you want to demolish the tower, if you don't mind my asking? It's rather lovely, in a strange way.'

'Well, I do mind you asking. These past hundred years have evidently ravaged good manners, but if you must know I wanted to rid us of all the ridiculous ghost stories and fairy tales that attached to it. You Sisters of Antares were cutting back on the magic side of things, so I thought I'd do my bit.'

'Oh,' said Shelia, still not sure what to make of this funny little creature who appeared so brusque and yet had a reputation for acts of kindness and goodness.

As they neared the top of the hill, they could hear hooves cantering towards them from the far side of the tower. They reached the apex just as Tara-Zed and Procyrion came into view. The judge let out a gasp.

'Good heavens. Sister Rigela Kent. What are you doing here?' said the judge, his eyes narrow and his voice venomous, just before he slipped off Sunbeam's back and landed in a heap on the ground.

Tara-Zed looked taken aback.

'You are mistaken. I am Judge Tara-Zed. You must be the good judge from the legend. How honoured I am to meet you,' she said, dismounting and walking towards the struggling heap of man.

The judge made a strangulated sound and reluctantly took Tara-Zed's hand.

'So the children were right. They did let a woman become a judge. Ridiculous. No wonder the standards have slipped since my day,' he muttered.

Tara-Zed clenched her fists.

'I am also a Sister of Antares and I have the wand entrusted to me.'

She withdrew it from its sheath. Ralph and Alba quietly dismounted.

'Wow,' said Ralph. 'Can you zap something? Like Alba,' he said.

More like the judge. But Alba only thought that.

'I agree,' said Ralph out loud, before he realised that Alba hadn't actually spoken.

'Where is Giena?' said Tara-Zed.

'I still can't believe it. Miss Cygnus. A Sister of Antares? She's my teacher. It's weird enough Mum being one,' said Ralph.

'Well, she is, and she should be here,' said Tara-Zed, shielding her eyes from the long rays of the lowering sun, searching the landscape for any sign of her friend. 'If the witch attacks it's her against me and judging by the fact she's already mastered a broomstick and commanding crows to do her bidding, there's not going to be much of a contest.'

Tara-Zed relayed details of the attack of the crows to the weary group and how she had seen the witch flying at speed up the valley, the crows following.

'She's probably gone to get some rest,' said Shelia.

'And recruit some more crows after Tara-Zed killed so many,' said Ande grimly.

'Still, you do seem quite awesome with the wand. I mean zapping all those crows on your first attempt, well, that's crucial, Your Worship,' said Ralph. He could feel himself redden as soon as the words came out of his mouth.

Tara-Zed smiled.

'Well, you three must have had a time of it in the cave. Did the witch say anything at all?' said Tara-Zed.

'Not really,' said Alba. 'She cackled horribly quite a lot, made a sort of grunty snuffling sound. The only word I thought I heard her say was "revenge", presumably for being stuck in a cave all that time. But who does she want revenge on? I mean, everyone from that long ago is dead. Sorry, Judge, except for you.'

The judge had remained quiet during this conversation, but kept sneaking sidewards glances at Tara-Zed, who now looked directly at him. He averted his eyes.

'Dear Judge,' said Tara-Zed, 'is there anything you can remember that may help? What was she like before the murders?'

The judge looked directly into Tara-Zed's face. His features grew more pliant and when he opened his mouth, he spoke quietly.

'She was quite exquisite, the most considerate creature you could ever meet. She moved to the village a year before it all happened. Rigela Kent had got her an appointment at the school. She became engaged to Coran Stalwart, a goodly young man from a fine village family. She was delightful. Radiant. And then… nobody knows why she turned so bad. I tried to help her, but she wouldn't turn from the darkness. She just wouldn't.'

Tears welled in the corners of his eyes. Tara-Zed placed a hand on his shoulder.

'Thank you, Judge. I know that was painful, but it tells us she was compassionate at one time. Perhaps there is a remnant of good in her that we can appeal to,' said Tara-Zed.

'Very much doubt it. I saw the bodies of the victims. She is a monster,' said the judge, shaking his head and resuming his more familiar look, as though he had just eaten a sour plumpberry.

'For once I agree with the judge,' said Ralph. 'She was pretty relentless in the caves. Goodness knows what she would have done if she'd caught us.'

'Yes, but she didn't, did she?' said Alba. 'I mean before she had the wand she couldn't have done much, but afterwards, well, if I were her I'd have just got a stalactite to fall on our heads.'

'Err, Ingleborough calling planet Alba. What was she doing with those boulders and that rain of straw stalactites?' said Ralph.

'I know, but, well, she missed us, didn't she?' said Alba.

'Oh for crying out loud, Alba, she was trying to kill us!'

'I know, but…'

'Look, never mind that now, you two,' said their mother patiently. 'We're all tired and we must accept the witch is a danger. Now we have to work out how to defeat her.'

'There won't be any time for that,' said Ande, looking down the valley. A black mass was moving rapidly towards them. 'The crows. Try and take cover as best you can.'

'They'll target the horses first,' said Tara-Zed.

'Can you use the wand again?' said Ande.

'Of course,' Tara-Zed replied.

Ralph tried to lead Polaris to the side of the tower, but he stumbled.

'His shoe has just fallen off,' said Ralph. 'Come on, Polaris, you can make it.'

The horse limped over to the wall of the tower and stood with his haunches facing out, the stone building affording some protection for his face. The birds would not be able to fly too close to the wall without damaging their wings. Procyrion was led to the wall and Sunbeam was placed in the middle of the two black horses.

Shelia had taken the judge by his hand and placed him in the doorway of the tower, pulling his robe over his head so only his bulbous nose was clearly visible. She wondered at his garments as she adjusted them. They felt like animal skin in her hands.

The twins stood between the horses' heads, holding the reins, quite protected from the impending attack. Shelia and Ande stood either side of Tara-Zed.

'You must take cover,' said Tara-Zed.

'No, Sister. We shall help you,' said Shelia.

'I may not have a wand but I do have some fists I can use,' said Ande.

'Well, I won't let them get so close this time,' said Tara-Zed, withdrawing the wand, which was already cracking with anticipation.

The crows were now less than a hundred metres away. There were about three hundred of them, flying in a chevron formation, their preferred shape of attack, thought Tara-Zed.

She aimed her wand at the lead bird and gave a firm flick of her wrist, concentrating hard as she did so. Ande and Shelia staggered back with the unexpected force that the wand issued. A straight line of silver spat out and just as it reached the birds, split into three forks of lightning, knocking about twenty birds to the ground. The flock kept on coming, closing together to reform the 'v' shape.

'Crucial,' said Ralph. He had stepped forwards and he and Alba were picking up small stones, hoping that their parents would not notice.

Tara-Zed had time for one more attack. This time, she held the line of lightning for a fraction longer and added another fifty birds to those already stupefied, but now the crows were upon them.

Ande covered his face with his left arm and punched and grabbed with his right until he felt it make contact and disable a bird. Then he swapped arms, attacking with his left until another bird fell. He kept up this alternating method of defence and wrung a few necks as well, despite the birds raining pecks and tearing at his head, back and legs.

Shelia stood firm for the first wave of the attack but, realising she could be of no use fighting at that moment, withdrew to the horses. Whereas most creatures would have lashed out, these three brave horses stood quietly protecting their humans. Tara-Zed had been correct. The horde were concentrating their attack on the horses, who were being struck relentlessly by the birds' shiny beaks. The birds would swoop down, hover with wings flapping whilst they took one or two tugs at the poor animals' hides, before flying off to let another bird take its turn.

Alba and Shelia took it in turns to flap their arms to shoo the crows away, before retreating between the horses to stroke their soft noses. Then either mother or daughter would rush out and swat as many birds as their arms would reach.

Tara-Zed was firing her wand as quickly and accurately as she could but was not making sufficient headway to fend off the attack before serious injuries were done to horses and humans alike. She also knew, from her instruction on the wand's healing powers, that it could not be used indefinitely to restore the same creature before its power started to reverse. This was the safeguard built in so that people in possession of the wands could not live forever, along with anyone they chose. Procyrion had already had one healing touch and she didn't want to have to use many more on him.

Ralph had been throwing stones, which from time to time connected with a crow, but not enough to make any impact on the attack.

'Sis, we've got to help,' said Ralph.

'How?' said Alba.

'Follow me. Be quick,' he said and ducked beneath Polaris's stomach. He sprinted to a small outcrop of limestone and gorse, followed closely by Alba. Their father was still taking well aimed punches and knocking crows out of the air to join the pile of stunned birds surrounding him, but his progress was barely penetrating the flock and their relentless attack continued.

The twins reached the pile of rocks. Alba yanked up a large sprig of gorse and, running back towards the horses, used the branch as a crow swat, batting the birds out of the way of the horses' hides as best she could. In the meantime, Ralph had knelt down and rummaged amongst the coarse grass between the rocks. He found a cluster of stones, fragments which had broken away from the parent rock through years of water freezing and melting. These were sharper then the pebbles he had been using. He stuffed two fistfuls into his waistcoat pocket and, from his crouched position, started to throw the stones at the crows. It was easier now he had some distance between him and the attack. At first his aim was not good as the crows were constantly moving, but after a couple of misses he got his eye in and started picking them off one by one.

Despite the increasing piles of feathered bodies twitching or struggling weakly off down the hill, too shocked to fly, the attack of the crows was unremitting and the humans were beginning to tire. Tara-Zed had attempted an umbrella defence, but the crows were attacking from all directions and choosing separate targets so they were more spread out, and her effort was not as successful as before. Ande's fists were starting to miss the birds. He drew closer to Tara-Zed.

'We're losing this battle, Tara-Zed. I suggest we group together and try one joint attack on the birds,' said Ande.

'I agree. You call…' Tara-Zed's voice trailed off as her attention was drawn to a movement down the hillside. 'Is that…'

'Arfur Sendal,' said Ande. 'What's that weasel doing here? He never reports on anything dangerous. He's in a hurry though.'

And indeed, Arfur was scurrying up the hillside, his face crimson with effort. As Arfur ascended, the attack of the crows subsided and they began to fly back down the valley.

'Well. Who'd have thought Arfur would have been our secret weapon?' said Tara-Zed, allowing herself a wry smile.

Arfur was now close enough for the group to hear his wheezing and a strange whistling sound, which was emerging from his nasal passages.

The rest of the group, except for the judge, had gathered round. All had suffered at the beaks of the birds, and blood was leaking from open wounds on their faces and backs of their hands.

'Looks like you're too late for the story, Arfur,' said Ande, staring coldly at the reporter.

'Story? Story? I saw you were in trouble and thought I might be able to offer assistance, didn't I now?' said Arfur, still wheezing. His eyes appeared glazed.

'Well, there's a first time for everything,' said Ande. 'The crows have gone, probably to rest and regroup.'

'Is the good judge with you, by any chance?' said Arfur who was looking at the sky then at the ground and then at the tower, in fact anywhere other than making eye contact with another person.

'Yes he is. Why do you ask, Arfur? Why not enquire after the health of my children?' said Ande.

'Oh I, well, of course. How are they? I just wanted to secure an exclusive with him, if possible. I mean over one hundred years...'

'You really are a weasel, aren't you? No, that's an insult to weasels. You...' Ande's voice trailed off as Shelia's hand gripped his arm.

'Ande. Look,' said Shelia, pointing with her free hand down the valley.

Alba let out a shriek and Ralph's face turned ashen. Flying up the centre of the valley was the witch, her tattered garments flowing behind, her cat crouched low on the end of the broomstick. Following her was the black murder of crows, already positioned in their chevron attack formation.

'Ahem,' said the judge, who had joined the group, straightening his robes and adjusting his wig. 'And to what disaster have you embroiled me in now?'

'Excuse me, Judge. My family and friends have been defending you from a vicious attack, and very well too,' said Shelia. 'Look, you haven't a mark on you thanks to our defences.'

And indeed it was true. The judge had been unscathed during the battle.

'She's coming, Dad,' said Ralph.

The group watched as the witch, who had now swung her broomstick up the side of the valley, headed straight towards them, followed by the army of birds.

'Everybody stand firm and fight the best you can,' said Ande. 'Tara-Zed, may I ask you to concentrate on the witch? We need to stop her.'

'I'll do my best,' said Tara-Zed.

The group were standing between Arfur and the judge. Arfur started to edge around the people towards the pompous man, just as the witch passed over them, knocking Arfur to the ground. She flew straight to the top of the tower, hovered for a few seconds and then dismounted. As she leant through the ramparts the wand could be glimpsed dripping blue particles of ice, which showered the wall of the tower and bounced off the grass at the base before melting with a hiss, narrowly missing the horses. The cat stood on top of a turret, its back arched and tail stiff. Moments later the crows began their assault, this time harrying and pecking with even more ferocity than before.

The judge cowered beneath his robe as Ande, Shelia, Ralph and Alba punched and thrashed the air trying to push the wretched crows away. The poor horses, without the closeness of a human to reassure them, reared and bucked, wheeled and bit, in an effort to repel their feathered tormentors. Tara-Zed could not stand firm enough to take a shot at the witch atop the column and had to be content with striking crows.

A fearful cracking noise echoed across the valley and the red, pink and orange of the fiery sunset were tinged purple as a blue bolt of ice issued from the top of the tower. The strike landed less than a metre from Ralph and knocked several birds from the sky just above his head, where they had been about to attack his eyes.

Just as well she's not that great a shot, thought Ralph.

Give it time and she will be, replied his sister, although her lips never moved.

Another line of ice crashed down in front of Ande's feet, instantly killing several birds who were attacking his knees.

'That was close,' said Ande.

'Too close,' said Shelia. 'Tara-Zed, you have to try and hit her.'

'I know. I'll line up for a shot,' replied Tara-Zed.

Whilst the attack was taking place, Arfur had crept, with shoulders hunched as if this would make him invisible, towards the judge. As he reached him, Arfur stood his thin frame upright. The judge peered at him.

'So you are the one chosen to be my servant?' said the judge.

'Yes. I have been called,' replied Arfur, with a look of admiration across his ferret-like face.

As this short exchange took place, the crows lessened their attack by circling the tower, coming in for an occasional nip which the humans fended off quite easily. The view of the witch was obscured by the density of the rotating birds. The horses stood in an uneasy stillness, stamping the ground with their hooves and exhaling through flared nostrils. The attention of the group was drawn towards Arfur and the judge.

'You have it, my servant?' said the judge.

'Yes, Your Worship.' As he said this, Arfur bowed on one knee and with a flourish withdrew from his corduroy jacket a shining silver stick.

'The third wand,' cried Ande.

'Is that Giena's wand? What have you done to her?' Shelia's voice was shrill.

'I'll take that,' said the judge, extending his portly arm towards Arfur.

Arfur placed the wand in the judge's dumpy hand, who immediately pointed it at Shelia.

'Don't come any closer. I have no experience with these instruments and wouldn't want to use too much force,' he said with a leer. 'I might burn you to a cinder by accident. After all, this is the fire wand.'

'I knew you were an evil creature,' cried Ralph, his father grabbing him by the shoulders to stop him running straight at the judge.

'You and the witch were in it together all along. You rotten pig,' shouted Alba.

'Calm down, love,' said Shelia, as they all stood staring at the judge holding the inert rod.

As this had been going on, the crows had been attacking less and circling higher. Gaps began to appear in the formation and the top of the tower where the witch, who still stood peering over the top, came in and out of view. Ande motioned to Tara-Zed with a slight nod of his head. Tara-Zed gave a quick blink to show that she had understood. She could take a strike at the witch through the separated crows.

Whilst the stand-off between the judge and the rest of the party was taking place, Tara-Zed kept glancing at the top of the tower. She saw a pattern in the crows' flight and suddenly spun round, pointing her right arm to the top of the tower. A streak of lightning cracked forth and sped towards the turrets, but the bolt never made it. Instead a thin red streak, with flames running along it, came out of nowhere and intercepted the streak of lightning, sending it into a group of hapless crows who immediately dropped to the ground. Tara-Zed's hand jerked sideways with the momentum.

'What happened?' cried Ande.

'I don't know. A streak of fire came out of nowhere and knocked my shot out of the way,' said Tara-Zed.

'Look. The witch is on the move,' shouted Ralph, pointing towards the top of the tower where the witch was now hovering on her broomstick, her cat crouched low on the brush.

'Stop! All of you,' screeched the judge and he started flicking his hand in which he held the silver stick as fast as he could, stabbing at the air.

Nothing happened. No sparks emerged nor fire brands nor shards of ice.

'What is the meaning of this? What have you brought me, you imbecile?' he squawked at Arfur, all the time shaking the would-be wand as if it were an empty salt cellar.

The sound of rustling grass and plodding hooves made the group divert their attention down the hill.

'It's Miss Cygnus. And she has a wand,' shouted Alba.

Giena Cygnus was approaching in her cart, recognisable by the outline of her grey trilby. She was not alone, for a small figure dressed in black, not dissimilar in appearance to the judge, sat next to her. Stardust was taking strong, deliberate steps as she pulled her load up the hill, her nostrils wide and her head low.

'Jasper Corvus is with her,' said Alba.

'What's he doing here?' said Ralph.

As Giena approached, the judge turned to Arfur and started prodding him with the false wand.

'You idiot. Was there no better specimen than you?' screeched the judge.

'I did exactly as the crow commanded me. It's not my fault if that thing has no power. Perhaps you got it wrong,' he said, curling up into a ball to avoid the digging.

'Well, that woman who you were supposed to dispose of seems to have a working wand,' said the judge, spit coming from his mouth.

Giena and Jasper had by now reached the group. Ande rushed forwards to help Giena, but Jasper was already holding her hand as she stepped from the cart. The crows were still circling, as if waiting for a command to attack. The witch was poised above them.

'Quick, Tara-Zed. We must get rid of the crows, together,' said Giena, extending her wand arm. Tara-Zed followed suit. The tips of the two wands touched and a line of fire and lightning extended upwards and became caught up in the circular current the birds were making. The birds cawed and shrieked as they flew around their statically charged vortex, one touch of a spark of lightning and flame sending them squawking away in every direction. The smell of singed feathers whipped around in the turbulent air. Gradually, the birds dispersed across the countryside until just one large crow remained, who flew up and rested on the ramparts. At this the witch flew down.

'What's going on?' said Ralph.

Giena and Tara-Zed lowered their wands and turned to the judge, who was glowering, a look of menace in his beady eyes. He turned towards Arfur, who was cowering as if he was trying to push away an unseen foe. Suddenly, Arfur got up and ran down the hill, the arms and legs of his gangly frame moving with a complete lack of co-ordination. Before the wands could be used, Ralph spotted Polaris's missing shoe, picked it up, lined up his shot, breathed in and then launched the horse shoe, exhaling as he did so. The horse shoe rotated through the evening air and caught up with its target, hitting Arfur Sendal firmly between his shoulder blades. The reporter collapsed to the floor, unable to move, looking like a squashed, four-legged spider. Polaris's shoe had bounced upwards when it had hit its target and now landed firmly on Arfur's head, rendering him fully unconscious.

'Good shot, Ralph,' said Alba.

'Perhaps all that quoits practice wasn't such a waste of time,' said Shelia.

Whilst these events had been unfolding, the sun had sunk below the horizon and a fearsome sunset was the only thing stopping it from being quite dark. Giena Cygnus walked towards the judge and drew a large circle on the ground around him, with her wand. Fire combusted into life where the wand had marked the grass, so the man was imprisoned by flames. They were not close enough to burn their prisoner but they did provide warmth and light to the now weary battlers.

'Look at the ring on his finger,' said Alba, pointing at the judge's hand. He was standing in the midst of the fire, turning the ring on his finger.

'It's a ruby, but in the cave it was black stone,' said Ralph.

'He probably stole it and disguised it. He was always messing with it. He's completely deceitful,' said Alba.

'What happened to you, Sister? Why did Arfur bring a false wand?' said Tara-Zed.

The witch circled above them with absolute calm and no appearance of menace.

'I went to my wand's hiding place, the Old Abbey,' said Giena. 'I entered the crypt using the key given to me by my mentor, Sigma Octantis. But she had told me that there were two hiding places and that I should retrieve the false wand first. You see, when Altair had chosen her original hiding place, she noticed a flock of crows following her. One in particular, like the large one up there,' she pointed to the black bird sitting high up on the turrets, 'seemed particularly nosy, in an almost human way, and Altair knew her hiding place had been compromised. Three nights later, she returned with a false wand and a sophisticated locking mechanism, both of which she had asked the trusted blacksmith to forge for her. She then hid the false wand, which is just a bit of scrap metal, in the more elaborate hiding place. I'm glad she took that precaution. Arfur turned up and set the crows on Leo Gammacom and Canis, so I handed him the false wand. The only problem was I became locked in with only a thread of candlelight and hundreds of spiders. I would have been here sooner, but I took my time feeling my way around the crypt to the right spot.' Giena gave a shudder.

'So where was the true wand?' asked Shelia.

'In a simple coffin containing the bones of Coran Stalwart,' said Giena.

They looked up, for when Coran's name had been mentioned the witch had given a cry, full of anguish, the cat clutching to the broomstick tightly as she sought to steady herself.

'But how did you know that the judge isn't all he seemed?' said Ande.

'Arfur seemed to be under some sort of control. I mean he was unusually brave and even more odious than usual. Then I thought about what he had said. He never mentioned the witch, just "our noble leader". I remember the judge being described as noble and then things started to fall into place. I used the wand to blast myself out.'

'What of Leo and Canis?' asked Shelia.

'Well, I have to admit I expected the worst. The crows sounded pretty murderous and Arfur was acting really strangely, revelling in the thought of blood, but,' here she turned towards Jasper Corvus, who had been standing in dignified silence, his hands clasped behind his back, gazing intently at Giena, 'well, I was surprised to find Jasper. At first, I'm ashamed to admit I thought he was part of the evil plan, and had betrayed Tara-Zed, what with Corvus being Latin for "crow", but then I saw that he had seated Leo in a pew and was tending his wounds with holy water and had already bandaged poor Canis's paw with strips torn from the altar cloths, well…'

'Jasper, how did you manage to be there especially after you left in such a huff from the meeting?' asked Shelia.

'Forgive me. My demeanour lends itself to my looking ill-tempered, but I am generally quite content. In any event, my feelings count for nought. I realised that there was danger about. Judge Tara-Zed told me as much and, well, I took the liberty of following Miss Cygnus as I thought she may need some assistance. I was wrong, of course. She was her usual brave and resourceful self, qualities I have long admired in her.'

Jasper suddenly reddened and looked away from the group.

'Leo and Canis were glad you were there, and so was I,' said Giena.

The court usher, usually so correct and austere, turned even more crimson.

'I remembered my training and gave them each a touch of the wand. We left Leo dancing a jig and Canis was leaping around like a puppy, chasing butterflies.'

'Well, Judge. Is this true? Are you malign?' said Ande, staring through the fiery circle at the man, who returned the look with his face distorted by the ghastly shadows cast by the dancing flame.

Before he had a chance to speak, the onlookers felt a gentle draught on their faces. They looked up and saw the witch descending until she and the cat alighted the broomstick and stood between them and the judge. She was grotesque and gave off a foul smell of decay. Her eyes glowed orange and Alba shrank back behind her father as she remembered how they had penetrated the darkness in the cave. Ralph took a step forwards as if to attack the witch, but she looked straight at him and he saw there was no malice in her face. In fact, she reached her wart-covered hand towards the boy before withdrawing it quickly. Her cat, with its peculiar black and white markings, gazed intently at Ralph.

'Please forgive my abhorrent state,' said the witch with a rasping voice.

'It's the voice from the village hall,' said Ande.

'I knew I'd heard it before, but how…' said Alba.

'Please, Alba, do not be afraid. I would never harm you,' said the witch.

'What?' said Ralph. 'You were pelting us with rocks and making things come alive out of walls. What would you have done if you had wanted to harm us?'

'I am sorry. I was trying to stop the judge from leaving the cave. I knew once he was out he would be able to command the crows and manipulate people just like he used to.'

The witch stared at the judge, who held her gaze before turning away to study the ground.

'You see,' she tried to continue, but had to pause as a bout of coughing rose in her throat. 'I'm sorry. I feel I have little time left.'

Tara-Zed stepped forwards and gazed at the witch. With her left hand, she held the witch's gnarled chin, and with her right hand, she placed the wand on her paper-thin lips. The gentle sparkles drifted into the ancient mouth and could be seen circulating through the tired body. As it did so, the witch seemed to unfold from her hunched stance. The filthy matted grey locks became strawberry-blond tresses and her skin became as smooth and pale as alabaster. Hazel eyes stared out from a pretty, youthful face. Even her rotten rags fell to dust to be replaced by a simple brown frock, with an embroidered waistcoat.

'Aster, welcome,' said Tara-Zed, replacing her wand in its holster and embracing the former witch. 'A great wrong has been done to you. But why?'

'I shall tell you. But first I must give one of you this.'

Aster turned to Shelia and placed the wand from the cave in her hand.

'My intention was always to bring this to you. You see, the Sisters of Antares had chosen me to be a successor before... well, I'll get to that. That's how I knew how to use it so accurately in the cave and just now against the crows. Anyway, I must continue, for although my body is restored, I am still weak. And I really will not be with you long.'

And so she began her story.

CHAPTER 17

'My parents were killed in the Global War. I was taken as a baby to Skipton Castle. I remember growing up surrounded by love and happiness. Rigela Kent, Altair and Deneb were always playing with me, and I had two lovely fairies as my best friends, Willis and Elle. They'd stayed with me long after their own kind had returned to their kingdom.' Aster stared at the judge. 'They taught us how to live closely with the magic of nature, not to exploit it. Rigela Kent even let me have a go with her wand.

'When I was nineteen, I became a teacher in Ingleset. I also grew flowers and herbs for remedies. For the first few months I was so happy. You see, I soon met Coran, son of Marsha and Stalwart Woodkeeper. They were a wonderful family. So like you,' she smiled at the Milway family, who were standing with their arms around one another, 'handsome and kind. Good people.'

Shelia sniffed loudly.

'Anyway, Coran and I became engaged and went to see dear Bishop Roland to arrange our wedding. The judge happened to be there. He took a keen interest in our arrangements, but kept saying horrid remarks about Coran's family only being wood cutters and how one shouldn't marry beneath one's true social standing. After that, he would visit me every day either at home or at school, letting me know how well he was thought of and how he would go far in the judiciary.

'Then, one day, not long before I was due to marry Coran, the judge proposed to me. Of course I turned him down and told him exactly what I thought of him. Do you remember that, Judge?'

The creature clasped the lapels of his gown, podgy thumbs turned upwards, feigning disinterest by looking into the night sky, as the flames performed their danse macabre around him.

'The next day, I was due to meet Coran at the abbey for our wedding rehearsal. We were getting married there because people from the whole region were going to turn up and the village church would never have coped. We arranged to meet there early and pick some flowers for his mother. But he never turned up. A search party found his body that evening, face down in the river. His lips had a purple tinge. He had been poisoned and as he lay unconscious was pushed into the stream, where he drowned.'

'You poor dear,' said Shelia, stepping forwards with tears in her eyes, her arms outstretched to Aster.

Aster held up her hand to halt Shelia's movement.

'Please, I must continue. My time is short. I was distraught, as were Coran's parents. I could not leave my cottage. The next day, Willis and Elle brought me some food. I wish you could have seen them. These tiny creatures fluttering on wings more delicate than a butterfly's, carrying a picnic basket between them as if it were a feather. Pies and fruit. Bread and cheeses. Cakes and buns. I didn't have much of an appetite, but they were so kind that I ate some. They continued to do this for several weeks. I looked forward to their food. I craved it. But the more I ate, the more haggard I grew. Bishop Roland was still paying me regular visits and one particularly beautiful day he told me he had walked a longer route through the woods, and overheard a conversation between the judge and the fairies. It turned out that the judge had asked the fairies to bring me the food, explaining that I would be too upset to see him or accept gifts of kindness from him, as I was in love with him all along. I'm amazed Willis and Elle believed him, but they were such trusting little things and they had no reason not to.

'Seeing my demise, the bishop realised that the food was enchanted and that the fairies were being unwittingly used to poison me. Rather than take this matter to the Sisters of Antares he summoned the judge to the abbey where the judge stabbed him in the heart with one of my knitting needles, which he had stolen from my cottage.

'The judge then went to meet the fairies under the pretence of delivering a special food parcel, and murdered those sweet innocent creatures by strangling them one in each hand – they were tiny little things.'

The judge let out a chuckle that rattled the phlegm in the back of his throat.

'The fairies went "pop" when I squeezed them. Most amusing, ahem. It was highly satisfying to stop their ridiculous chit-chat,' said the judge.

The group stared at him, their faces showing a mixture of anger, pity and resignation. Aster looked away and continued her story.

'He then cut out their hearts and placed them in a jar, which he planted on a shelf in my kitchen. It was found when the village council came to arrest me. Nobody believed the story of a once lovely young girl turned into a vile crone through her own evil acts, against that of a distinguished man of the law. They could barely understand me, my voice was so damaged by the poison I had been ingesting.'

Aster finished her story. She looked even lovelier, as if telling the truth of her wrongful conviction was a weight from her mind.

'So what made you drag him into the cave?' said Alba.

'He was so evil. I couldn't stand the thought of him destroying more lives, as he surely would. I saw the right moment and with the help of Pusskin here,' she tickled behind her cat's ears, 'we managed to make him partake in the eternal punishment which was rightly his all along.'

'And what have you got to say to this, Judge?' said Tara-Zed.

'Oh, it's quite true,' he said, staring at Aster. 'Every last detail of it. Except two things.'

His lips thinned into an evil sneer.

'What is it? What don't I know?' said Aster.

'Well, your parents didn't die because of the war. I killed them. You see, I had wanted to marry your mother but she spurned me, just like you did. War is the perfect cover for murder, you see. I shot them with arrows that I had taken from an enemy.' He sniggered to himself.

Ralph rushed at the judge without thinking of the flames, but as soon as he ran into them he was thrown backwards. Still, he rushed a second time and was repulsed again.

'You evil little man. You deserve to die. Let me kill him.'

'Ralph. No,' said Ande, placing a hand on his son's shoulders, which were smouldering slightly from his impact with the fire. 'That is not our way. We shall take him back to the village for a trial.'

'But that's not fair, Dad. Look at Aster. He destroyed her life. He murdered good people and fairies.'

Aster broke in to laughter, surprising everyone.

'Oh, Ralph. You are so like your very great uncle in looks and deeds. You see Coran would have been yours and Alba's uncle back down the family line. But your father is correct. The judge must be put on trial.'

Alba looked at her mother.

'Why didn't you tell us that we were related to Coran? It seems so obvious now,' said Alba.

'The baby girl, your great-great-grandmother, born to Marsha, never spoke of it. Never even mentioned magic, by all accounts. I only discovered the connection when I became a Sister of Antares. I can only think she didn't want this hanging over the family like a curse,' said Shelia.

'What about the villagers? Surely they must have gossiped. They can't be any different than today,' said Alba.

Giena stepped forwards.

'They were different times then, Alba. Humankind nearly didn't survive. The wands were hidden for a reason, to make people trust in their own resources and not always rely on magic. They couldn't deny the Concert of Singing Flowers, but even that was put down to science,' said Giena, glancing at Aster. Alba furrowed her brow, still looking puzzled, before looking at Aster.

'How did you survive down there? Surely it must have driven you mad. All that blackness and silence?' said Alba.

Aster laughed, like the sound of tinkling silver bells.

'It's not as quiet as you think down there. You know how loud the water is and that would get even noisier in early spring when the snows melted. Then there are the drips. I had one stalagmite which dripped right next to my ear for fifty-five years. I also had the cave dwellers…'

'What are they?' asked Ralph.

'Don't interrupt, Ralph. It's rude,' said his mother.

Aster smiled again.

'I don't know for sure but they've certainly evolved from the primordial mud down there…'

'I said that,' said Ralph, as his mother shot him a look that silenced him once more.

'They have evolved to their surroundings. They are transparent, have no bones and yet can turn rigid if they need to. They can breathe in or out of water, stretch to four times their length and communicate through touch. They show no malice, are intelligent and kind,' continued Aster.

'Well, they helped us enough,' said Ralph.

'Yes, but they never really helped the judge, did they?' asked Alba.

'Oh and they are good judges of character,' said Aster, and everybody, except the judge, laughed. 'There was one other thing that did keep me very amused.'

'What?' asked Alba.

'When I lived in the village I kept a garden. I was keen to extract healing properties from the plants. Just as I fell into the cave, some seeds shook from my clothes. The wands implanted just enough magic so that I could breathe music into the roots of the flowers so that once a year they might perform for you and remind you of what had taken place. One day I knew we would be found.'

'That was you?' cried Alba. 'How amazing. I knew the concert was caused by magic, not some scientific freak of nature. Thank you, Aster. It was brillig.'

'Erm, does that mean that there won't be any more concerts, now you are out of the cave?' said Ralph.

'I'm afraid not,' said Aster.

Alba groaned but Ralph looked at the ground and then at the sky and simply said, 'Oh.'

'Were you also the voice in the village hall? How did you get there? How did you know about the parchments?' asked Shelia.

'The force of the wands propelled Pusskin and myself right into the cavern where Ralph and Alba first saw us. The judge had dropped like a stone almost as soon as we entered the cave. The wand's force wasn't *that* strong.'

Alba giggled as she saw a look of dismay cross the judge's sour face and he tried to hold his stomach in.

'Sadly, the judge was also touched by the magic. We probably would have stayed where we landed and died,' continued Aster, 'but then I realised the Meteor Table...'

'The what?' said Ralph.

'Shush, Ralph. Later,' said Shelia.

'Anyway, once you've touched the table, as I did during my training,' said Aster, 'you can feel when it is activated, like a ripple on a pond, and I realised there would be a prophecy. Parts of it came through to me. I knew we would remain in suspended animation for one hundred years and then I'd have the chance to put things right. Thanks to the bravery of these two, that has been allowed to happen.'

Ralph and Alba exchanged glances, both slightly embarrassed and yet proud at the same time.

'I was able to be at the meeting because a little moonlight had entered the cave. It was just enough to give the power to project myself and Pusskin. It was Pusskin who disturbed you outside your window. I knew that a blood relative needed to be made aware, or else there would be no one to stop the judge if I failed. As it happens, there were two relatives to help.'

Aster smiled at the twins.

'You said there were two things we didn't know, Judge. Tell us what the other matter is. It may help you in your trial if you have told us the whole truth,' said Tara-Zed.

'Oh, I doubt that anything I say will help me,' said the judge, 'but out of the goodness of my heart I will bring a little comfort to someone.'

He sneered and looked directly at Ralph. 'You are a stupid creature. Did you not notice that when you were laying the charges you were not alone?'

'What do you mean? Of course I was alone. There was nobody around,' snapped Ralph, and then more sullenly he said, 'I was trying to prove that I could do the job on my own this year. Not that I did that.'

'Quite right there was no person, but what about another creature?' replied the judge.

The large crow, which was still perched on the ramparts, let out a staccato caw, like an evil laugh.

Ralph's brow furrowed. Then he looked up and said, 'Of course. That crow was circling above me and then it was joined by others. They went round and round. I felt quite dizzy because I could see their shadows. They made me feel sick. I couldn't even face my sandwich when I got home.'

'Well, let me tell you,' the judge stabbed a fat finger at Ralph, 'that you did faint for a few moments, and when you came to, there was an extra nought on your figures, wasn't there? And you laid your charges accordingly, like the idiot boy you are.'

'So I did see the extra nought. It was you tricking me just so you could be blown out of the hole. You had no thought that people might get hurt. You really are evil,' said Ralph.

'How did you know about the prophecy?' said Alba quietly.

'Relatives in high places,' said the judge, and then he thinned his lips like a bullfrog.

'Judge. I suggest you keep quiet now. You have caused my family and its ancestors enough pain and I will not be held responsible for my actions if you continue with these taunts and insults,' said Shelia, through gritted teeth. 'I believe you are what my daughter would call "skank".'

The large crow flapped its wings vigorously and took off from its roost. Aster narrowed her eyes as she watched its progress, framed like a giant bat in the moonlight.

'So who or what is that crow and how is he controlled?' asked Alba.

'Well, Silas Morte resembled a crow and I suspect he went missing after the trial,' said Aster.

'It would take some hefty magic to transfigure a man into an animal,' said Tara-Zed, curling a lock of hair in her fingers as she spoke, 'but it's not impossible. Crows don't usually fly at night, so something's got that thing up there bothered. Just be aware of it. Wherever that crow has been, there is always trouble. Also, I don't believe the judge is the main controller.'

'Why?' said Alba.

'Well, for one he's not that clever and secondly he wanted the wands but doesn't really seem to know why. I think someone else is controlling the crows and other dumb animals,' said Tara-Zed.

'Like Arfur?' said Ralph.

'You said you didn't have much time,' said Alba, looking at Aster. 'What did you mean?'

'Although I am restored, I feel I am being called elsewhere,' said Aster.

'Well, none of us are going anywhere until morning,' said Ande. 'It's too far to walk in the dark, and the horses need to rest in any event.'

'I'll see what food and drink we have left,' said Shelia, moving towards the horses. 'Giena, perhaps you would kindly light another fire for us. At least we'll get some warmth, but I think it's going to be a pretty uncomfortable night.'

The group murmured their agreement and Giena helped Shelia rummage through the saddle bags for whatever scraps were left. Suddenly a beam of light fell on Aster as if she were caught in a searchlight. It came from the top of the tower, although there was no visible source. Pusskin mewed loudly and Aster picked the cat up and handed her to Alba.

'Take care of dear Pusskin for me. It's not her time yet,' she said.

'What do you mean? Where are you going?' said Alba, as she cradled the mewing cat in her arms.

Aster turned towards the door of the tower, which was now wide open, her flaxen hair swaying in a gentle draught. Everybody, including the judge, followed her gaze. Ralph made towards the door, but Ande placed a hand firmly on his shoulder.

'This is not for you, son. Stay put,' he said.

Aster looked back at her new-found friends, a smile on her beautiful face interrupting the tears of joy that were spilling from her eyes.

'I knew it was them calling to me,' she whispered. 'Thank you for all you have done. I know we shall meet again. God bless you all,' she said.

She turned to the judge, whose face was that of a monstrous gargoyle, through the flickering flames. 'And may you find forgiveness in God's mercy.'

The judge narrowed his eyes and gave her a look of contempt.

The beam of light moved towards the door and Aster moved with it. Voices could be heard from within the tower. Laughter, merriment and the sound of a violin playing a cheery reel floated on the still night air before evaporating, like bubbles. Lights flickered in all the windows of the tower and silhouettes of people dancing, laughing and raising glasses were momentarily glimpsed. As Aster neared the door she gasped and put her hands to her mouth. Around her head hovered twenty silver lights. She raised her hands and two of the lights rested in each palm, which she raised to her face. With barely a whisper she said, 'Hello, Willis. Hello, Elle.'

The fairy lights flew into the tower and Aster strode through the doorway with arms outstretched. Her voice could be heard exclaiming, 'Mother! Father! Marsha! Stalwart!' and then the most exuberant of all, 'Oh, my love! Coran!'

As she disappeared into the tower, the door swung gently shut behind her and the lights at the windows faded away. Ralph rushed to the door and pushed hard, but it was shut fast. He placed his ear against the wood and then backed away.

'I can't hear a thing,' he said. 'Where did she go?'

'This tower holds many mysteries,' said Tara-Zed. 'It also holds many answers, but only for the people who need them. It is not your turn, Ralph. But it was Aster's and now she can have the happy future she deserves. But that's not your story anymore, Ralph. You were just a small part of hers as she was of yours. Although I would have loved to have asked her what the original Sisters were like,' she added, almost to herself.

'Come on, son. Let's settle down for the night,' said Ande.

As he guided Ralph back to the group, there was a loud creaking behind them and once more their attention was drawn to the tower. The door was again open, but this time there was no warm light or sounds of festivity. Instead there was a gaping blackness as deep as anything the twins had experienced in the cave, perhaps deeper for the darkness had a viscous quality, as if it were alive. The terrible blackness seemed to peer out, as if wishing to spill through the windows to engulf them all.

Cold air gushed through the doorway. The air felt as if it were filled with knives. The onlookers flinched and wrapped their arms around their bodies. The horses shook and whinnied. The flames of the judge's prison burnt stronger and bluer. Then there came an awful sucking noise, as if too much water were trying to drain down a too-small plughole. The flames flickered behind the judge and now extended away from him, making a flame-lined pathway to the door. The judge screamed as the flame behind him started to push him towards the door, singeing him when he failed to move.

'No. No. You can't make me go in there,' screeched the judge, as if he were talking to an unseen foe. 'I'll change my ways. I'll do anything you ask. Just name it. I have some money. And silver. Don't send me in there. No. No! Help me, Silas. Help me, Mother!'

With that, the large crow came diving down and placed its claws on the back of the judge's robes. It tried to pull backwards, beating its wings so hard they blurred into one. The judge dug his heels into the ground, but he continued to be dragged closer and closer by the blackness, whilst being pushed by the blue flames. The heels of his feet left two parallel furrows in the grass.

The group looked on in horrified fascination as the judge and bird edged towards this gaping void beyond the door.

'Dad? Can't we do something?' said Alba, clutching her father's strong arm.

'The flame was made by a wand. It is as if the wand itself is forcing him onwards. It is not our story, but his,' said Tara-Zed.

Even so, Ande moved towards the flames, but as he approached, a devilish face leered out and belched a column of red embers, which sprinkled over his face, causing little puffs of smoke to rise from his skin. Ande stepped back, flicking the singeing motes from his face.

The judge reached the doorway and clung to the frame with all his might, his chubby hands grasping and clawing, his fingernails leaving scratch marks on the stone. The flames seemed to rise higher as the crow's flapping wings fanned them into renewed mayhem. The screeching and cawing of the bird and the pitiful wailing of the doomed man reverberated across the valley until, as if fed up with waiting, there came a dreadful, hollow moan from within the tower as if it were inhaling a never-ending breath.

'Don't leave me, Silas!' screamed the judge. His legs were lifted from the ground as he was sucked, surrounded by flames, into the void.

Before the bird relinquished its grip, unwilling to be part of the punishment, it grasped the ruby ring in its beak, and tore it from the judge's finger. The judge's final yell of terror was silenced as the heavy door slammed shut.

The Welsh Lagoons

Lady Anna had sat mesmerised by the drama that had played out before her through the lens of the ruby eye in the centre of the cross. Her free hand rested on the urn.

'It was clever of me to give my son to the hobgoblins – he is so steeped in magic. Those foolish hobgoblins thought they'd own a human forever, but they're gone now. We outlived them all,' she said. 'And sending Anthony's ruby ring to him was a stroke of luck. I have watched him all this time, even in the dark of the cave.'

But as the door of the North Tower opened and the flames pushed the judge towards the opening, she squeezed the cross so tightly her hand bled. A strangled scream caught in her throat.

'No! I cannot lose another child!' As she saw the tower consume the judge, she slumped in her chair. She found a final strength and flung her arm across the table by her side. The photo of her firstborn son and his urn of ashes crashed to the floor, broken glass and ash mixing in a heap.

When the guard brought in her supper of baked fish and carrots, all he found on the cushion of Lady Anna's chair was the ruby from her wooden cross in the centre of a pile of dust.

The crow flew away into the night sky, its progress easily tracked by the flaming tail feathers set alight as it escaped, bobbing like a firefly into the darkness.

The group stood in stunned silence before realising that without the flames they were illuminated only by the light of a crescent moon.

Giena Cygnus suddenly pulled out her wand and flicked it after the fleeing crow, but the bird had gone too far and the flaming line faded into the night air.

'If it is Silas Morte, then he has nowhere to go but a nest in a tree. Perhaps that is his fate,' said Giena.

'Oh, Mum! That was horrible. What happened?' sobbed Alba into Pusskin's furry skin.

'I hope we never find out. But I think the judge's actions in life have determined what judgement awaited him in death. Try not to worry, love.'

'Anyway,' said Ande, clapping his hands together in an attempt to distract them from the macabre theatre that had just played out before them, 'Giena, I don't suppose I could trouble you to provide some more flames for us, otherwise I think we'll freeze.'

'Of course, but I don't think there will be any need,' said the teacher, pointing towards the mysterious door, which was once again open.

'I'm not going in there. No way,' said Ralph.

'I'm sure it will be all right,' said Shelia, who was already at the threshold. 'Come and see.'

The group peeked into the tower, none of them quite sure what to expect having just witnessed two completely different facets of this peculiar structure. Each of the party let out a gasp as they saw what lay inside. There were no parties or groups of dead relatives to greet them, no gaping black voids to engulf them; instead, around the edge of the room there were seven beds sumptuously covered in purple velvet throws and billowing gold cushions. A roaring fire in an open hearth was opposite them, its orange and yellow flames dancing gaily, plumes of smoke drifting up the chimney stack. To the side of this was a little gold weaved cat basket with a purple blanket, a monogrammed 'P' stitched on it. A bowl of thick yellow cream and a plate of fish steaks was placed next to this. Pusskin leapt from Alba's arms and headed straight for this, undaunted.

Ralph and Alba broke away from the group, who were still huddled in the doorway, and ran to the back of the tower, where a chimney stack should have been. There was none and neither was there a curl of smoke escaping into the night air.

That is so weird. Where is the smoke going to? thought Ralph.

I don't know. It's like that room belongs to another building in another world, replied Alba, by thought.

Alba, thought Ralph, *are you reading my thoughts?*

'Yes. It's been really easy since you saved… well, since the cave,' said Alba. 'Look at those little trees. A miniature elm, ash and there's an oak and a sycamore. Birds must have dropped seeds on this hill.'

As they walked back round the base of the tower, they saw a figure, like a drunken crane fly, stumbling up the hill, emitting an odd high-pitched groaning.

'We forgot about Arfur Sendal,' said Alba, stifling a giggle, but she and Ralph went to help him despite his earlier treachery.

'Where am I?' he whined, rubbing the back of his head. 'How did I get on this hill? It's dark. What's the tower door doing open?'

The adults had entered the tower and Alba and Ralph were about to lead Arfur in when Tara-Zed appeared in the doorway.

'There are only seven beds. I do not think the hospitality has been extended to you, Arfur,' she said, not unkindly.

'What hospitality? What's going on?' he said, trying to leer over her shoulder, into the interior.

'Arfur, I feel sure a good night's sleep will revive your memory and I believe that your night is to be spent here.'

Tara-Zed indicated to just outside the doorway. The children hadn't noticed a wooden bench, upon which was placed a canvas bag filled with straw, for a pillow, and a crude woollen blanket. A pitcher of water and a clay goblet, some fresh bread and cheese and a bright green apple were set on a pewter tray, resting on the ground.

'You will be comfortable enough there, Arfur, probably more so than you deserve,' said Tara-Zed. 'Come along now, children. Good night, Arfur.' And they turned away from the dumbstruck man who was staring at the bench as if it were an object from another planet.

'I just want to see the horses,' said Ralph.

They were standing by the small stone outcrop. Ralph expected to see them munching on grass, shivering in the chill night air. Instead he found all four beasts bedecked in thick purple horse rugs with gold braid fastening them. They each had a bucket of honey-scented oats, which they were devouring enthusiastically, next to which were four pails of water and a pile of sweet-smelling hay.

'You're all right then,' said Ralph, patting Polaris on the neck, who purred contentedly through his munching. 'But don't expect this treatment when you get home,' he said, returning to the tower barely noticing a large circle of brown toadstools that had formed near the horses.

Once inside, Ralph saw that in the centre of the room was a low table covered with a flimsy gold cloth and laden with fruits and cheese, breads and meat, nuts and honeycomb, wine and water so cold and clear it could have been drawn from a mountain glacier.

'Wow,' he said, as the door shut behind him.

A look of alarm crossed his face, for he feared he had trapped them within. He examined the door and was relieved to see a latch on the inside. He lifted it up and the door opened easily, although there was no corresponding latch on the outside. They could leave whenever they wanted, but no one uninvited could come in.

There was not much talking amongst the party. They had not realised how cold, hungry and exhausted they were. Once their hunger and thirst were satisfied they each lay on their cots, snuggling under the luxurious bedspreads and sinking their heads into what felt like clouds. Despite the terrible things they had seen and experienced, and none more so than the twins, each one of them slept deeply and dreamlessly until the creaking of the door, well after sunrise, awoke them.

CHAPTER 18

Alba was the first to open her eyes, puzzled by a scratching in her ear. She stretched her arms above her head, gave a silent yawn and sat up.

'Mum! Dad! Wake up! Look what's happened.' For the luxurious beds they had fallen asleep on were now wooden planks, balanced on logs. Their velvet quilts had turned into canvas. All that remained of the roaring fire was charcoal, and the beautifully laid table was now a simple bench with fresh bread, cheese and a jug of water and seven clay goblets. The scratching that had awoken Alba was caused by a stick of straw poking through a sack pillow.

'Well, I'll be blowed,' said Ande, rubbing his eyes and expanding his chest. 'What do we make of this?'

'The tower. It's met our needs,' said Alba, looking at Tara-Zed. 'It gave us what we needed last night and all we need this morning is a simple breakfast and we are free to go.'

'We need no more than this, now,' said Tara-Zed, pouring the water.

Ralph leapt to the door and tugged on the handle. The door opened with a whisper.

'Crucial,' said Ralph as he stepped on to dew-soaked grass.

Arfur Sendal was still fast asleep, snoring loudly, but was now lying on the ground, his bench having disappeared. His breakfast was to be a cup of water and some bread.

'His punishment must still be ongoing,' said Ralph with a grin, until he remembered that he did things that deserved reprimanding as well.

The horses were munching on the wet grass, the soft blankets from the night before gone, although Ralph noticed how warm their rumps were as he patted them. Even the saddles and irons were glistening, as if some magical polish had passed over them. The toadstool ring had disappeared.

He looked across the valley. The floor was covered in fluffy mist. A group of baby harebits were tripping over their ridiculous ears, the adults lopping on their ungainly back feet, making the strange flicking motion with their heads. A flock of sheep lazily munched nearby. There was an almost tangible serenity to the day. It smelt as if it would be warm again. Ralph smiled and turned back to the tower.

After breakfasting, the group left the building. Tara-Zed was the last to leave. As she swept through the frame she turned her head round and whispered 'thank you' to the unseen force that had met them in their need. The door shut behind her with a gentle thud, making a hiss that sounded like 'well done'.

Arfur was by now sitting up, leaning against the tower wall, still groaning.

'I kept dreaming of crows attacking me,' he wailed, 'and my head hurts like anything. What's going on, eh now?'

'Oh dear, Arfur, you really don't remember do you?' said Tara-Zed. 'It's probably for the best, although it would have been a great story. You'd have sold lots of papers.'

'I didn't think you could be so wicked, teasing the poor man like that,' said Shelia.

'Well, who is going to believe this story?' said Tara-Zed.

'Mum. Come and see these little trees before we go. I saw them last night,' said Alba. Shelia walked with her daughter to the rear of the tower.

'What trees, love?' said Shelia.

'They were here yesterday. Four of them. I'm not making it up,' said Alba.

'It's probably just another of the strange things that have happened. Now let's get home.' Shelia placed her arm around Alba's shoulders as they walked back to the others, who were already on their horses.

They mounted up. Alba sat behind her mother on Sunbeam, and Ralph joined his father on Polaris. Arfur Sendal was left to walk. Giena had offered to let him ride in the cart along with Jasper Corvus and Pusskin, but Arfur refused, not trusting Stardust not to bolt off with him in it.

Thanks to the unexpected sleep and nourishing food, the travellers felt exhilarated as they made their way back to the village. The horses pranced and snorted as their hooves trod across the springy ground. During the night, Polaris's shoe had been retrieved from the hillside and fitted securely to his hoof by the mysterious helpers. Ralph chuckled to himself as he recalled the expert shot that had stopped Arfur Sendal in his tracks. Alba hugged her mother tightly, inhaling the scent of plumpberries from her jacket.

After the gloom of the cave, Alba could not believe how green and vibrant the countryside was. Even the bark of the trees had a richness to it and the streams and little waterfalls surged with bright, white foam. The smell made her nostrils tingle with its freshness. How she loved her home.

The sun was high in the sky as the group rode into their valley. Ahead of them, riders and a horse-drawn wagon came into view.

'Better late than never,' said Ralph with a grin on his face, which suddenly faded.

'Ralph, please don't be sarcastic,' said Shelia, as Alba stifled a giggle behind her.

The rescue party consisted of Bishop Guy, Simon Beer, Roger Baker and his son Davyd, May and Davis Bellows and their children Murgus and his younger sister Lulu. Finally, Farmer Matthews sat upon his wagon, which was filled with rescue equipment and enough provisions to feed a small army. Two handsome shire horses pulled the cart sure-footedly.

As soon as Murgus and Davyd spotted their best friend, they let out a whoop of delight and pushed their ponies into a canter, with Lulu urging her smaller charge on behind them with a cry of 'wait for me!'

They soon intercepted Ralph and Alba.

'Hello, mate!' cried Murgus.

'Whoa, Ralph! You look different. Older. Is that fluff on your chin? It wasn't there two days ago.' Davyd snorted.

'No way, mate. You disappear for a couple of nights and when you get back you need to shave. Awesome!' said Murgus.

'Oh, hello, you two. I'll tell you about it sometime,' said Ralph, looking at the ground.

Just then the remainder of the rescuers arrived.

'Praise be! How marvellous to see you. We feared the worst when night fell and there was no sign of anyone,' said Bishop Guy.

'Was she there?' said May Bellows. 'Did you see her, the witch?'

'May, let them have a break. They must be exhausted and hungry,' said Farmer Matthew.

'Actually, Matthew, they are two things we are not,' said Shelia.

'No, we had a generous meal last night and a good night's sleep,' said Tara-Zed.

The rescue party looked bewildered.

'I don't think he did,' said Lulu, pointing up the valley, and there, just rounding the bend, came the pitiful figure of Arfur Sendal.

'Ah, yes. His story took a slightly different turn to ours,' said Tara-Zed, winking at Lulu, who giggled, 'but I expect he won't say no to a cart ride home.'

'We'll tell you all about it when we've been to our homes, changed and had time for reflection,' said Shelia.

Once Arfur had caught up and accepted the lift on the wagon, the group returned to the village, largely in silence. Murgus and Davyd were confused and saddened that their friend was not more talkative, but for once had enough sense not to question him.

'Did you secure the hole in the hill?' asked Ande.

'Yes. There's a temporary fence around it. Actually, it won't be that difficult to open the cave again if we get the right equipment from Skipton,' said Davis Bellows.

Before they reached the village, Shelia asked Alba to ride alongside Farmer Matthews. Alba objected at first but relented when she saw that Tara-Zed and Giena had broken away from the group and were waiting for her mother. Jasper Corvus and Pusskin were reluctantly climbing on to the wagon, too.

The three women conferred quietly before Shelia turned round and said, 'We have to take a detour. We won't be gone long. I'll see you back at home. There's a pie in the larder.' And with that the three Sisters of Antares trotted off to the east.

News of the travellers' safe return spread throughout the village and during the day well-wishers delivered pies and buns, eggs and cheese and all manner of gifts to those returned safely home. That evening, a village meeting was held and Shelia, Ande, Tara-Zed and Giena relayed their version of the story, to an entranced audience.

Ralph and Alba were quiet throughout the meeting, neither really knowing how much to reveal of the danger they had been in.

'Can we just write it all down for you?' suggested Alba.

'That's an excellent idea,' said Shelia. 'Do it when you are ready.'

Tara-Zed sent a note to the seat of the High Council in York, requesting a meeting. It was arranged for three weeks' time, which gave the members time to assemble. She knew rumours about the events at White Scar would travel fast around the country, and wanted to ensure that the truth was told before fiction set in.

CHAPTER 19

Two weeks passed. Alba and Ralph were not their usual active selves. Murgus and Davyd stopped calling, as Ralph kept making excuses not to see them. Alba spent much time reading or taking Sunbeam out on errands that didn't really need doing. They would leave the room when Ande started to tell them how the hole in the hill was to be made safe and that there was now a way big enough for a person to crawl through into the main cave itself. Neither of them spoke of their adventure or wrote a word.

Ralph asked Lila Monkfish out again. He thought it was what a man might do. One overcast afternoon, they went for a walk along the riverbank. Ralph threw stones at leaves and twigs, shrugging his shoulders each time he hit the target as if to say, 'Huh, it's nothing.' He tried to tell Lila about the cave but the words wouldn't come out right and he felt as if he was describing a children's fairytale, so he shut up. Lila gabbled on about school and growing up and getting married. Ralph wasn't really listening. They sat on a log near a quiet pool. A kingfisher dashed by and a heron eyed them suspiciously from a reed bed. Lila turned towards Ralph, shut her eyes, tilted her chin and puckered her lips. Ralph thought she looked just like a monkfish. He ran home without saying a word. For all he knew, Lila was still sitting there, waiting to be kissed. He really wasn't being either a man or a boy.

The evening of Ralph's failed date, Tara-Zed came to their house.

'I have to visit my home in Skipton Castle. I should like some company for the journey. Would Ralph and Alba like to come along?'

Ralph kicked an imaginary piece of fluff with his foot and Alba stared out of the window.

'The reason I'm going is to collect two horses. They are Procyrion's offspring, a mare and a stallion. They might suit a couple of brave children I know.'

Alba grinned and Ralph stared at Tara-Zed.

'Ralph, close your mouth, you'll catch a fly,' said Alba. 'Sorry if we've been rude. We'd love to come along and not just because of the horses…'

'Speak for yourself, sis,' said Ralph.

'… as I was saying, it's not the horses. It's just, well, we're both having difficulties thinking about the events. It's all so strange. As if it never happened and yet it is so vivid,' said Alba.

'I understand. Come along with me. It will do you good to get out of the village. And it's okay. I'd be going just for the horses,' she said, smiling in Ralph's direction.

They rode with Farmer Matthews the following day, as he took produce to Skipton market. Tara-Zed rode alongside on Procyrion.

Arriving at the castle, they found two wonderful horses standing in the courtyard. The stallion was as black as Procyrion, but with a white star on his forehead. Next to him was a pretty palomino mare, the hair covering its body a dark gold, the white mane and tail flecked with black.

'They are crucial,' said Ralph, stroking the stallion's muzzle.

'Are you sure they're for us?' said Alba as she buried her face in the mare's silky mane. 'I can't see Mum and Dad agreeing to such an extravagant gift.'

'Actually they were in full agreement. You have been through so very much. And these horses deserve noble owners,' said Tara-Zed.

Procyrion neighed in agreement.

'Yours is called Polestar,' she said, looking at Ralph, 'and, Alba, yours is named Sungold.'

'Thank you,' said Alba.

'Yes, thanks. When do we get to ride them?' said Ralph.

'You're so rude,' said his sister.

'Well, it's getting a little late now, so I agreed with your parents you could stay the night and then ride back with me tomorrow. Come on,

I'll show you to your room and then you can explore the castle if you want to.'

Judge Tara-Zed took them up the spiral steps to the private chamber that the Sisters of Antares had used for a century. Alba and Ralph both hesitated in the doorway as if frightened to enter. Their eyes seemed to absorb the décor of rich colours of gold, magenta and purple. A display of red roses placed on an ornate cast iron stand, added a soft, sweet, scent to the room. Food and drink were laid out on the low table in the centre of the room. Tara-Zed eyed them with a quizzical look.

'It looks like… somewhere else,' said Ralph.

'It's like the room in the North Tower,' said Alba.

'It is, but the décor doesn't change on a whim. It's always like this,' said Tara-Zed.

The twins crossed the threshold and looked around with open mouths at their surroundings. Alba pointed at the gilt candelabra, still suspended from the high ceiling. She walked over to one of the bureaus and let her fingers touch the quill, making the plume sway as if rippled by a gentle breeze. Rich parchment sat on the tilted desk.

'Who are they?' said Alba, looking at three portraits of women, one white-haired, one red-haired and a dark lady with black hair.

'Deneb, Altair and Rigela Kent,' replied Tara-Zed.

'The judge was right. You do look like Rigela Kent, but…' Alba's voice trailed off as a sad look crossed her face.

'This is a portrait of my mentor, Lady Eta Carinae,' continued Tara-Zed, seeming not to notice Alba's melancholy.

A proud-looking woman with a slender nose and auburn hair stared back.

Ralph wandered over to the stone table, which had a plum-coloured velvet cloth across it.

'Wow! Is this it? The actual table where the Sisters got the prophecy from?' said Ralph.

'Yes, it's the Meteor Table and also where Rigela Kent hid the lightning wand,' said Tara-Zed, peeling back the cloth to reveal the crystal surface. Alba came over.

'It doesn't look like very much could happen in it,' said Ralph, trying to mask his disappointment as he ran his fingers across the solid surface.

Alba peered into the crystal and placed both hands in two of the grooves. As she did so, the surface shimmered and a circle of ripples broke to the edge.

What was that, sis? thought Ralph, pulling back his hand.

I don't know, thought Alba.

The siblings looked at each other. Tara-Zed watched their expressions.

'Do you know what we just did there, sis?' said Ralph out loud.

'We haven't thought read since the… well for two weeks,' said Alba.

'Come and rest now. We'll talk about this tomorrow. I have some knowledge of telepathic communication and can give you some training. After all, you don't want each other knowing all your thoughts, I'm sure,' said Tara-Zed, whilst replacing the cloth over the stone table.

'Tara-Zed, can you read thoughts?' said Alba.

'No, but part of the Sisterhood's training is on such matters, so I may be of help. And you must take instruction from your mother. Also, Alba, please don't touch the table again, not yet anyway.' And with that, Tara-Zed gave them each a plate.

'I have some matters to attend to. I'll leave you to eat and come and see you later.' And with that she left the room.

'That was weird, sis, I mean the way you made the crystal on that table turn to liquid. Quite crucial,' said Ralph.

'I know. It was like something awoke inside me. I don't want to think of it now. Let's eat.'

The children tucked into the feast provided. A pageboy came and stoked the fire in the great hearth so it was soon blazing and the day turned to night through the windows. When Tara-Zed returned, both children were fast asleep and so she placed fur throws over them, snuffed several of the candles out and left them, a curious smile on her lips.

All night the children dreamt of the events of their strange adventure, starting with the concert of the singing flowers, the explosion, the adventures in the cave, the attack of the crows, up until the morning after the night in the North Tower.

Each child saw it first from their own perspective, and then it was as if they could see the events through their sibling's eyes. When Alba recalled nearly drowning, she also felt the fear emitted from her brother as he dived into the water to save her. Yet despite the trauma of the events they were recounting, both slept without stirring and when the story was told they continued to sleep dreamlessly until the sun was well risen in the morning sky. Not even the ceaseless scratching of two quill pens dancing across the antique desks, etching ink on to their parchments, had disturbed the children from their slumber.

The smell of freshly baked bread, sperryberry jam and hot honey milk awoke them. Tara-Zed was in the chamber and poured them both a drink.

'Did you sleep well?' she enquired.

'Yes, but I dreamt of our adventure,' said Ralph, stretching his arms and yawning, 'and so did you, sis, didn't you?'

'Yes,' said Alba, rubbing sleep from her eyes, 'but I feel really rested. Like a great weight is off my mind.'

'Well, it is, actually,' said Tara-Zed, walking to one of the desks where a neat pile of parchment was not only stacked but bound in green leather and secured with a red velvet ribbon. She picked the document up and passed it to Alba. Walking to the second desk she passed a similar tome, this time bound in red with a green velvet ribbon, to Ralph. They undid the ribbons. The writing was spidery, but easy to read.

'It's my dream,' said Alba, after a page.

'Mine too,' said Ralph.

'But how is that possible?' said Alba.

'A lot seems possible in this room,' said Tara-Zed, looking around. 'Your account is now recorded. You can talk about it now or leave it written and never speak of your adventure again.'

'Funny. Now it's written down, I don't mind talking about it,' said Alba.

'Me neither,' said Ralph, 'in fact, Tara-Zed, can the telepathy instruction wait? I'd rather like to get back home. There are some people I'd like to see.'

'Of course,' said Tara-Zed. 'The horses are already saddled.'

The horses were wonderful to ride, well-schooled, but full of life and mischief and the children knew they would all be lifelong friends.

The journey back to Ingleset was one of the best experiences of Ralph's life. They cut across country, jumping logs and splashing through streams. Their parents were in the garden as they trotted up and joined in making a fuss of Sungold and Polestar. But then Ralph disappeared into the wood shed where he remained for the rest of the day.

The following morning Ralph walked to the village. He saw Murgus and Davyd sitting by the well, each with their carved Global War figures lined up next to them. They turned away from Ralph as he approached them.

'All right, you two?' said Ralph.

'Did you say something, Murgus?' said Davyd.

'No, not I,' said Murgus. 'A pompous superhero adventurer, who is too important to spend time with his mates, may have spoken.'

'Oh yes, Murgus. You are quite right. No doubt he has come to brag about his new superhero horse, which I saw him pass by on yesterday afternoon.' The two friends continued sorting out their carvings.

'Look, you two. I'm really sorry. I have been an ass, but I have really missed you. And I've brought these.'

Ralph pulled a leather pouch from his belt and unrolled it. On it were several carved figures, characters from his adventure.

'This is the judge and the witch. Here are the three original Sisters of Antares and this is a crow,' said Ralph.

'Wow,' said Murgus, forgetting his apparent disinterest. 'These are well crucial.'

'They're part of my story. There are loads more to carve. If you like, I'll tell you all about it. But I'll understand if you don't want me around,' said Ralph.

Davyd rolled several of the carvings between his fingers.

'I suppose the Global War figures are a bit boring now. We could do with something new,' said Davyd, smiling from ear to ear.

'Great. Thanks.' And to the cries of 'crucial' and 'awesome', Ralph recounted his adventure to his two best friends. The world of adults could do without him for a while longer.

Shelia accompanied Tara-Zed to York. They travelled on horseback. Giena Cygnus decided to remain in Ingleset. She was still feeling tired from the adventure and her back was constantly aching; she had refused a touch from the wand.

'It's for life and death cases, not a twinge in one's back,' she had said.

The roads which had once been surfaced with tarmac or concrete were now covered with a thin layer of grass and had become bridleways, although as the ladies drew closer to York they saw that roads were being excavated and repaired. Several of the solar-powered vehicles passed them. These were homemade craft, made from salvaged tyres and other items salvaged from cars, lawn mowers… in fact, anything that had once moved. The solar panels had been retrieved from homes once advanced enough to have such equipment for heating and hot water. The drivers waved at the two ladies as they chugged by.

Once, in the distance, they heard a low grumbling and, straining their eyes, saw a sleek metal object, not like the homemade solar vehicles, moving quickly away from them, a thin trail of white vapour emitting from a tube at the rear.

'That's a car. I've seen them in a book,' said Shelia.

'They've made a fuel from vegetable leftovers,' said Tara-Zed.

'What a pity they didn't think of that a couple of hundred years ago,' said Shelia.

'Well, as much as I love this old boy, those *cars* look a lot drier and warmer,' said Tara-Zed, leaning forwards and patting Procyrion on his shoulder, just as it started to rain.

They lodged in a former department store. Two boys were paid in harebit skins and four jars of honey to tend to the horses in what had once been a storage bay. The ladies lounged on sofas that had been too heavy for the looters to carry off in years gone by, slept in beds whose mattresses had not been ransacked by vermin and breakfasted on provisions Shelia had packed for the journey.

The High Council still met in the museum buildings in front of Clifford's Tower. Shelia had only been to York twice before and had never visited these premises. They entered through the entrance to the

Debtors' Prison. She stared open mouthed at the dust-covered models of ancient convicts in the gloomy interior, but Tara-Zed ushered her to the airy conference room where business people had once gathered and wedding guests had danced in celebration.

'Good morning,' she said to the eleven members already seated at tables arranged in a square. The council members, seven men and four women, stood in greeting. 'May I present Shelia Milway, a fellow Sister of Antares.'

At the mention of the Sisterhood, two of the male members huffed and rolled their eyes. An extra place had been set for Shelia. They sat down.

'We have read your report, Tara-Zed. It was highly... creative,' said a short, middle-aged man, with a large nose. He was dressed in slacks, a V-neck jumper, a blue shirt and a yellow tie and spoke with rounded vowels.

Tara-Zed's skin darkened. Shelia flicked her thumb nail against her finger.

'What part did you find particularly *creative*, Vaston Varmer?' said Tara-Zed, leaning forwards. Several council members fidgeted in their chairs.

'Did I sound facetious? I apologise. The bit I found most creative was when you recovered a wand from a mythical hiding place to the point where you saw a *witch* enter a tower,' said Vaston Varmer, with a sneer.

Tara-Zed dug her nails into the table. Her hair flopped across her face.

'You see our dilemma, Tara.' A thin woman in her twenties spoke. She had mousy brown hair twisted into a bun and wore tortoiseshell glasses.

Tara-Zed pushed her hair from her face and glared at the woman, before forcing a smile on to her lips.

'My name is Tara, with a Zed. And no, Brugella, I do not see your dilemma.'

The woman adjusted the arm of her spectacles.

'Well, anyway. Your story makes us sound a bit, well, parochial. We meet in Europe soon to discuss trade and communication routes.

There is to be discourse about opening air waves, now the static has subsided, and even talk of trading using a common currency, rather than bartering with goods and services,' said Brugella.

'That's all well and good, but what I reported in Ingleset is the truth,' said Tara-Zed. Vaston Varmer snorted.

They all jumped as Shelia slammed her palms down on to the table and stood up.

'My children risked their lives for you. If the judge had not been stopped and Aster not restored, I can promise each of you would not be sitting here now. You lot have forgotten the magic that helped humanity survive. It was the pursuit of riches through the exploitation of science and nature that brought this planet to its knees, barely a century ago. Do not ignore faith and things that cannot be explained by logic again!' Shelia sat down and looked at each of the council members.

A gentleman with grey hair and wearing a well-tailored black suit, collar and tie raised his hand.

'Of course we appreciate what your children risked, and no one at this table doubts your story.' He spoke with the voice of a classical actor. He glared at Vaston Varmer. 'What I propose is that the wands be brought to York for safekeeping in these very buildings. After all, we have stored the Crown Jewels safely, and many other treasures of this great country.'

'Lord Brinkham. The Sisters of Antares are guardians of the wands,' said Tara-Zed through clenched teeth.

'I agree with Tara-Zed,' said a man of Indian origin, sporting a beard and wearing a green turban and matching Nehru suit.

'Thank you, Steven Smith,' said Tara-Zed, nodding towards the man.

'If there is no magic, and the strange events can be explained by some other means, then this council has nothing to worry about. But if there is no explanation other than magic, then one day, we may be more grateful of the Sisters' intervention than we can ever know.'

'Shall we vote?' said Lord Brinkham, gruffly. 'All those who think the wands should be brought to York, raise your right hand.'

Six hands were raised. In the event of a draw the vote always went in favour of the proposer. Tara-Zed shook her head, but then Brugella adjusted her glasses with her right hand and lowered it to the table. Lord Brinkham glared at the woman, who ignored him.

'All those in favour of the wands remaining with the order known as the Sisters of Antares, raise your right hand.'

Six hands were raised. Brugella rested her hands in her lap. Lord Brinkham stood up, glared at Tara-Zed and Shelia and strode out the room.

The ladies stood up next.

'I'll see you all in Europe,' said Tara-Zed.

They rode out past York Minster, its gothic dominance of the city now softened by the surrounding tall grasses. Creepers covered the scaffolding once used in the renovation of its magnificent stonework.

A man, dressed in leather trousers and jerkin, went by holding a pack of baying domesticated foolfs on leashes. They would catch rats and mice and bring them to their master's feet for a tasty titbit of squirrel meat or pigeon offal.

Children played in the open space in front of the cathedral on shiny hundred-year-old bikes, newly retrieved from a local warehouse. They jumped over humps where pavements were now covered in grass and pedalled alongside the horses, trying to get close enough to pull their tails, before they got bored and cycled off to taunt the foolfs with sticks.

'I can't wait to get home,' said Shelia.

'The Council are a bit jittery. There's a lot at stake, but even so I was surprised at their hostility to the wands' reappearance,' said Tara-Zed. 'Still, they are ours for the time being, and hopefully won't be needed ever again.'

They rode in silence for a while, passing buildings, some empty and hollow, whilst others such as shops, kitchen showrooms or medieval merchants' houses had been turned into unlikely homes. The people they saw were healthy and waved greetings to the women. They wore clothes taken from the many fading shops, so a woman in a ball gown walked along the street with a friend dressed in designer jeans, a leather jacket and an elegant hat.

When they reached the city outskirts, Shelia turned towards her friend.

'What would you have done if the vote had gone against us?'

'To use Ralph's phrase, *I would have got the wands and zapped them*.' Both women threw their heads back with laughter, as if it was a great release. Once the laughter had subsided, they fell quiet again.

'I would send my wand back into the Meteor Table before surrendering it,' said Tara-Zed.

'Me too,' said Shelia, as she urged Sunbeam into a canter.

The next day Alba sat with her mother, Giena Cygnus and Tara-Zed around the kitchen table, as the smell of plumpberry pies filled the air. The sound of the grandfather clock nudged into the kitchen, but the family had easily adjusted to its mesmerising rhythm. Ande had not been able to alter the time mechanism, so it had become a curiosity as the hands moved backwards and nothing more.

The women had just finished admiring Giena's amethyst engagement ring, which Jasper Corvus had given her the day before. Pusskin slept undisturbed next to the oven.

'Alba, there is something we Sisters wish to ask you. We have long thought that you would make an excellent member of the Sister of Antares and eventually succeed one of us. This was confirmed to me, following the reaction of the crystal when you touched the stone table. Training can begin now. Please think about it, especially in the light of what has happened,' said Tara-Zed.

'Oh!' said Alba, a look of surprise on her face. 'I'd be taught the secrets of the Meteor Table, the whereabouts of my wand and even some of the mysteries of the North Tower. It would be brill. Thank you.'

Shelia folded and unfolded a napkin. The faces of the three women looked grim.

'What is it?' said Alba.

'Now the High Council have confirmation that the wands exist, they are not convinced that they are safe anymore,' said Tara-Zed.

'We only narrowly won the vote to keep them under our control,' said Shelia.

'Nonsense,' said Giena. 'Only we know where our own is hidden and I'm not about to tell anyone.'

'What if someone threatened Jasper? Or Alba? Would you tell then?' said Tara-Zed.

Giena twisted her new ring.

'Yes, put that way, I would,' said Giena.

'No, you mustn't,' said Alba.

'Alba, it could be any one of us who are threatened,' said Shelia.

'The wands have been safe with us for a hundred years, so a few more weeks won't matter. I'm unaware of any real threat, so I'll talk to the High Council again. They're just a bit twitchy because of the trade talks that are coming up. I'm off to Europe,' said Tara-Zed.

'I heard we might be able to trade our harebit skins for cocoa beans and make chocolate,' said Alba.

'I'm sure it will all be okay. And in the meantime, we have a wedding to plan,' said Shelia.

'Can you believe Arfur's offered to take the photos?' said Giena.

'He's been quite nice lately, by his standards. I suspect a guilty conscience,' said Shelia.

The ladies laughed, and Shelia flopped the napkin over Giena's head like a mock bridal veil. A clink followed by a gentle thud came from the side of the house.

'Ralph's practising for the county quoits championship,' said Shelia as she adjusted Giena's veil.

They didn't notice Ande shooing the large black crow from the kitchen windowsill, the creature squawking along the valley, its newly grown tail feathers spread out like a fan and its ruby eyes glinting in the sunlight.